STORM RISING

IT HAS ALREADY BEGUN...

A NOVEL BY
GARY NAIMAN

Cover Art by: Todd Aune
Spokane Valley, WA

ALSO BY GARY NAIMAN

Heartland

P.P.M.

Omega

The Response

From the Void

The Warriors

The Battle

From the Depths

Vengeance is Mine

Robosapiens

White Tiger

Electron

THE SMALLEST INSECT
CAN BRING DOWN THE BIGGEST TREE...

CHAPTER 1

FREEDOM SQUARE

Makely crawled against the cracked wall and stared at the sunlight beaming through the collapsed doorway. He clutched his M27 and huddled against his four comrades. Nothing was said. Nothing had to be. The only sound was their strained breathing.

His nostrils stung from the acrid stench drifting into the gutted room, a toxic brew of cordite, charred wood, and burnt human flesh. He'd never forget that stench. He'd remember it to his dying day.

His fingers dug into the M27. *Dying day? Quit dreaming, Marine. The way things are, you'll be dead before noon.*

He dragged off his helmet and rested his head against the wall. Hard to believe everything was so quiet. Forty minutes ago, the ground shook from artillery blasts and rocket hits. Debris rained down from the night sky. Star shells ignited the darkness, accompanied by bursts of small arms fire.

And there was that other sound, barely audible through the explosions and sniper fire. A terrifying sound. A heart-wrenching sound. The muffled screams of men, women, and children.

He glanced at the four men crouched beside him. Forty minutes ago, there were seven. Yesterday, nine. A month ago, twenty-six. Now just Joey, Edgar, Rafael, and Terell. Four Marines trying to survive another day.

He heaved a nervous breath and wiped the sweat off his face. Twenty-two men snuffed out like candles, their surviving brothers cowering on the floor of a gutted house in the middle of hell.

For what, dammit? To shoot at ghosts darting between burned buildings? To hit the dirt with every burst of small arms fire, praying it wasn't your last second on earth?

He buried his face in his hands. *No more, goddammit! I'm not an animal! I'm a human being!*

"On your feet!"

Makely's head snapped up. Sergeant Hoffman had ducked through the blown out doorway, his black eyes glaring at them.

Hoffman slung his M27 on his shoulder and shuffled into the gutted room. "You guys deaf? I said on your feet!"

No response. They stared at him from the debris-strewn floor.

Hoffman lunged at them, his face seething with anger. "Move!"

For a moment, the only sound was the small arms fire echoing off the buildings. Then a grunt as Joey pushed off the floor on shaky legs.

It took a few seconds for the others to follow. They rose to their feet and leaned against each other, their eyes fixed on Hoffman.

It was a miracle they could stand. None of them had slept more than a few hours since their chopper landed at the city's outskirts a month ago. Not easy to close your eyes in a fire zone. That's when you relive the artillery concussions, tracers, and charred bodies. If you're lucky enough to doze off, some ghost opens up from a rooftop and your eyes snap open to the bitter truth. The only way to sleep in Tehran is to die in Tehran.

Hoffman knelt down and yanked a map out of his shirt pocket. He spread it on the floor and waited for the five Marines to gather around him before shining a penlight on the map. He aimed the beam of light at a red circle and stared at them with those shark eyes.

"This one's gonna be rough. G-2 says we got eighty insurgents holed up in this mosque." Hoffman tapped the red circle with his finger. "They got AK-47's, RPG's, and hell knows what. We got orders to take them out before they deploy their weapons to neighboring cells." He paused and eyed the Marines. "No prisoners. You see any wounded, smoke the bastard."

Hoffman ignored their muffled curses. "We're going in at 0700 with six squads from A Company. The strike signal will be…"

What was wrong? Makely could see Hoffman's gnarled finger jabbing at the map, but he couldn't hear his voice. Everything was spinning. His gut churned. He gripped his forehead and heaved a deep breath, but the nausea kept coming. He couldn't hold it any longer. He broke away from the circle and bolted for the doorway.

"Hey, where are you going!"

Makely gripped the splintered wood and dropped on his knees. Then came the puking and firm hand seizing his Kevlar vest.

"What the hell's wrong with you!" Hoffman jerked Makely to his feet and spun him around, his black eyes aflame. He jabbed his gnarled finger into Makely's chest and spit out the words. "Damn you, Marine! Don't you ever walk away from me!"

"Sergeant, I—"

"Shut up!" He shook Makely's vest. "You tryin' to cause trouble? You tryin' to shake the men? Damn you, Makely! You walk away like that again and I'll blow your head off!"

Hoffman shoved Makely to the floor and glared at the trembling Marines. "Now listen close. You grunts volunteered for this. Big heroes and all that. Bet you thought it would be like them recruitin' ads. Well, it's too late now. No turnin' back. You're in it up to your scrawny necks and I'm gonna make sure you don't disgrace me, your country, or the Corps. Now get ready cause we're movin' out!"

Makely crawled off the floor and felt his finger slip over the M27's trigger — and something weird happened.

He wasn't afraid. It was like a wave washing everything clear. If he was going to die, it wouldn't be in a firefight with a bunch of brainwashed beggars. Not after a year crawling around the Middle East with its suicide bombers and roadside mines.

He wiped the puke off his mouth. *What a joke. We elect a president to change things and four years later I'm stuck in Iran because some fanatics blew up a skyscraper in Chicago. So much for the war on terror. A hundred thousand GI's fighting a bunch of madmen in the most god awful place on earth. Don't our leaders know what's going on? Don't they care?*

His finger tightened on the trigger. *That's it, fool. They don't care. They never cared. That's why they sent us here. Forget the patriotic crap. It's the fucking oil and those hefty reconstruction contracts for the fat cats. They're the puppet masters and we're the fucking puppets!*

He stepped back from the others and raised his M27. *Well, this puppet's had it. They're gonna care from now on cause I'm gonna light a fire that'll burn those fat cats out of their trees. It starts right here, dammit. The shot heard round the fucking world. Right here. Right now. Compliments of Corporal John Makely.*

"What are you doing, Makely? You crazy or somethin'?"

Makely aimed the M27 at Hoffman. "Go to hell, Sergeant."

Hoffman stepped back and unslung his M27, his eyes on fire. "You better lower that piece or so help me god, I'll blow you away."

Makely's face twisted in a sneer. *Yeah, it's real clear now. The enemy is standing in front of me with his weapon raised. Another pawn in the fat cat's army, protecting their investment while they stuff their pig wallets with the spoils of our blood.*

Our blood, dammit! Joey's blood! Edgar's blood! Rafael's blood! Terell's blood! My blood! Young men that will never see their families because a perverted scum named Hoffman carries out orders from his pig masters!

Hoffman stepped toward him. "You got three seconds, Makely. One! Two!"

Someone slammed into Makely, but he was already shooting. The last thing he saw was a shadow crouching in the doorway as the sergeant's bullets ripped into him.

CHAPTER 2

GHQ

First word of the incident reached GHQ in the Elburz Mountains at 0714 hours. Sergeant Waldo Hoffman had been assassinated by one of his own men while conducting a pre-strike briefing in Tehran's Freedom Square.

General Malcolm Taylor put down the e-mail printout and stared at Lieutenant General Farley Morell who was standing across the desk. "You're sure about the reporter?"

"Yes, sir."

Taylor stroked his chin. "This is bad. We can't let it leak out."

Morell looked down at the printout. "Sir, maybe we should contact the Pentagon."

Taylor's head snapped up. "Are you nuts? That's like putting a gun to your head. The top dogs don't like bad news, and mutiny tops the list. They'll fry us both."

Morell nodded at the three red flags on the map behind his commander. "Sir, that's the third incident in twenty-four hours. We have rumors of more trouble in Qom and Isfahan. I don't know what's going on, but it's spreading."

Taylor snatched the printout and read it again. "What about the reporter?"

"He got the whole thing on a digital camera. Carnage shots of the two dead soldiers, their guns still smoking. Interviews with the four witnesses, the whole nine yards."

Taylor glared at Morell. "For god's sake, how?"

"He was embedded with a fire squad from A Company across the street. They were getting ready to hit a mosque when he heard the shooting and broke for shelter along with the others." Morell shrugged. "Bad luck for us. The reporter crawled through the doorway in time to see Makely and Hoffman blasting away at each other. That's when he started taking pictures."

"Damn."

Morell rested his hands on the desk. "There's more, sir. The reporter was a real pro. Got damaging interviews from the four Marines before our guys broke in and dragged him out."

Taylor crushed the printout in his fist. "He broke the rules!"

"Yes, sir, but the media boys don't care about that. In a court-room, they always fall back on the first amendment. Besides, that recording is a dagger."

Taylor slammed his fist on the desk. "Confiscate the damn thing!"

"We did, sir, but the reporter transmitted a copy to WNN."

Taylor's face went blank. The only sound was the warbling coming from the communications equipment on the table beside him.

Morell looked at his commander. "Sir, we only have a few hours. By noon, this mess will be on every TV screen on the planet."

Taylor nodded and took a deep breath. "Thank you, Farley. You can go." He stood and returned Morell's salute. When the door closed, he turned to the red flags and listened to the message coming in from Isfahan—

"This is Lieutenant Manuel Bogart. We have an incident at intercept 0933-C114. At least seven dead from friendly fire. The shooter has been taken out. Situation tenuous but stable. Need medical assistance for nine wounded. All wounds inflicted by M27 rounds from deceased Marine. No explanation at this time. No warning. Consider situation volatile."

Five minutes later, General Malcolm Taylor placed an urgent call to the Pentagon.

CHAPTER 3

WNN

Sid Rubin was in the midst of a typical twenty-hour work day when his cell phone went off in WNN's front lobby. He sank into a guest chair and yanked the phone out of his pocket. It was pushing midnight in Atlanta.

He frowned, his eyes squinting at the ID on the phone's illuminated screen—

"Ambrose"

Rubin had learned phone calls from that name meant trouble. He pressed the talk button and held the plastic phone against his ear. "Go ahead."

"That you, Sid?"

Rubin glanced at his watch. "Make it quick, Perry. I'm short on time. I have a midnight teleconference with Carlton in New York."

"I was just thrown out of Tehran."

Rubin stiffened. "You what?"

"I managed to transmit a video recording before they took away my camera. You can access the images from our data bank."

Rubin's frown became a scowl. "Dammit, Perry, quit talking in riddles. What happened out there?"

"I walked into the biggest story since we started this bloody war. The whole thing's coming apart. A corporal assassinated his sergeant and died in the exchange. I have video of the bodies and interviews with the witnesses. It's all in our data bank."

Rubin lowered the phone and stared at the empty lobby. He'd fought the executive committee's decision to assign Perry Ambrose to the Iran campaign, but was overridden by CEO Franklin Carlton's fascination with Ambrose's blind ambition. Just the guy we need for the sweeps, Carlton had told him. Now, Carlton and his committee would pay for their decision.

"You there, Sid?"

Rubin raised the phone. "Do you know how hard we worked to get you in there? You just cost us our eyes and ears in Iran."

"Listen to me, Sid. It's the beginning of the end over here and I've got it on video. No other network has what we have. We need to go live with it before they catch up."

Rubin clenched the phone. "You done?"

"Yeah."

"Then listen closely. I want you to write a formal letter of apology to the military and fax it to me. I'll see about erasing your video and submitting a written guarantee of nondisclosure to the joint chiefs.

"Rubin waited for a response. "Perry?"

"I can't believe what I'm hearing. This thing's huge, Sid. We can't back down now."

Rubin ignored him. "Where the hell are you?"

"Waiting for a chopper outside Tehran. They'll probably drop me at the border."

Rubin glanced at his watch. "Tell them you talked to WNN and we've arranged your transfer out of there. Tell them we're contacting the Pentagon to resolve the misunderstanding."

"Misunderstanding? Sid, do you know what you're saying?"

Rubin pressed the phone against his mouth. "Listen, dammit. You just cost us embedded news coverage of the fight for Tehran. Do you know what that means? We have the sweeps coming. We need those firefights on the evening news. I have a meeting with Carlton in twenty minutes. What am I supposed to tell him?"

"The bloody truth, dammit! We've got footage of the first break in our ranks. It's mutiny, Sid. Biggest mutiny of all time. People will be glued to their TV's when that footage hits the screen. Our share points will go through the roof."

Rubin fought his anger. He knew Perry's story would quickly fade without follow-up. A few days after it broke, the government's public relations apparatus would squelch the damn thing. Without an embedded reporter, viewer attention would quickly shift to other networks covering the latest firefight or suicide attack while WNN sat on the sidelines. All because an overzealous reporter tried to make a name for himself by creating a story that was over the top.

"Sid?"

Rubin stared at the WNN logo above the lobby. "I have an idea. We'll edit your story to take out the mutiny. I'll work out the details with the Pentagon. Just get me that letter of apology and throw in an admission you stretched the truth."

"What?"

"Do it!"

Ambrose hesitated. "Sorry, I can't do that."

Rubin pushed out of the chair, his face hot with anger. "Mark my words, Perry. This assignment was your last chance. If I don't have that letter in twenty minutes, you're finished at WNN, and every other news organization."

The phone clicked.

"Perry!"

No response.

Rubin jammed the cell phone in his pocket and headed for the elevators. It would take two minutes to reach the teleconference room. It would be the longest two minutes of Sid Rubin's life.

CHAPTER 4

THE PRESIDENT

"**M**r. President, may I speak with you?"

The President nodded at his chief of staff and pushed up from the most powerful desk on earth. He raised his forefinger and smiled at his secretary of commerce seated across from him. "Hold that thought, Peter. I'll be back in a minute."

But the President didn't come back. He was too shaken by the news from the Middle East. Firefights were raging in Tehran, Qom, and Isfahan, but not with the insurgents. Shooting had broken out between American soldiers. Over a dozen incidents of outright mutiny had been recorded in the past thirty hours, and the number was increasing.

The President stared at the top-secret communiqué in his hands, unable to accept its words. He looked at the television monitor on the conference table and lifted the paper toward the military officer on the screen. "What is this, General?"

General Augustus Cook took a deep breath and forced out the words. "At 0655 this morning, one of our men went berserk after a firefight in Tehran's Freedom Square. Before we could intervene, he killed his sergeant and was himself killed in the exchange of fire."

The President leaned forward. "But why? It says here Corporal Makely was a good Marine. He'd fought in the Afghan campaign for nearly a year before we transferred him to Operation Scorpion."

Cook shook his head. "I don't know, Mr. President. Makely crossed a line that's different for each soldier. No warning. No symptoms. The killing and carnage suddenly become too great to cope with, like a pot of overheated stew boiling over."

The President dropped back in his chair. "Stew?"

"Yes, sir."

"And the others?"

"Same thing, sir. With our moves into Iran and Syria, we've been forced to extend duty tours by several months." Cook hesitated. "We must be hitting some kind of threshold."

The President looked down at the paper. "Do you know what you're saying? If you're right, the whole Middle East campaign could collapse."

Cook folded his hands and glared at the President. "I'm sorry, sir. We asked for additional funding to beef up recruiting and psychological counseling, but we were shoved behind the education stimulus program. We'll just have to clamp down until this mess blows over."

The President crumpled the paper in his fist. "Are you telling me there's no solution?"

Edwin Hammel cut off Cook before he could respond. "We'll manage, sir. The city is almost ours. In thirty days we'll occupy the country from Tabriz to Bandar Abbas. We just wanted to let you know before this mess hits the news."

The President felt an icy chill while staring at his secretary of defense. "News?"

"Yes, sir."

"What news, Edwin?"

Chief-of-Staff, Jack Wiley leaned toward the President. "One of their reporters smuggled out a video of the incident. It should hit WNN's global network within the hour."

The President jumped up and flung the crumpled paper on the table. "What's the bastard's name?"

Wiley looked down at his notes. "Perry Ambrose, sir."

"I want their CEO on the line!"

Wiley raised his hand in a calming gesture. "We're already in contact with Franklin Carlton, sir. It sounds like he wants to cut a deal."

"Deal?" The President eased down in his chair after hearing the magic word that soothes the savage political breast. He watched Wiley dismiss Hammel and Cook while shutting off the video screen.

The President leaned toward his chief of staff. "Jack?"

Wiley sighed. "Good thing we caught them before the sweeps. Gives us a large bargaining chip."

"Go on."

Wiley held up a piece of paper. "This is an apology from WNN. They're prepared to work with us to edit the recording so it doesn't impact national security, if you get my drift."

The President breathed a sigh of relief. "What about the reporter?"

"He's a loser, sir. An egomaniac searching for a Pulitzer Prize. They'll cut him a deal and cut him loose. All they're asking is reinstatement over there in time for our big push."

"And their sweeps?"

"Yes, sir."

"Who replaces Ambrose?"

"Josh Barden, sir. A real patriot. He'll rally round the flag and do us proud."

The President nodded and pushed up from the table. "Well done, Jack."

"Yes, sir." Wiley stood and shuffled his papers into a folder.

The President was almost out the door when he turned around. "One thing, Jack."

"Sir?"

"That jerk, Ambrose. I never want to hear his name again."

"Yes, sir." Wiley watched his boss leave the room.

CHAPTER 5

PERRY AMBROSE

"What the bloody hell!" Perry clutched his throbbing head while listening to the high-pitched beeps. He groped for the alarm clock on the nightstand and slammed his fist on the snooze button.

He leaned toward the clock and squinted at its blurred digits. Seven twenty. The alarm had been beeping for twenty minutes.

"Blast." He crawled off the bed and hesitated when his hand struck something. He looked down at the empty bottle of *Jack Daniel's* on the blanket. "Great ... bloody great." He sat on the edge of the bed and buried his face in his hands.

This has been the worst nightmare yet, a suitcase nuke vaporizing the nation's capital while he stared helplessly at the timer's final countdown.

Two nights ago, he was having a drink in the John Hancock Building's ninety-sixth floor *Signature Lounge* when a hijacked 767 slammed into the famed Chicago skyscraper. Just enough time to guzzle his martini and activate his camera while the building shuddered under him. Pulitzer all the way, a breathtaking video of the restaurant's eleven hundred foot plunge to hell.

Three nights ago, he was covering a Mideast peace conference in the United Nations Building when terrorists broke into the general assembly hall and began assassinating the attending world leaders. He was almost to the exit when one of the terrorists opened fire with his AK-47, and he woke up in a cold sweat.

He stood up on shaky legs and stumbled to the dresser. The unshaven face in the mirror wasn't pretty. He stared at the face and stroked his tangled black hair. *Blast, it's getting worse. Used to be a nightmare a week. Now it's every bloody night. You need help, man. You're at the end of your rope.* He yanked off his briefs and headed for the bathroom.

He was stepping out of the shower when his cell phone went off. He wrapped the towel around his waist and snatched the buzzing phone off the dresser. "Yeah?"

"That you, Ambrose?"

He winced. "Mr. Caliento?"

"Where are you?"

He hesitated. "Just pulled up to the Mount Oread campus. The place is packed."

"Bull! You're still at the motel."

"Motel?"

"I called the motel to see if you checked out. The manager said your car is outside the door, along with a do not disturb sign."

"I can explain, Mr.—"

"Damn you, Ambrose! You get to the university and catch her when she steps out of that limo or our deal is off!"

"Mr. Caliento, I—" He grimaced from the loud click.

The next twenty minutes were a blur. He remembered slipping on some deodorant and clothes. No time to shave or brush his teeth.

His rented Toyota skidded out of the motel parking lot and sped toward downtown Lawrence and its tree-covered hill known as Mount Oread, home of the University of Kansas.

The media was there in force when he pulled up to the security blockade on Massachusetts Street. He was about to drive around the blockade when a scowling state trooper stepped in front of the Toyota and pointed a hard finger at the windshield.

He fumbled through his frayed sport jacket, praying he hadn't left his press badge at the motel. Thank god, it was nestled in his pocket. He breathed a sigh of relief while extending the plastic badge to the trooper.

With no parking left, he was forced to abandon the car and make a dash for the approaching caravan. His ears filled with sirens as Minton's black stretch limo pulled up to the sea of reporters, accompanied by a phalanx of motorcycle cops.

He caught a glimpse of her exiting the limo. *One chance, idiot … go!* He made a futile rush toward her, but was pushed back by the secret service agents. He watched her and her protective wedge of state police disappear into the sea of reporters, en route to the university's auditorium atop the hill.

In that brief moment, Perry Ambrose realized Claire Minton was no longer a political curiosity. Her unexpected performance in the primaries had triggered mandatory secret service protection. At eleven percent, she could no longer be taken lightly.

She was clear of the reporters now, standing at the auditorium's glass doors behind her protective screen of state police. She waved to the cheering crowd at the base of the hill while Perry adjusted his zoom lens and snapped away.

Her photos didn't do her justice. At a slender five foot nine, Claire Minton conveyed the stature of a leader. Her short black hair was cropped neatly above her ears. She wore little makeup and her deep-set blue eyes burned right through you. Add the taut lips and military countenance, and Claire Minton was the perfect warrior.

Senator Adam Clayborn had learned that painful lesson on national television last year. Claire Minton was wearing a uniform then, its army blue plastered with medals from her heroics in both Gulf Wars. Clayborn was hammering her with innuendos about her lack of patriotism in light of her recent attack on the President's bungling of the Iran campaign.

When Minton dodged a loaded question, Clayborn rose to his feet and pointed a trembling finger at her, accusing her of selling out to the anti-war movement. She gave him a minute to vent his wrath before spotting an opening and firing back.

"You look like a puppet standing there, Senator. Who's pulling the strings?"

"What did you say?"

"You heard me, Senator. Please zip your fly and act like the man your constituents voted for."

Clayborn was caught off guard by Minton's bold retort. As it turned out, his fly was quite zipped, but his downward glance was enough to turn him into a buffoon on national TV. He collapsed in his chair amidst a rush of laughter, and all the while she glared at him with those penetrating blue eyes, the perfect sound bite to launch her campaign for the presidency.

Perry watched her disappear through the auditorium's opened doors followed by a select band of reporters, each flashing their VIP badge at the security guards. He looked down at his restricted press badge and frowned. Six months ago, that badge would have been stamped with the same "VIP" initials, but times had changed. He sighed and snatched the buzzing phone out of his jacket pocket.

Caliento's voice crackled in his ear. "Well?"

Perry watched the auditorium's doors close.

"Ambrose?"

"I'm on it. I'll get her when she comes out."

"You didn't get her going in?"

Perry hesitated. "Better to wait until she comes out. I can intercept her at the limo."

Caliento's voice sharpened. "You didn't get there in time?"

"Don't worry, I've got it covered."

"Damn you!"

The phone clicked. It didn't take a rocket scientist to know the Caliento deal was off.

Perry collapsed against a tree and stared at the reporters scrambling down the hill with their video cameras and cell phones. By the time Minton exited the hall, the world's television networks would have ample video footage to broadcast the event on their 24/7 news.

He heard cheers and looked up at the loudspeakers on the auditorium's roof. A retired general named Harland was introducing her to the auditorium's eight thousand roaring supporters.

Perry spent the next five minutes listening to her speech on the loudspeakers. Clouds had moved in and a light rain was falling.

He was about to call it quits when Minton's voice rose in a fiery condemnation of the President, both political parties, and the apathetic American public.

"It's more than an unjust war. We're at the most important crossroads in our nation's history. The planet's last great hope for democracy is about to fade into oblivion because you don't care! My fellow Americans, you have given up! They're taking away everything you have, and you don't care!"

Perry stared at the loudspeakers in disbelief. Was she daft? She had just condemned the American people for their apathy. Claire Minton had just committed political suicide.

He pushed away from the tree and heard the roar. They were bloody cheering her.

Her voice rose above the cheers. "Listen to me, all of you! I didn't enter this race to win a hollow victory. I entered it to get the message through, and here it is. Our nation has been sold out to global corporations. They control the media, the government, and the courts. They will do anything to advance their quest for power … anything!"

Perry listened to the cheers. The sky flashed with lightning. His ears rang from a deafening thunderclap, and the cheering went on.

"We spend more on cosmetics than education for our children. We spend more on perfumes than clean water. Our richest billionaire has more money than the poorest thirty million Americans. Both spouses work multiple jobs, but we're falling deeper into debt. Our health insurance is failing. They're replacing us with machines. We can't even afford a decent burial, and you don't care!"

She waited for the cheers to subside. "Well I care! We can stop this mess before it's too late, but I need your help. There are still good people in government who will rally with me to confront the President, the Congress, and their fat-cat puppeteers. But we can't do it without you!"

She hesitated, her voice drowned out by the cheers. Then the chant.

"Minton! Minton!"

She milked it before throwing in the clincher. "They call me an imposter, an egomaniac who's only in it for the short haul.

Well, my friends, the March primaries are over and we took eleven percent. So much for the short haul!"

The auditorium exploded with cheers.

"I've come home to my native Kansas and my beautiful Lawrence to ask your help in the days ahead and to make you a promise. I'm going to stay in this fight right up to the November election!" She raised her voice above the screaming crowd. "Yes, my friends, I'm in it for the long haul. With your help, we'll take our country back and set a new course for a better world. May God give us the strength and wisdom to pick up the torch and carry it to the White House!"

"I'll be damned." Perry collapsed against the tree and stared at the booming speakers.

Minton was nearly to her stretch limo when she noticed a man waving a small placard. Not very creative from the scribbling. She was about to duck into the limo when the words caught her eye—

I have something you need.

"Please, Ms. Minton. It's getting hard to keep them back."

She ignored her security agent's plea and stepped toward the man holding the placard. He extended it toward her and nodded at the small envelope clipped to the placard's lower corner.

She snatched the envelope just in time. The man was shoved backward and bullied away by two secret service agents.

Minton's limo was almost to the Eldridge Hotel when Jess Wilkin leaned toward her. "What was that about?"

Minton smiled at her campaign manager.

Wilkin nodded at the envelope. "We should check it."

Her smile became a grin. "Why … anthrax?"

Wilkin frowned. "You've entered dangerous ground, Claire. You're a celebrity now. Never know who's out there trying to strike you down."

She slipped the envelope into her jacket pocket. "I'll be careful."

Claire Minton didn't open the envelope until late that night. She'd retired to her penthouse suite at the Eldridge Hotel and was about to crawl into bed when she recalled the folded envelope in her suit jacket pocket. A quick trip to the closet and she was carrying the innocent looking white envelope to the bathroom sink.

She slipped on the mask and gloves provided by one of the secret service agents while recalling the agent's warning when she refused to hand over the envelope.

Open it under a faucet, Ms. Minton. Use this mask and gloves. Douse the envelope with cold water. Same for the contents. Then close the bathroom door and call us.

How can I read it?

Please understand, Ms. Minton. We prefer you let us handle it. This sort of thing is routine for us. We just want to screen it for germs. We won't read the contents. We're holding the man who gave it to you. He seems okay, but these people are well-trained in terror tactics. Please, Ms. Minton. Let us handle it—

She took a deep breath and ripped open the envelope, exposing a small business card, which dropped into the washbasin. A quick check of the torn envelope revealed nothing else. She stared at the name on the card—

PERRY AMBROSE
JOURNALIST

She picked up the white card and read the scribbled writing on the other side—

> Are you for real? If you are, I can give you the
> presidency. I have a video of the Tehran mutiny
> … Perry Ambrose (999-313-9499)

She read the card several times before slipping off the mask and gloves. Claire Minton would not sleep tonight.

CHAPTER 6

PANIC

It was a beautiful spring day in the nation's capital. The cherry trees were in full bloom, their brilliant reds and pinks luring the city's bureaucrats from their stuffy offices to a pleasant lunch in the warm sun. Plenty of grass and park benches to relax with friends while wolfing down a sandwich and beverage before marching back to the grind.

For the power brokers, it was more exotic with lunch at one of the swank restaurants lining Embassy Row, or perhaps a raw steak at the *Capital Grille*, or something more intoxicating at the *Monocle.*

For the nation's elected officials, a light workout and massage were in order at the Capitol's gym, followed by lunch in the congressional dining room, or maybe a touch of intrigue over martinis at *The Watergate* with its sweeping view of the Potomac.

Unfortunately, the President wasn't enjoying the sun today. He was seated at his desk in the oval office, his brown eyes glaring at the television screen beside Lincoln's portrait.

"Don't break it, sir. Our furniture budget's exhausted."

Jack Wiley waited for a response, but the President ignored him. "Mr. President?"

No response.

Wiley snatched the remote off the desk and pressed the "off" button.

"Hey, what are you doing?"

"It's over, sir. That's a commercial you're watching."

The President frowned and sank in his chair. He had spent the past hour watching a rerun of Claire Minton's impassioned speech at the University of Kansas. At one point, he turned off the volume to silence the cheers and applause while calling her every name in the book. Not very presidential for the nation's leader.

Wiley watched Lincoln's portrait slide over the darkened screen. He looked across the desk at his friend of thirty years while forcing a smile. "Well, at least she's declared herself. Now we have something to work with."

The President shook his head. "Damn her to hell."

"Yes, sir."

The President eyed his chief of staff. "Now what?"

Wiley leaned back in his chair. "We face facts. At the rate she's going, she'll take sixteen percent."

The President glared at him. "And I'll be history."

"Not necessarily."

The President's glare softened. "Come on, Jack. If she gets sixteen percent, three fourths of it comes from me. I'm only ahead of Hawley by four percent."

Wiley shrugged. "It's only April. She still has to get on the ballot in twenty states. That's not going to be easy. Lots of things can happen between now and November."

The President pushed out of his chair and turned to the three windows facing the south lawn. The only sound was the clock ticking on the mantle. He folded his arms and looked down.

"Nice picture."

"What?"

"You look like Kennedy in the missile crisis."

The President shook his head. "Not funny, Jack. If that bitch gives Hawley the election, everything we've built goes down the drain. She'll set the clock back fifty years."

The next five minutes were dead silent except for the ticking clock. The two men seemed frozen in time, the President standing at the window, his chief of staff gazing at him.

The President sighed and turned to his friend. "What about the debates?"

Wiley shrugged. "From the look of things, there will only be one and she'll be in it."

"There's no way to stop her?"

Wiley patted the desk. "Maybe we shouldn't try."

"Are you nuts? She'll eat me for lunch. You saw what she did to Clayborn."

Wiley shrugged. "This is different. She's in the big leagues now. The gloves are off."

The President waved his hand impatiently. "Cut the hyperbole. Do we have anything?"

Wiley smiled. "Remember Nixon?"

"What?"

"There are no recorders running, right?"

The President gave him a puzzled look. "Of course not."

Wiley leaned toward his boss. "I always figured Hawley would give us a good fight. Probably beat him fifty-two to forty-eight." He paused. "Minton changed that."

The President frowned. "That's it?"

"Not quite." Wiley looked his boss in the eye. "She might have an Achilles Heel."

The President's face brightened. "Yes?"

Wiley shook his head. "I'm still unclear, but if my sources come through, it could cost us some money."

"How much?"

"Three million. Maybe four."

The President dropped back in his chair. "For what?"

Wiley glanced at his watch. "We'd best not discuss it further."

The President glared at him. "What the hell do you mean? You're not going to leave me hanging?"

Wiley raised his hand in a reassuring gesture. "I'd better get going. Damn League of Women Voters is trying to push their way back into the debates. I have a meeting with their rep in five minutes. No sense ruffling any feathers." He turned for the door.

"Jack?"

"Yes, sir?"

"Give me something for god's sake."

Wiley smiled. "We want her in the debate, forked tongue and all. When the time is right, you'll crush her in front of the nation while Hawley looks on like a bump on a log, and we'll spend the next four years in this really nice room."

The President watched his chief of staff disappear through the oval office's double doors. He turned to the windows and stared at the south lawn.

CHAPTER 7

WARNED

"**Y**ou're free to go."

Perry squinted at the blue-suited man standing at the cell door. He recognized the man's gaunt face from last night's interrogation.

The man pulled the cell door open and dropped Perry's shoes on the cement floor. "Let's go."

Perry crawled off the cot and stretched his aching back. He slipped on his shoes and shuffled out of the cell into the shadowed corridor, his hand tucking in his denim shirt.

The man handed Perry a small plastic bag. He watched Perry pull out his cell phone and wallet before shaking the empty bag.

Perry held up the empty bag. "Where are my car keys?"

The man frowned. "You won't need them. We paid for your car rental and motel room."

"Paid?"

The man glared at him. "You only had twenty dollars in your wallet and your credit card was spent. Now let's go." He gripped Perry's arm and led him toward a metal door at the rear of the corridor.

Perry felt a chill. "You're secret service?"

"Not important."

"Show me your ID. I have a right."

"Shut up."

"Where are you taking me?"

"The bus station."

"Bus?"

The man reached into his pocket and handed Perry a white ticket. "One way to St. Louis."

Perry gawked at the ticket.

"Good place to consider your future. There's three hundred bucks in your wallet to cover your expenses while you figure things out." He jerked Perry's arm. "I suggest a new career."

The man led Perry through the jail's rear security door to a waiting black sedan. A light rain was falling and the morning sky was blanketed with gray clouds. The rain felt good on his face.

A second man stepped out of the sedan and opened the rear passenger door.

Perry froze. "Where's my camera?"

The blue-suited man nodded at the car. "Lying on the back seat with a nice clean memory."

Perry glared at him. "You scrubbed my pictures?"

The man shrugged. "What pictures?"

"Damn you!"

The blue-suited man seized Perry's collar and yanked him close until they were nose-to-nose. "I don't think you get it, Mr. Ambrose. Now listen good cause I'm not going to repeat myself. If you try to contact Claire Minton, you'll spend ten years in a maximum security prison." He gave Perry's collar a hard twist. "Clear?"

"Quite."

"Good, we have an understanding." The man released his death grip and retreated into the jail.

Perry felt a firm hand on his shoulder as the second man pressed him into the car. He slid across the rear seat beside his camera. It was eight a.m. in Lawrence, Kansas on Friday, April 17th, 2020.

CHAPTER 8

CONTACT

Perry's bus pulled into St. Louis' 13th Street terminal at four p.m. It was raining hard and there was talk of severe weather.

He grabbed a map at the terminal and checked out the nearest cheap motel. With three hundred bucks to his name, it was time to tighten the old belt.

Not the best location, but the *Hi-Huckleberry Hostel* had warm water and a bed. He grabbed a sandwich at a bar down the street and headed back to room "111" with a pint of *Jack Daniel's*.

Six months had passed since the incident in Tehran. In that time, Perry Ambrose had been blacklisted by every major news organization in the country. Of course, it was done with utmost subtlety to avoid legal reprisal, but the results were devastating.

The best Perry had managed was a series of contracted assignments with four *paparazzi* sleaze rags, with no money given until the required photographs and interviews were delivered to the editors.

Bad choice. In his four assignments, Perry had been paid once, and that was half the amount promised. The other three rags were still "reviewing" his submissions.

The deal with Caliento was Perry's first venture into the world of political action groups. Whoever Caliento represented, one thing was clear. Caliento's backers were out to nail Claire Minton. Had Perry succeeded in getting that interview with her, Caliento's technicians would have distorted her words and image into a hate commercial for release to prime time television. So much for 21st century journalism.

Perry went easy on the booze while watching the news on his favorite network. Josh Barden had become WNN's top news anchor after his stellar performance at the Iranian front. With the face and frame of a movie star, Barden had just published his best-selling book, *Memoirs from Hell,* a stirring account of the battle for Iran and Barden's front line heroics with our gallant troops.

Perry purchased Barden's five hundred-page masterpiece at an Indiana book store en route to Lawrence. He almost got a chance to confront Barden who was doing a signing at the store, but the famed reporter fled the store in a huff when he spotted his old friend glaring at him from the autograph line.

Perry took a swig of *Daniel's* while recalling the scene at *Higgin's Bookstore* when Barden ducked out the side door with his agent. Barden must have left fifty unsigned books on the signing table, with at least that many people standing in the autograph line. Perry could still see their stunned faces when Barden rushed out the door.

Perry took another swig, his eyes trained on the TV. Blast, all he needed was another five minutes. Just five more minutes and he would have been in Barden's face. Oh, what a story that would have made. Imagine the crowd's reaction when a stranger assailed Barden with battlefront questions the famed war correspondent couldn't answer, and for good reason.

Josh Barden was an imposter, a sycophant who replaced Perry when the military ran him out of Tehran six months ago.

Barden was in Iran only one month when WNN pulled him out after their successful performance in the sweeps. In his brief stay, Barden was sheltered in protected areas except when flown to battle locations for contrived interviews with the weary troops. There were even rumors of make-up artists smearing Barden's face with dirt and grease before the interviews were recorded. Must look like you just crawled out of a bloody firefight — right?

It worked like a charm. WNN cleaned up in the sweeps and Josh Barden rocketed up the promotional ladder until he was named WNN's top news anchor only two weeks ago. Hell of a ride for the ambitious dirt bag.

Perry took a long swig and pressed the remote's off button. The only sound was the rain spattering against the hotel room window. He put the bottle on the nightstand and stared at the ceiling.

You really messed up, chum. You're lying in a bloody flophouse with two hundred sixty-four bucks in your pocket, an exhausted credit card, a used bus ticket, and an empty camera. Seventeen years of hard work for nothing. So much for the great American dream.

He took a deep breath while recalling his dad's pub in Cardiff. Not the best locale, but it was honest work and a father's legacy to his son. He could still see the Welshman's scowl when he told his dad he was off to the states to seek fame and fortune.

His old man socked him pretty good when he pulled out the offer letter from the *Hartford Courant*. Bloody near took out the whole line of bar stools when he slammed into the counter.

Can't blame the old guy. Perry's dad was dead-set on passing the pub to his son. Instead, his namesake was headed for America with stars in his eyes and no money in his pocket, and of all things to become a parasite reporter who would make his money off the pain of others.

His dad cursed him plenty on that Sunday in Cardiff. Perry's ears still rang from the old man's tirade that America was a deteriorating nation that had seen its best days. That he was about to give up everything his father worked for to become a slander merchant.

And that final warning when his dad chugged his glass of bitters and shattered the empty glass on the counter.

You'll be back, Perry, but it'll be too late. Mark my words boy, you'll be back with your bloody tail between your legs, but it will be too bloody late!

He was nearly asleep when his cell phone went off. He fumbled with the ringing phone and dropped it on the floor. Hell with it, probably some bloke trying to collect a bill.

He tried to close his eyes but the bloody thing kept ringing.

"Blast." He rolled on his side and groped for the annoying phone. When he finally snatched it off the floor, the ringing had stopped.

He rolled on his back and placed the phone beside him. If the cursed thing went off again, he'd throw it at the wall. Nothing but bad luck anyhow. Like when Sid gave him the axe at WNN. Or when those sleaze-bag editors told him they were still reviewing his work. Or when Caliento chewed him out. Vermin! Dirtbags!

He felt his eyes closing. *Get some sleep, man. Tomorrow's another day. You'll figure something out. Just go to sleep. Nothing like beautiful ... numbing ... sleep...*

His eyes snapped open. The phone's message alert was chiming. He sat up and snatched the phone off the bed. "That's it, phone! Go to bloody hell!"

He was winding up to throw the phone at the wall when the speaker went off. He listened to the garbled message and slowly lowered his hand.

"If you're interested in picking up where you left off yesterday, I'll call back in five minutes."

Perry gazed at the phone. He didn't recognize the man's voice, but it might be one of Caliento's stooges trying to make amends.

Blast, no surprise there. Hard to find a washed-up reporter at the end of his rope. Maybe Caliento had reconsidered his ultimatum. After all, Minton would be in Denver next week. With a little luck, he could still get that interview.

He stared at the phone. *Blast, that's it. The bloke's reconsidered. Well, this time it'll cost him. No more promises, Mr. Caliento. This time we play it my way.*

The phone rang five minutes later and Perry Ambrose stepped into hell.

"Yeah?"

"Hello, Mr. Ambrose. Were you serious in that card?"

Perry looked down at the phone in shock.

"Mr. Ambrose?"

"I'm here."

"Were you serious about the video?"

Perry gripped the phone. "I have some questions."

"So do we. Where can we meet?"

Perry froze while recalling the agent's threat at the jail.

"Mr. Ambrose?"

"Who is this?"

"An interested party. Where are you?"

"St. Louis."

The caller hesitated. Perry could hear him mumbling to someone.

"Didn't expect that, Mr. Ambrose. It will take us a couple of hours to get there. Where are you staying?"

Perry hesitated. *It's a bloody setup! It's that goon at the jail checking on me. Watch it, Ambrose. One wrong word and you're toast!*

"Mr. Ambrose?"

Perry struggled for words. "Who are you?"

"Can't say."

Perry glanced at his watch. "Meet me at the thirteenth street Greyhound Terminal at midnight. Front entrance."

The man mumbled something in the background. "Can you get there without being spotted?"

"What?"

"We think you're being tracked, Mr. Ambrose. It's critical they don't trace you to us. Very bad if they do."

"Bad?"

"For you, Mr. Ambrose."

Perry felt a chill. "You're with Minton?"

"Can't say. Please answer my question."

"Not until you answer mine."

The man hesitated. "It's your decision, Mr. Ambrose. If you're not at the terminal at midnight, you'll never hear from me again."

Perry sighed. "You're not giving me much."

The man chuckled. "About the same as a card with a promise scribbled on it."

Perry hesitated. "I'll be there."

"One last thing. Before you come, check your clothes for a bug. It'll look like a pin or staple. Maybe a laundry tag or shirt button. If you see anything like a black dot or filament, rip if off and leave it behind. Check your personal possessions too.

Remove anything that looks out of place. It's imperative they don't trace you to us."

Perry slumped on the bed. "You know this is hard to take."

"Believe it! You're playing with fire."

Perry listened to the click. He lowered the phone and stared at the rain spattering against the window.

He spent the next hour probing his clothes for the phantom bug. Nothing so much as a loose hair. Even his underwear was free of anything resembling a transmission device.

At 10:45, he got desperate and started checking his camera. It would take an hour to reach the bus station on foot and he still hadn't figured how to pull that off.

He was detaching the lens assembly when he glanced at his watch. "Hell with it." He slipped on his sport jacket and jammed his wallet in the inside pocket. No time to check the camera. No time for anything. He reached in the closet and snatched his raincoat.

He was nearly out the door when he realized his shoes were still in the closet. He took a nervous breath and ran for the closet in his stocking feet.

He was slipping on his left shoe when it hit him. *My shoes! They took them from me during the interrogation.* He stared at the shoe. Was he going paranoid? *Put on the bloody shoe and get out of here.*

He started to slip on the shoe and froze. *What the hell is that bloody rattling?* Next thing he knew, he was yanking at the heel. He ran into the bathroom and slammed the shoe on the toilet bowl. *Again, dammit!* He slammed the heel against the porcelain and watched it fly into the bathtub.

What's wrong with you, Ambrose? You've lost your bloody marbles. That's your only pair of—

He stared at the exposed sole and the black, metallic object dangling from it. "Blast." He slumped against the toilet bowl and grasped the object in his hand.

The black sedan had been parked on 12th Street for three hours, its two bored occupants trying to stay awake while monitoring the *Huckleberry's* front entrance. A small black box rested on the console between them, its electronic map emitting a flashing red dot.

Agent Shackleton poked his snoring colleague. "You still with me?"

"Huh?"

Shackleton frowned. "Wake up."

Agent Kravetz yawned and reached for the cup of cold coffee on the dashboard. He took a sip and squinted at the tramp staggering through the *Huckleberry's* glass entrance doors.

Shackleton nodded at the tramp. "Bet they throw him out."

"Why?"

"They're full. The last guy barely got in. I saw him pleading with the desk manager."

Shackleton focused his night vision scope on the *Huckleberry's* glass doors. He couldn't see the tramp, but the desk manager was yelling at someone.

Kravetz stared at the glass doors. "Bet they keep him."

Shackleton gave his colleague a dirty look. "Never mind the tramp. How's our friend doing?"

Kravetz glanced at the screen. "No change. Take my word for it. Our man's fast asleep from that bottle of booze. He's not going anywhere." He squinted at his watch. "Another hour of this crap and I can see my wife and kids."

"Think they'll recognize you?"

"Not funny."

Shackleton lowered the scope. "I win."

"What?"

Shackleton nodded at the tramp backing out the front door. The poor creep yanked up his parka hood and headed north on 12th.

Kravetz stared at the staggering drunk. "One more hour. That's all I can take. Think of it, Phil. All that money out there and a flophouse turns away a homeless drunk. And I'm sitting here watching it like a sicko." He frowned. "Makes you want to get out."

Shackleton shook his head. "Better wait for that pension before you get brave. You don't want to end up like that poor dude."

The two agents watched the pathetic creature fade into the rain while their beeper continued its boring ritual. And while they sat in their car, a nameless tramp stretched out on the vacated bed in room "111", his hand clutching the fifty dollar bill Perry gave him for his parka and shoes.

The tramp swigged the half-empty pint of *Jack Daniel's* Perry included in the bargain. He smiled and looked down at his toes poking through his torn socks.

No need for shoes. Easy enough to pick up a pair at the shelter. Yeah, it felt real good snuggling in a warm bed on a night like this. And with a TV too.

The tramp drifted off to sleep, unaware of the broken shoe under his bed, and the tiny micro-transmitter lying beside it.

CHAPTER 9

KEY TO THE KINGDOM

The wind had picked up, driving the rain into his face. He turned away from the stinging drops and squinted at his watch. Ten minutes to midnight. The bus terminal was thirty minutes away.

"Blast!" He tightened his hood and ran up 12th toward Tucker Boulevard where a yellow taxi sat beneath a lamppost. The light had turned green for the oncoming traffic, but this was no time for caution. He sprinted off the curb and dodged two speeding cars.

"Watch it idiot! What the hell's wrong with you!"

He ignored their blaring horns and curses while charging across Tucker toward the parked taxi. He dodged a third car and ran alongside the taxi. The service light was off.

He crouched beside the driver's window and peered at the man asleep behind the wheel. He rapped on the window, but the driver didn't budge. An empty pint lay on the seat.

"Wake up, you bloody lush!" Perry yanked the door open and glared at the stunned driver.

"What the hell?" The driver leaned away from the opened door while fumbling for the wrench under his seat.

Perry leaned toward him. "I need a ride."

"Go to hell." The driver lifted the wrench and waved it at Perry. He tugged the door closed and started the engine. He was about to pull away when Perry flashed a twenty at the windshield. The driver eyed the twenty and gunned the engine.

The second twenty did the trick. The driver rolled down his window and poked his head into the rain. "Where to?"

"I need to make the Greyhound Terminal by midnight."

The driver snatched the twenties. "Get in."

Perry was halfway into the taxi when the driver floored the accelerator, sending his passenger sprawling across the rear seat.

"Hey, watch it!"

The driver glanced at the rear view mirror. "You want to get there or not?"

The yellow cab skidded away from the curb and raced up Tucker Boulevard toward North 13th Street and the Greyhound Terminal. Seven minutes later, it splashed to a stop at the terminal's deserted entrance.

The driver glanced at the mirror. "You got one minute."

Perry scrambled out the door onto the curb as the cab skidded away, spraying him with dirty water. He pulled up his hood and scanned the rainswept sidewalk. No one in sight except a homeless dude lying beside the terminal's glass entrance doors, his body covered with cardboard and plastic.

Perry eyed the glass doors through the rain pelting his face. *Inside, idiot. They won't be out here.*

"You him?"

Perry spun around and stared at the black SUV that had pulled up to the curb.

"Mr. Ambrose?"

Perry squinted at the shadow inside the opened window. If it was the creep from the jail, he was toast. He clenched his fists and nodded.

A hulking man in a raincoat stepped out of the SUV and waved him aboard. "Please hurry."

Perry shuffled toward the SUV and winced from a cold sensation. He looked down at his stocking feet. "Blast."

"What's wrong?"

"My bloody shoes are gone. I must have run out of them."

"Forget that." The man backed away and watched Perry crawl into the rear seat. It was three minutes past midnight.

Nothing was said for the next few minutes. They cut across town and hopped on the I-70 North. An airport sign flashed past Perry's window.

Perry leaned forward. "We're going to the airport?"

The man nodded. "We have a small plane waiting. Only an hour to Kansas City."

Perry glanced at the rain-streaked window. "We're flying in this?"

"We'll be fine, Mr. Ambrose." The man turned toward him. "You are Ambrose?"

Perry nodded. "What's left of him."

The man eyed Perry's parka and shoeless feet. "Looks like you've had a rough time."

Perry ignored him.

"Can I see your ID?"

"What?"

The man glared at him. "I need to be sure."

Perry slipped out his wallet and removed his driver's license. He handed it to the man and watched him give it the evil eye.

The man handed it back to him. "What's in the bag?"

Perry frowned and slipped the leather bag off his shoulder. He watched the man open it and study the camera.

The man held up the camera. "You used this in Tehran?"

Perry nodded.

The man closed the bag. "I'll give it back to you when we're done."

"No need for that. The bloody thing's empty."

"Just protocol. Nothing to worry about." The man placed the camera on the seat and stared at the windshield.

The SUV took the airport exit and veered toward the charter terminal. They were almost to the terminal when the driver pulled up to a guardhouse and extended a badge.

The guard made a quick phone call before waving them through the opened gate. Perry could see a *Gulfstream* parked on the rainswept tarmac.

They were about to board the plane when the hulk pulled out an electronic wand and ran it across Perry's body.

"What the bloody hell."

"Sorry, just proto—"

"Get on with it." Perry raised his arms in anger and looked up at the falling rain.

The flight took a bit longer with the bad weather. Perry stared at the flashing sky while his host sat across the aisle, his stubby fingers working a laptop computer. No words were spoken between the plane's only passengers.

The *Gulfstream* touched down at an airstrip near Kansas City and taxied to a stop beside a parked limo. Perry followed his host down the exit ramp and shuffled toward the limo in his shredded socks. He watched a uniformed chauffeur step out of the limo and open the rear passenger door. It had stopped raining.

Perry slid into the car's rear seat and stared at the attractive woman seated across from him.

"Mr. Ambrose?" Claire Minton leaned forward and extended her hand.

Perry clasped her hand.

She smiled and looked down at his torn socks. "Nice touch."

He frowned. "Not funny."

Her smile faded. "Were you serious about this?" She handed him the card.

Perry stared at his writing. He returned the card and looked her in the eye. "I'm very serious, but quite expensive."

She pulled an envelope from her jacket pocket. "A thousand dollars to show our intent." She leaned forward and placed the envelope on his seat. "We need to see what you have before we go further."

Perry looked down at the envelope.

"Something wrong?"

He sighed. "I don't quite know how to put this, but you're asking me to hand you the bloody key to the kingdom for a thousand dollars. How do I know you won't take the video and dump me?"

She shrugged. "If you have what you claim, it would be worth a great deal to me. I would be willing to offer you more than money."

"More?"

"I need a good press secretary, Mr. Ambrose. We have six months before the election. With your help, I can drum up enough votes to reach twenty percent. That means a lot of press coverage in the months ahead." She locked her blue eyes on him. "From what I know about your history at WNN, it would be a real slap in their face, if you get my drift."

Her words lingered. It sounded so damn good. A chance to get even with Carlton, Sid, and their pathetic excuse for an anchorman. He stared at the envelope.

"You okay, Mr. Ambrose?"

He frowned. "Why are you doing this?"

She shrugged. "To win."

"Win?"

"The presidency."

His frown deepened "You expect me to believe that?"

"Yes."

He shook his head. "I need to know the reason, Ms. Minton."

"I just gave it to you."

He leaned toward her. "No … the real reason. Negotiating leverage for your backers? Appointment to the winner's cabinet? Advance publicity for a book? Power trip?"

She smiled. "We don't have time for that. Maybe after you show us the video."

He eased back in the seat. "I need to know."

Her smile faded. "Why should it matter? You get what you want and I get what I want."

Perry felt a rush of anger. "You make it sound like I'm a bloody sleaze-bag looking for a handout. That this is all for money."

Her smile returned. "We do what we must."

He nodded, his black Welsh eyes gleaming. "Looks like you know everything about me."

"Pretty much."

"Then know this. Before I give you that video, I need to know what you stand for."

She shrugged. "Why?"

"If you're serious about using me, I need to believe in the cause. You should know that by now."

She leaned back in her seat and folded her arms. "You're a strange one, Mr. Ambrose. A real renegade. Had the world by the tail and lost it because you wanted that Pulitzer."

Perry's face reddened. "Fuck the bloody Pulitzer." He leaned closer. "It's more than money, Ms. Minton."

"Yes?"

Perry clenched his fists. "It turns me on. Makes me feel like I'm worth something. Like I'm throwing a punch for the underdogs." He paused to let his words sink in. "That's why I need to know about you." His black eyes burned into her. "If you're a fake, I just might go after you."

Her eyes flickered. "You're pushing, Mr. Ambrose. I suggest you shut up."

He dropped back in the seat. "I need to know."

She stared at him like a wolf eyeing its prey. The only sound was the air conditioning rushing through the vents. The door swung open.

"I'm sorry, Ms. Minton. There's another front coming in. If you need the plane—"

She turned toward the young man, her eyes aflame. "Shut the fucking door."

The stunned young man backed away and closed the door while Claire Minton composed herself. She locked her blue eyes on Perry and took a calming breath. "It's late, so I'll give you the thirty second version."

She hesitated. "I grew up on a farm outside Lawrence. My dad was a good farmer, but the government and their corporate backers didn't care. My dad lost his farm when I was twelve. It killed him and my mom. I saw my brother give up. He died of a drug overdose, and I—"

She looked down. "Real personal ... sorry."

Perry nodded.

She composed herself. "I had no options, so I joined the army after high school. They were good to me. Put me through college and taught me leadership."

Perry nodded at her ring. "War college?"

"Yes."

"Impressive."

She leaned forward and glared at him. "Everything has a price, Mr. Ambrose. I lost some good friends along the way. Saw the darker side of life. They gave me more medals than I deserved because I was a woman, but that didn't matter. I'd chuck them all if I could bring back my dead comrades." She took a deep breath. "I owe it to them and my family. If I can shake things up in that cesspool called DC, we might turn things around." She blinked a tear. "That's why I'm running."

Perry looked down at her clenched fists. "You know you can't win. They'll never let a third party run this country. Too much at stake."

She eased back in her seat and glanced at her watch. "You asked for a reason."

Perry sighed. "I need a couple days. You have my number." He started to open the door and felt her hand on his wrist.

"Do you believe me?"

Perry looked down at her hand. "I want to believe you, but it's not easy. Maybe I've seen too much."

Her grip tightened. "Then consider this. If I get twenty percent, both sides will be forced to cut deals for my support. That means ironclad guarantees to pull out of the Middle East … money that can be channeled into health care, education, and jobs. And that's just the beginning." She slid her hand off his wrist. "We don't have to win to get the job done. Don't fail me,

Mr. Ambrose. If you mean what you say about shaking those trees, we can do it together."

Perry frowned and opened the door. "Goodnight, Ms. Minton." He snatched the envelope and stepped out of the car.

She watched him climb aboard the *Gulfstream,* accompanied by her security man. It was four a.m. in Kansas City and she was dead tired. She pressed the intercom and watched the plane taxi toward the runway.

"Yes, Ms. Minton?"

"We can go, George."

"Yes, ma'am."

She was nearly asleep when her cell phone went off. "Yes?"

"He wants us to drop him in Indianapolis. Insists on working alone. I tried to explain the bodyguard is for his safety, but he got pretty upset."

She rubbed her tired eyes. "Give him some decent clothes and tail the hell out of him. Under no circumstances is he to be exposed."

"Yes, ma'am."

"Keep in touch." She pressed the off button and closed her eyes.

CHAPTER 10

SOUTH CENTRAL

Julia Kramer gripped the rusted iron railing and pulled herself up. She stood motionless on the tenement's front steps, her eyes trained on the uniformed soldier who had stepped out of the taxi.

She pressed her hand over her mouth and fought the tears. Yes … it was him. Maybe a little thin from the bad food and desert heat, but it was him.

The Marine slung his duffel bag over his shoulder and started toward the tenement. He paused and looked at the woman on the steps.

A year had passed since he last saw her. She looked the same except for a worry line or two. Even wore the same blue dress and white apron she'd worn on that sad day last year when he went off to war.

He rested his hand on the railing. "Hi, mom."

She sobbed and held out her arms. "Oh, my Terell. Praise the Lord, my Terell's come home."

He dropped the bag and rushed up the steps. They clung to each other and wept while the sun set over the tenements. Nothing was said. Nothing had to be. Terell Kramer was home.

That night, Julia phoned family and friends while boiling up enough food to feed an army. There would be time for tears, but first let's celebrate this wonderful day. With so many dead and dying, so many maimed and broken, the Lord had brought Julia Kramer's son home.

It was a night of gaiety and laughter at the Kramer's South Central LA apartment. Aunts, uncles, girl friends, and school chums showed up to welcome their Terell home. A few hood brothers even popped in for a quick toast to their old bud from the streets. "I'll be damned, that you Terell? What kinda suit is that? You look like a cop."

They danced and drank and ate and talked while Terell Kramer tried to grasp how much life could change in a few hours.

The hardest part was fielding the ignorant questions.

"Pretty rough, huh?"

"So, how we doin' over there?"

"Goin' back?"

He smiled and gave them canned replies while clutching the tattered card in his pocket.

The party broke a little after midnight. They could go on all night, but everyone could see mom Kramer and her son were exhausted. Besides, it was Saturday night in LA with places to go and people to see. So be well, brother Kramer. Maybe we'll see you at "Freddy's" tomorrow night. We'll have a couple of cold ones and talk about the war and our hell-raisin' times in the hood. And for god's sake, get out of that uniform before one of the brothers takes you for a cop and starts shootin'.

Julia was nearly asleep when her son plunked down on the couch beside her. The TV was tuned to WNN where the latest grim news was coming from the Middle East. Terell pressed the off button and stared at the blank screen.

"That you, son?"

He rolled his head to the side and smiled at his mom.

"Bet you're beat. I'll fix you some warm milk. Help you sleep."

He patted her hand. "I'm fine, mom. Get some sleep. I'll finish cleaning up."

She grasped his hand and smiled through her tears. "My boy's come home … my Terell … my son …"

He watched her eyes flutter and close. When he was sure she was asleep, he slipped his hand away and eased off the couch. He lifted the flannel comforter off the couch's arm and draped it over her. "Sleep well, mom." He leaned forward and kissed her on the forehead.

Terell didn't sleep much that night. Too many bad memories flaring up in his psyche. He saw the bombs light up the night sky and the tracers cross paths while streaming toward their targets. He heard the cries of dying men, women, and children, and felt the hot blasts against his face. And while he relived it, his hand clutched the tattered card.

Mom Kramer awakened the next morning to find her son sitting on the front steps in a T-shirt and jeans. He was just sitting there watching the morning traffic on Crenshaw.

"You okay, son?"

He looked up at her and smiled. "You're up early."

"I'm always up early." She sat on the steps and wrapped her arm around him. "You look awful tired."

He shrugged. "Guess I'm not used to the time change. I'll be okay in a couple days."

She looked at him with concerned eyes. "Maybe you should see a doc."

"I'm fine, mom." He patted her hand and stared at the passing cars.

They sat together looking at the cars before she finally forced out the words. "They say it's real bad over there."

He shrugged. "It's war."

"They say we're losin'."

He smiled. "Just a lot of news talk. Can't believe anyone these days."

She nodded and looked at the cars. "Lose anyone close?"

He shook his head. "No time to make friends. Better that way." He stood up and smoothed down his jeans. "Think I'll take a walk. Looks like a nice day."

She slapped her apron and stood up. "Good idea. I got some laundry, so leave out anything you need washed." She paused. "Some of the guys said you might be hangin' out with them tonight."

He shrugged. "Maybe a beer or two, but we can have dinner first. Maybe talk a little."

She didn't like the way he said it. She nodded and gripped his arm. "You plannin' to move on?"

He gave her a hug. "We'll talk later." He walked down the steps and headed up Crenshaw.

She pressed her hand against her mouth and watched him fade into the morning sunlight. God, how many times she'd watched him take that treacherous walk. The streets of Tehran might be deadly, but South Central wasn't far behind. They were finally reining in the gangs, but the root causes were still here.

She glared at the sunlit tenements. *Damn them in Washington. Thirty billion dollars wasted each month on a war against phantoms. Good money that could be used to rebuild our hood and give our young men hope. Heck, the only ones rakin' in that money are the rich corporate dudes on TV. Damn them. Damn them all!*

She caught herself and lowered her head. "Forgive me, Lord. Don't make me bitter. I have no right. You brought my boy home." She wiped away a tear and climbed the steps.

Terell turned right on Florence and headed toward Eddie Reefer's gas station where he worked as a mechanic before joining the army. He smiled to himself. Old Eddie had taught him everything about cars. Hard to tell if Eddie was blowing smoke last night, but if he really needed a mechanic, Terell was his man.

It was a beautiful spring morning in South Central. Terell soaked up the sun before stopping at his favorite deli to grab a sandwich and coffee from his old buddy, Billy Bob. They shared a few minutes together while Billy Bob ranted about his days in Vietnam.

Billy Bob changed the subject when he noticed Terell's face covered with sweat. He knew that pained look from his days in recovery. Best to let it go.

"Sandwich and coffee's on the house, brother. Welcome home." Billy Bob patted Terell's shoulder and watched his young friend walk out the door.

Terell was almost to Eddie's gas station when the nausea overtook him. He ducked into an alley and threw up, his body wrenching in pain. He staggered to the trashcans and dropped beside them, praying for the panic attack to pass.

He cowered beside the cans, his mind trapped in Tehran. He clutched the tattered card while three ghostlike faces flashed in his eyes.

Edgar, Joey, and Rafael were dead, taken out last week in a deadly crossfire near Isfahan. The official word was they walked into an insurgent trap, but Terell knew better.

He saw the tracers streak over his head while his three comrades lay dead beside him. He relived his desperate escape through the gully until he'd cleared the incoming fire. Then that quick look through his night-vision goggles at the insurgents poking the three corpses with their automatic weapons. He heard their voices in the darkness. They were speaking English!

He staggered to his feet and leaned against the brick wall. It was clear now. Six months ago, he and his three comrades witnessed a shooting that never happened. If word of the Tehran mutiny ever reached the press, it would unleash a wildfire that might bring the war to a grinding halt. No way could that be allowed. Too much money at stake. Too many powerful interests involved.

He rubbed the sweat off his face and felt the same icy chill he'd felt for the past six months. *I'm the last one, dammit. The last one who can speak out. The last one who can hurt them. They're gonna kill me for sure. No turning back now. It's them or me.*

His eyes filled with tears. *Oh, mom … I'm so sorry. I'm so damn sorry.*

He lifted the tattered card and stared at it—

PERRY AMBROSE
JOURNALIST

He squinted at the phone number. In the past six months, he must have read that number a thousand times while praying for his life and the lives of his three comrades.

They had been ordered to say nothing about the Tehran shootout under penalty of court-martial. The embedded reporter who interviewed them was removed from Iran and his recording confiscated. No word of the shootout had reached the media. No contact with embedded reporters had been allowed for six months while Terell Kramer and his three comrades were thrown into the worst battle conditions imaginable.

He crumpled the card in his fist. Well, the bastards finally did it. After six months of futile tries, the CIA had killed his three comrades, and now they were going to kill him. Last chance, man. Take the shot.

He groped for his cell phone and punched the phone number on the tattered card. Ten minutes later, he walked out of the alley and headed toward the Arco station on the corner. He was almost there when someone called his name.

"That you Terell?"

He squinted at the youthful face smiling at him from the SUV parked at the curb.

"It's Ralph. You don't remember me?"

"Who?" Terell walked toward the SUV.

The young man threw up his hands. "It's Ralph … I mean, you are Terell Kramer?"

"Yeah, but I—"

Terell never finished the sentence. The last thing he saw was the young man pointing the *Uzi*. He tried to run for cover, but the bullets ripped into him before he took a step. He collapsed on the sidewalk, his body spurting blood while stunned pedestrians ran for their lives. He was crawling toward the alley when the young man jumped out of the SUV and ran beside him, his *Uzi* pointed at Terell's head.

The young man squeezed the trigger and blew away Julia Kramer's son. He backed away and glared at the terrified onlookers, his *Uzi* pointed at the sky. "No strangers in my hood!" He fired a burst in the air and dived into the SUV.

The shaken witnesses watched the SUV skid away from the curb. They stared at the lifeless body lying in a pool of blood on the sidewalk. Slowly, deliberately they eased closer and bent over the man's blood-stained body.

An old man knelt beside the body. He gripped the young man's wrist and felt for a pulse while his friend looked on.

"Why you doin' that? Can't you see he's dead?"

"Never know." The old man backed away and snatched the cell phone from the dead man's bloody hand. "Better call the cops. Guess he won't mind me usin' his phone."

The old man's friend stared at the bloody scene. "I'll call the cops. That phone's no good with a bullet hole in it."

The SUV veered onto the Harbor Freeway and sped south toward the 405. The young assailant had already stripped off his sweatband, wig, and afro-shirt. The driver glanced at him and smiled. "A bit heavy with the sixties crap."

The young man ignored him while punching a security code into his cell phone. He pressed the phone against his ear and stared at the road.

A robotic voice crackled in his ear. "Authenticate."

The young man hesitated before speaking. "Romeo … Zebra … Alpha … Bravo … Two … Asterisk … Gamma."

"Cleared."

The young man sighed. "Target spotted and terminated. Returning to cleansing area."

"Well done, Gamma. Message confirmed."

The young man closed the cell phone and leaned back in the seat.

The driver glanced at him. "Who the hell was he?"

The young man shrugged "Not a clue. They said he was important." He closed his eyes and went to sleep.

59

DECLARATION

Claire Minton groped for the annoying phone and dragged it off the nightstand. She fumbled with it and pressed it against her ear.

"Sorry to pull you out of bed, but it's almost ten and we have a visitor coming."

She rolled on her back and stared at the Eldridge's ornate ceiling. "Ambrose?"

"No ... Seth Hawley."

"Who?" She sat up and clutched the phone.

"Yup ... in the flesh. He has a fund-raiser in Kansas City. Guess he wants to drop by to say hello."

She ruffled her hair in the nervous gesture she'd carried from childhood. "Are you nuts? I can't be seen with that red neck. He'll finish me."

"I don't think so."

She slammed her fist on the bed. "Tell him I'm sick or something."

"Too late. His staff already put out the word. The Eldridge will be swarming with reporters in an hour."

She glared at the receiver. "How could you do it, Jess? You'll destroy everything we've built. If that bastard shakes my hand in front of the press, I'm history."

"If you would just listen—"

Her fingers dug into the receiver. "No, you listen! Hawley can kill two birds with this move. He'll fire up the other side and make me look like a spoiler who's willing to trade votes for concessions. That's the kiss of death for a third party candidate. You should know that by now."

"Will you please calm down."

She collapsed on the pillow. "I don't believe this. You're the one person I'm supposed to trust."

His voice sharpened. "Enough, Claire. Shut up and listen."

Claire Minton's campaign manager spent the next two minutes explaining his reason for agreeing to the meeting. He waited until his final sentence to drop the bomb.

"No, it's too risky. We're not ready."

"I think we are."

She stared at the ceiling, trying to grasp his words.

"Claire?"

"You're insane."

"Insanity's good. Keeps the other side off balance."

She rubbed her tired eyes. "I need to think it through."

"No time for that. Trust me, Claire. This is your moment. Seize it. You'll never have a better chance."

She sat up and stared at the sunlight beaming through the parted drapes.

"You still there?"

"Yeah."

"Wear the black pin-stripe with the white blouse and red tie. Looks presidential."

She listened to the click and stared at the sunlight.

Seth Hawley's limo pulled up to the Eldridge Hotel at 11:15, accompanied by a cordon of wailing motorcycles. It took a few minutes for the police to push back the army of reporters and spectators.

Hawley looked particularly presidential when he stepped out of the limo with that gray hair, tanned face, and beaming smile. He wore a gray suit over a white shirt and red tie. Oh, how they loved those red power ties.

Governor Hawley waved to the cheering throng and dived into the sea of shouting reporters. He was nearly inside the Eldridge's revolving door when he suddenly stopped beside Kathyrn Greeley, WNN's top political reporter.

"Here to make a deal, Governor?"

Hawley laughed. "With Claire Minton? Now that would be the day. Let me tell you something, Ms. Greeley. Claire Minton has been through too much to succumb to a deal, as you phrase it. I'm just here to extend my congratulations for her stunning performance in the primaries."

"So, no deal?"

Hawley gave her an annoyed look and waved to the crowd before disappearing through the revolving door. He followed his screen of secret service agents to a waiting elevator and rode it to the penthouse.

Claire had never met Hawley face-to-face. The South Carolinian was a tall man at six foot three and in tip-top shape from a vegetarian diet and lots of running. She stepped into the living room from her study and extended her hand while flashing that curt smile she was known for. "Governor…"

Hawley clasped her hand. "Pleasure to meet you, Ms. Minton. Sorry to be so abrupt, but we were close by and I thought—"

"No problem, Governor. Wish I'd known earlier. We could have had breakfast together, or maybe a jog."

He smiled. "You're a runner too?"

"Got used to it in the army. Clears the head and all that." She gestured toward the study. "How about some coffee?"

He nodded and followed her through the opened double doors. She flashed a smile at their campaign managers and closed the double doors while two secret service agents took positions to either side.

The meeting lasted forty minutes. Hawley came out first, his face beaming. He said nothing while exiting the suite with his campaign manager. The two men stepped out of the hotel five minutes later amidst a crush of reporters.

"How did it go, Governor?"

"Anything positive, Governor?"

Hawley dodged the reporters while following the wedge of secret service agents to his waiting limousine. When he was clear of the crowd, he paused at the limousine for a final wave.

As if on cue, Kathryn Greeley broke through the security screen and rushed toward Hawley, her microphone extended. "Anything for WNN, Governor?"

He smiled at her. "Great meeting. We have much in common. We promised to meet again in the summer."

"Any agreement?"

Hawley patted Greeley's shoulder and ducked into the limousine which did an abrupt U-turn before racing away amidst a wail of motorcycle sirens.

The crowd had nearly dispersed when a straggler jumped on a bench, his finger pointed at the Eldridge's revolving door. "It's Minton!"

The reporters spun around and stampeded toward the Eldridge while shouting into their cell phones. Claire Minton had emerged from the hotel with her entourage.

Disregarding safety, she broke away from her bodyguards and charged into the mass of reporters and their waving microphones.

"How did it go, Claire?"

"Did he offer anything?"

Minton smiled while pressing toward the deserted bench. She rested her hand on a reporter's shoulder and stood on the bench. Jess Wilkin eased beside her grasping a wireless mike.

"What happened in there?"

"You two going it together?"

"What did he mean about meeting again in the summer?"

She snatched the mike and raised her hands for silence.

"Any deal, Ms. Minton?"

She waited until their cameras were whirring before speaking. "I thought it best to let you know where I stand." She hesitated while they snapped away. "I told Governor Hawley what I am about to tell you. Eleven percent of the American people are prepared to cast their vote for a drastic change in government. In the weeks ahead, I intend to build on that vote of confidence by declaring in the clearest of terms what I stand for."

"But the primaries are almost over. You only have sixty-seven committed delegates?"

She glared at the reporter. "I don't care about the primaries. I represent the American people and their new party, the Heartlanders."

She waited for the rush of whispers to subside. "We must end this unjust war and bring our brave men and women home. The corporate fat cats have made enough money off the blood of our GI's. Let's take that thirty billion dollars a month and direct it to our health care, education, and jobs. And to hell with the special interest groups and their puppets in our nation's capital!"

The stunned reporters looked over their shoulders where cheers had broken out from the people in the street. Some were even hanging out of the store and office windows, their fists raised in support of the woman standing on the bench.

Claire raised her clenched fist to acknowledge their cheers. With the cameras locked on her, she glared at the reporters and fired a final salvo.

"Do you hear them, Mr. President? That's the American people crying out for real change." She shook her fist in the air as the cheering grew louder. "And to Governor Hawley and his corporate backers, I will not deal with you! I'm not in this race to bargain! I'm in it to win!"

She shook her fist and stepped off the stool. The war had begun.

CHAPTER 12

INDIANAPOLIS

It was drizzling in Indianapolis, but Perry didn't notice. He'd spent the past hour sitting on a park bench below the two hundred eighty-four foot *Soldier's and Sailor's Monument* that marked the center of town.

He took the call from Terell Kramer an hour ago, a desperate plea for help from the last survivor of B Squad, 6th Platoon, Fox Company, 1st Battalion, 2nd Brigade, 3rd Marines, Operation Scorpion.

Not surprising he recognized Terell's voice. The young Marine was seared in his memory from countless viewings of the *Freedom Square* incident — the incident that never happened.

Perry stared at the monument while reliving the terrible moment he heard the shots and dived into the gutted house to see Makely and Hoffman blasting away at each other. He'd never forget the smell of cordite from their discharged weapons as the two men collapsed on the cement floor, blood spurting from their wounds, their hands clutching their smoking M27's.

He could still see the others trembling in the shadows, their desperate faces glaring at him when he knelt beside the bodies. And now, only one was left.

Edgar Ramirez, Joey Matafuco, and Rafael Cambria were dead. Their surviving comrade cowered in an alley in South Central, Los Angeles, his voice quivering while he poured out his soul to the only other living witness of that horrible October morning in Tehran's *Freedom Square.*

Perry looked down at his clenched fists. Time for a painful decision. Either heed the bloke's warning at the jail or ride it out with Minton. He smirked while patting the envelope in his pocket. How about neither. Just get on a plane to London and lie low in Cardiff. He'd be safe there and it would buy him time to think things out.

Besides, he could finally visit his father's grave to pay him the respect he deserved. Blast, that was the least he could do after crushing his father's dream.

His smirk faded. Careful, chum. The old man might crawl out of the ground to throw a punch at his pathetic son. Hmmm, maybe not such a good idea.

A church bell rang in the distance. It was high noon in Indianapolis. He took a deep breath and pushed off the bench. Sorry, Ambrose, two choices are all you get and the clock's ticking. He slung his camera bag over his shoulder and headed up Washington Street toward *Hoosier National's* main office.

He'd stopped in Indianapolis last week after closing things down in Chicago where he'd worked as a bartender for the past six months. Good pay with all the tips. Bloody cold in the winter, but he had a decent room in Old Town and the bar's owner gave him an occasional free meal.

Yes, Chicago had been a good place to get by while working on the side for the *Whisperer.* Too bad the bar burned down and the bloody sleaze rag screwed him.

So he hooked up with Caliento and headed for Lawrence, Kansas, and the interview with Claire Minton. But first, a quick stop in Indianapolis where he rented his third safe deposit box in six months.

It only took ten minutes to reach *Hoosier National,* but it took twenty more to reclaim the duplicate box key he'd left at the bank for safe-keeping. The security hassle was worth it considering what had happened to him in Lawrence. If those agents got their hands on that key, all would be lost.

After providing the required identification, signature, and fingerprint checks, Perry followed a vault attendant to safe deposit box 0947. A quick insertion of their duplicate keys and he was alone in one of the viewing rooms, his eyes focused on the opened box and its sole content, a paper sleeve containing a silver CD.

He lifted the CD out of the box while reliving the terrible moment he dived through the shattered doorway and saw the two men backing away from each other with their weapons raised. Then the flashes from their discharging M27's as they blasted away at each other before collapsing on the stone floor in twin pools of blood.

He could still feel the camera whirring in his hand when he recorded the nightmare unfolding in front of him. He would never forget the young man's frozen eyes peering at him from the floor, blood spurting from his forehead, his hands clutching his spent M27. Then the interviews with the four shaken men in the shadows.

Joey Matafuco was in the worst shape. When he tried to speak, he dropped on the floor and vomited. The audio picked up his cries of anguish while he puked his guts out.

Ramirez snapped next. He pushed away from the others and spewed out his hatred of the political scum that had sent him and his comrades to hell.

They don't give a damn about us. We're the expendables, the losers who can't find a job. So they pay us like mercenaries and send us here to kill a bunch of lunatics. And for what, dammit? To get oil and reconstruction contracts for their pig bosses.

Hell, I don't care what they do to me. Just send those pigs over here to see what it's like. I'll show the bastards. I'll show them all!

Perry was interviewing Terell Kramer when "A Squad" stormed into the room, led by their sergeant. The sergeant lunged at Perry's camera just as Perry pressed the transmit button. Too late, sergeant. Transmission complete…

Perry slipped the CD out of its paper sleeve and inserted it in the camera. Then came the partial download to the camera's flash memory. It only took a few seconds to make the abbreviated copy, but it was long enough to recall Sid Rubin's tirade when he broke the news about the video.

He frowned while reliving his trip back to the states after refusing to write the letter of apology. He would never forget his ten-second confrontation with Sid in WNN's executive conference room. Eleven words that ended his career—

You're fired, Perry. I never want to see your face again.

He returned the CD to its paper sleeve while recalling his final walk through WNN's lobby under security escort, the ultimate embarrassment for a dismissed employee — and that last look at WNN's massive world globe before taking a taxi to his Atlanta apartment.

He placed the CD in the box, his eyes flickering with anger. The fools thought they had things under control, but they'd ignored one minor technicality, a duplicate image transfer to his home computer when he got off the transmission to WNN.

He would never forget his mad dash up the steps to his apartment while praying they hadn't broken in. Then the frantic CD download and race to the first safe deposit box.

He walked out of the viewing room and returned the safe deposit box and key to the attendant.

"All done, sir?"

"Yes."

"Everything in order?"

"Yes, everything's peachy." Perry forced a smile and walked out of the vault.

He was barely out of the bank when his cell phone went off. He yanked it out of his jacket pocket and leaned against the building. "Yeah?"

"Haven't heard from you. Thought I'd better see how things are going?"

Perry recognized the voice, the same man who had contacted him in St. Louis.

"Everything okay?"

"Peachy."

"Good, I'll give you a call at six. We need to arrange your flight back here. Lots to do and the clock is ticking."

Perry listened to the click and glared at the street. They were watching him! Every move! Every breath!

He stuffed the phone in his pocket and headed for a bus that had pulled up to the corner. A pedestrian brushed past him. Then another. He leaned against a lamppost and scanned the street and buildings.

Where were they? In that car parked across the street? In one of those windows behind him? He felt a chill. *Get away, man! They're going to kill you!"*

He pushed through the crowd and climbed aboard the bus as the doors closed. The driver gave him a dirty look, but he didn't care. He dropped in a vacant seat and stared at the driver's reddened neck. His eye stung from a bead of sweat. He flicked it away and clutched the camera bag. *Think, Ambrose! Be the reporter you were!*

He recalled the scene at Mount Oread when Claire Minton snatched his envelope. Before that moment, he was a pariah, an outcast who had been severed from his career by powerful forces.

Now, he was caught in the middle of a political war every bit as deadly as the war overseas, and it was just beginning.

"Nice camera"

Perry glanced at the shabbily dressed man who had squeezed into the bus behind him. From the look of the man's black stocking cap, sweatshirt, and gang-banger shorts, he was Indianapolis' version of a Crip.

The man nodded at Perry's camera bag. "Want to sell it?"

Perry's face twisted in a frown. "No."

The man bent toward him. "Come on, bro. Everything has a price."

Perry ignored him.

The man's face reddened. "Who the hell do you think you are? Show some respect, scumbag!"

Perry looked away.

The man gripped his arm. "You need to learn some respect."

The bus eased to a stop. Perry saw the doors swing open. "Sorry, I'm having a bad day."

The man glared at him. "So, you're gonna give me the camera?"

No time to think. Move! Now! Perry lunged off the seat and felt the man's grip tighten.

"Bugger you!" Perry slammed his camera into the man's face and charged for the opened door. He heard people screaming behind him, but he never looked back. He bolted past the driver and ran into the street.

CHAPTER 13

CADMORE

Zach Kingston leaned back on his favorite park bench and watched Jack Wiley walk toward him from the Lincoln Memorial. It was a bright, sunny afternoon in DC and a great day for a stroll along the reflecting pool. As always, two secret service agents flanked Wiley, their eyes scanning the park and trees.

Wiley sat beside Kingston and gestured for his two agents to step away. He waited until they were out of earshot before speaking. "Well?"

Kingston looked down. "We lost him."

Wiley looked at him in shock.

"We think Minton's involved. Something to do with the envelope he passed her at the Lawrence rally."

Wiley slumped against the bench. "My god, Zach. Do you know what you're saying? If he has something and she gets it, we're screwed."

Kingston felt his skin crawl. "I have my best men on it. We'll get him."

Wiley glared at him. "For Christ's sake, you're the FBI Director. You have to give me more than that. There are other players involved. They're not going to be pleased."

Kingston's gut churned. "We'll get him, Jack. I'm committing to twenty-four hours."

Wiley pushed off the bench and looked down at the shaken FBI director. "We can't let him get to her."

"I understand."

"How's Emily and the boys?"

"What?"

Wiley's eyes locked on him. "Emily and the boys. I bet they're enjoying the fruits of your labor. Nice house, nice car, nice life. Let's keep it that way."

Kingston grimaced. He watched Wiley turn away and walk toward the memorial with his security escort. The message was loud and clear.

✳✳✳✳

Perry wiped the sweat off his face and looked down at the swirling water. A quick glance at his map confirmed he was standing on a viewing platform overlooking the White River.

He leaned against the metal railing and surveyed the surrounding park. He could see Purdue's Indianapolis campus through the trees, its buildings reflecting the sunlight breaking through the clouds. He buried his face in his arms and closed his eyes. The only sounds were the river and children playing.

Twenty minutes had passed since he fled the bus. He still saw the faces flashing past him when he raced down Pennsylvania Street and veered onto Capital Avenue with its welcome crowd of fans waiting to buy tickets for tonight's basketball game. He recalled immersing himself in the crowd before heading down Maryland Street toward the river.

He rubbed the sore spot on his arm where the scum had clawed him before he broke away. He didn't know much, but one thing was clear. That bloke was no gang-banger. Not with those lucid eyes and contrived rags. He'd seen his share of street people and could tell the difference between a gang-banger and hit man. The pig was a professional all the way, but who did he work for?

He stared at the river. Whoever it was, they were very good. It was only a matter of time before they nailed him.

He squinted at the buildings. He needed answers and time was short. If he could get into the university's library, he'd have access to every major database on the planet. *Worth a shot, chum. Go for it.* He pushed away from the railing and shuffled toward the park.

It took some effort to convince Purdue's security police that he was a freelance journalist doing research on the city's political history. Then came the ID check and insistence that he turn over his camera until exiting the library. He nearly freaked out, but time wasn't on his side. He removed the flash memory stick and checked his camera at the security desk.

His first searches revealed nothing but redundant blurbs about Claire Minton's miraculous rise to power. Then came more dated articles concerning Major Minton's daring helicopter rescue of seven trapped GI's during the fierce battle for Basra. The 2004 article included a photo of her being transported to the states after taking enemy rounds in both legs. He zoomed on her giving a thumbs-up to the media, her stretcher flanked by the seven rescued GI's.

Minton was only a first lieutenant in Gulf War One, but her exploits were equally impressive. He found three 1991 articles covering her reckless charge across a minefield in Al Jarah to rescue three wounded comrades in her recon squad. Her photo included the three rescued GI's and a caption that summed it up—

"No one left behind."

The library's grandfather clock was chiming four when he leaned back in the chair, his eyes gazing at the computer screen. He'd spent the past hour searching in vain for earlier articles concerning Claire Minton. His last search was halted when the screen alerted him that anything prior to 1990 was stored offline.

He rubbed his tired eyes. Only two hours before the promised phone call from Minton's lackey. Don't quit now, chum.

Working on instinct, he pushed out of the chair and headed for the library's front desk. He would spend the next two hours probing various offline CD's in search of any reference to Claire Minton.

The grandfather clock was chiming five when he spotted an obscure 1976 article in the *Kansas City Star* concerning Bobby Minton's drug death. The article mentioned Bobby's teen sister, Claire, as the only survivor of the Minton tragedy.

The article went on to highlight the suicide deaths of Claire's father and mother two years earlier. It cited the loss of their Lawrence farm to powerful agricultural interests after the devastating storms of 1974. At fourteen, with her brother dead, the court ordered that Claire Minton be admitted to the *Cadmore Home for Girls* to await adoption.

Perry stared at the screen while recalling their meeting at the airport. In her tirade, Claire hadn't mentioned being sent to an adoption home, but he did recall her tearing up when she described her brother's death. It might be nothing, but it seemed so bloody important to her message. Why leave it out? Embarrassment? Abuse? Anger?

He nodded to himself. Whatever the reason, he needed to fill in the years that transformed a fourteen-year-old orphaned girl to a war hero running for President of the United States.

He printed the article and jammed it in his jacket pocket with the two military articles he'd printed earlier. Adoptions weren't public record, but he might find a link that could flesh out her stay at *Cadmore.*

He was entering the *Cadmore* search request when his cell phone went off with an annoying ring. He snatched the phone out of his pocket and stormed out of the library amidst a gauntlet of dirty looks from the angry students.

He walked onto the quadrangle outside the library and pressed the phone against his ear. "Yeah?"

"You okay?"

He frowned. "You said six."

"We have problems. Get out of there now."

He clenched the phone. "I don't like being followed."

"It's for your own good."

"Cut the bloody hype. If you keep this up, it's no deal."

"Idiot, they're going to take you out!"

The words echoed in Perry's ears. *He's lying. Anything to get that video.*

"Ambrose?"

"Give me your number. I'll call you in the morning."

"No, you'll be dead by then!"

"Call me in the morning. I'm staying here tonight."

"Dammit, Ambrose, you don't know—"

He pressed the off button and jammed the phone in his pocket.

Perry spent a final exhaustive hour on the library's computer. He was about to give up when he spotted a lone article on *Cadmore*. Not much except a brief paragraph that *Cadmore* had burned down forty years ago, claiming the lives of four young women and the headmaster.

He pressed further and noticed a reference to the school's history which included the only surviving record of *Cadmore's* successful adoptions. He was nearly through the photos when he saw her.

He slumped in the chair and rubbed his tired eyes. *You're hallucinating. Need to clear your head. Maybe some fresh air will help.* He stood up and walked out of the library.

The brisk night air didn't help. He could barely keep his eyes open. *Hell with it. Come back in the morning after a good night's sleep. Got to stay on that Cadmore search.*

He dug his fingers into his pocket and pulled out his wallet. Plenty of money with that thousand from Minton. Just find the nearest hotel and call it a night. Maybe grab a pint of *Jack Daniel's* along the way. He stuffed the wallet in his pocket and walked toward the security gate. It only took a minute to reclaim his camera.

It was nearly seven and the streets were deserted, probably because everyone was watching the basketball game. He flipped up his jacket collar and headed east on Michigan.

He walked a block before buying a hot dog and coke from a street vendor. The dog was cold, but it tasted like a filet mignon. He plunked down on a nearby bench and devoured the dog like a starving animal.

He flung the wrapper in a trash basket and sipped the diluted coke while trying to piece together the past forty-eight hours, but his mind couldn't focus.

His eyes fluttered. *Worry about it tomorrow. You're bloody wasted.*

He was snapped from his stupor by the vibrating phone. He yanked it out of his pocket and pressed it against his ear.

"They're on you, Ambrose. They must have you bugged. We're trying to get to you. Give me some help for Christ's sake."

Perry frowned. "Call me in the morning."

"Are you nuts? Do you know what I'm saying?"

Perry gripped the phone and let out a tirade. "That's it! The bloody deal's off! Now leave me—" He froze and stared the head-lights coming at him.

"Ambrose, you've got to believe me. They're going to take you out!"

Perry stood up and backed away from the bench. The car ran up on the curb and skidded to a stop a few feet away.

Perry stared at the hulk stepping out of the car, the same banger who'd confronted him on the bus.

"Hi, bro. Guess we got some unfinished business."

The banger lunged at him, but Perry was already running toward the university's security gate. If he could get there before they caught him—

A second car pulled up on the curb and two men jumped out, blocking his path. He could hear the banger's footsteps clos-ing from behind. They were coming at him from both sides.

"Blast!" He veered into an alley and screamed into the phone. "Running into an alley near the university's main gate! They've got me cut off!"

The first bullet ricocheted off the bricks above his head. He dived behind some trash cans and clutched his camera bag. He could hear their footsteps echoing off the alley's brick walls.

A quick glance to his rear revealed a passage to the next street. A hundred foot run, but it was all he had.

He sprang to his feet and felt a bullet whine past his ear. Another bullet struck the bricks above him, but he never looked back. He skidded out of the alley and ran south on Indiana Avenue. He could hear the man's voice crackling on the phone.

"Almost there. Where are you?"

"I'm headed south on Indiana Avenue! I think—"

Perry never finished the sentence. The bullet caught him in the left arm, dropping him on the sidewalk while two shocked pedestrians ran for cover. He writhed in agony and listened to the gunshots coming from the alley, and everything went black.

CHAPTER 14

UNHOLY ALLIANCE

Zach Kingston clutched the phone. "How could you lose him? Two teams? Best technology in the world? Slam dunk, for god's sake!"

The caller hesitated. "They closed on us when we were about to take him. Too much shooting to get caught. Last thing we want is the local police getting involved."

Kingston squeezed the phone. "Who were they?"

The caller's voice trembled. "We think it's Minton, sir. We think he linked up with Minton's people and is with them now."

Kingston grimaced. "Evidence?"

"We tapped his cell phone. He took a 1912 call from a cell near the university. The caller ID belongs to one of Minton's security men."

Kingston pushed back from the desk and collapsed in his chair. "I have a question."

"Sir?"

"How can you know so much and fuck up so bad?"

The caller hesitated. "I'm sorry, sir. We didn't figure on Minton's people getting involved. We thought Ambrose was working alone."

Kingston rubbed his forehead. "Listen to me, Vern. You find that bastard and make him pay. We warned him. Now he's going to feel the heat."

"Yes, sir."

"I want his head on a platter. I don't care what it takes."

"Sir, maybe we should let him go."

Kingston's face reddened. "Let him what?"

"The man's delusional. We think he snapped after they dumped him at WNN. He's desperate, sir. Trying to make a name for himself."

"You think so?"

"Yes, sir."

Kingston slammed his fist on the desk. "Goddammit, Vern! What the hell are you smoking? The man's poison ... the fucking angel of death. If Minton's interested, he has something. Now get that scum under a lamp and squeeze the truth out of him. You have twenty-four hours ... twenty-four!"

"Yes, sir."

Kingston slammed the phone in its cradle and stared at the portrait on the wall, a powerful rendition of J. Edgar Hoover, famed director of the FBI. He shook his head and thought of his wife and kids, and Jack Wiley's words.

✶✶✶✶

"Can you hear me, Mr. Ambrose?"

Perry squinted at the blurred face peering down at him. He tried to sit up, but a sharp pain stopped him.

"Easy does it, Mr. Ambrose. Nice 1and easy."

Perry clutched his throbbing head. "What happened?"

"You took a nine millimeter round in the arm. Passed clean through except for nicking an artery. No bones broken, but you lost quite a bit of blood."

"Where am I?"

"In a safe place."

Perry tried to focus on the man's blurred face. He couldn't make out the features, but he recognized the voice.

"We got there just in time. They ran like rats when we opened up on them."

Perry looked at the man. "Who were they?"

"I think you know." The man leaned toward him. "You came close, Mr. Ambrose. Another few minutes and we would have lost you."

Perry's face twisted in a sneer. "What do you want, a bloody medal?"

The man smiled. "Good to see you haven't lost your charm." He straightened up and walked out of the room.

Perry heard voices and saw a familiar face step into view.

"Hello, Mr. Ambrose." Claire Minton slipped into the chair beside him. "How's the arm?"

"It hurts."

She patted his shoulder. "A few days rest and you'll be fine. Just don't put any stress on that arm. Your artery required some surgery."

Perry fought a wave of nausea. He took a deep breath and stared at the ceiling. "We're in Lawrence?"

She nodded. "Outside of town. A little place I use for a refuge. Close to home, and all that."

Perry grimaced. "How long was I out?"

"Two days. You had quite a fever."

Perry squinted at the sunlit window beyond his feet. Through the trees, he could see a lake and boathouse. The sky was blue and streaked with clouds.

He was lying on a four poster bed with the distinct odor of perfume. He sniffed the pillow and looked at her. "Yours?"

"When I'm here."

"Hope I didn't mess it up."

She smiled. "I'll send you the bill."

He looked at the ceiling. "I'm pretty weak. We should talk later."

Her smile faded. She leaned closer and locked those blue lasers on him. "I need to tell you something that will piss you off."

"Piss?"

She nodded. "Temptation is a powerful force. We checked your video. It's a little thin without the interviews."

Perry's eyes flashed. He tried to sit up, but froze from the pain. "You messed with my camera?"

She raised her hand. "Your camera's fine. In better shape than you."

He collapsed on the pillow, his eyes gazing at the ceiling.

She shook her head. "Without those interviews, the shootout looks staged. The President's people will pick it apart." She hesitated. "You have to do better than that."

He stared at the ceiling.

"Are you listening?"

Perry looked her in the eye. "I have questions. When they're answered, you'll get the other half."

"Other half?"

"You only saw half of the video."

Her eyes burned into him. "We have a deal, Mr. Ambrose. It doesn't include halves."

"I need to know about Cadmore."

She glared at him and held up the three bloodstained newspaper clippings. "We found these in your pocket. I could have saved you the trouble. They're public record. Even the one about my brother. More dirt to be thrown in my face."

Perry watched her crush the articles in her fist. "How long were you at Cadmore?"

She looked away. "Not now."

Perry forced a smile. "Seems like a good time."

She lowered her clenched fist and stared at the crumpled articles. "Four years."

"And?"

She glared at him. "They gave me a high school education and protected me from the perverts lined up at the door. Do I have to paint a picture?"

"Sorry, I need to know."

She sighed and leaned back in the chair. "I learned some hard truths at Cadmore. No one wants to adopt a fourteen-year-old girl except a pervert. I hated Cadmore, but the alternative was hell."

Perry noticed her eyes glistening. "When did you enlist?"

"Nineteen eighty. It was the only way out of that hole. I could learn a trade in the army. Maybe build a new life."

Perry nodded. "Sounds like it worked."

She ignored him. "After I got out, I went to the University of Kansas on the GI Bill. Re-enlisted after that and walked into Gulf One."

"Why re-enlist? You'd done your job."

She sighed. "I loved the army because it gave me the home I never had. I spent three years training on the Cobra assault helicopter. When the mess broke out in the Middle East, I went over.

We were all stoked about Iraq invading Kuwait. Saddam was the perfect villain and we needed to kick some ass after that mess in 'Nam."

"The record says you re-enlisted twice."

She nodded. "After Gulf One, I spent two years at the Army's War College and one more at the Rand Corporation. After that, I went back to Lawrence and entered local politics. Worked my way into the Kansas legislature. Also headed a volunteer organization to help our impoverished farmers." She shook her head. "Why am I going through all this? You can check it on the internet. It's public record."

Perry ignored her. "What about Gulf Two?"

She frowned. "They told me I was going to Afghanistan. I believed in the cause, a chance to strike back at the bastards that took out the twin towers." She looked him in the eye. "I lost friends in those towers, good friends that had helped me along the way. I owed it to them."

"There's no mention of you in Afghanistan."

Her frown deepened. "Never went. That jerk in the White House had his own agenda, so they sent me to Iraq."

"In 2004?"

She nodded. "You know the rest. Now it's your turn."

Perry looked at the ceiling. "You have enough to knock them on their heels. When they catch their breath, I'll give you the second half."

Her face reddened. "We had a deal!"

"We never discussed that."

She jabbed her finger at his chest. "You're asking me to stick out my neck for something that might not exist. What kind of fool do you take me for?"

Perry brushed her finger away. "Nothing foolish about it. We put our lives on the table ... yours and mine. The perfect deal."

Minton glared at him. "That's it?"

Perry hesitated. "Not quite. You owe me for the first video."

Her face reddened. "We owe you nothing until we have it all."

"One million for the first half and one million for the second."

"What!" Jess Wilkin rushed the bed, his face flushed.

"Seems fair."

Wilkin went ballistic. "That's blackmail! Is this the way you repay the people who saved your life?"

Perry locked his black Welsh eyes on Minton's campaign manager. "I risked my bloody life for that video. I'm offering you the presidency for two million dollars. If you don't want it, I'll check with Hawley's people."

Wilkin was about to explode when Minton stood up and pushed him back. She took a deep breath and looked down at the reporter she had come to hate. "Why should I trust you? A vagrant who can't get a decent job in his own profession? A Judas who will sell his soul to the highest bidder?"

Perry smiled. "You don't have to trust me. It's the perfect deal. An unholy alliance between thieves. Remember what you said in the car? I get what I want and you get what you want."

She pointed a trembling finger at him. "I was willing to cut you in. To let you join the battle. Instead, you turn out to be a Judas Goat."

Perry looked at the window. His ears were ringing. Everything was spinning. A dark veil closed over his eyes. "If I'm Judas ... the match is perfect. He was Christ's friend ... wasn't he?"

She watched him drop off to sleep while cursing his name.

CHAPTER 15

CHARLESTON

All warriors need a refuge from their battles, a special place where they can clear their heads while planning their next move. For Claire Minton, it was a secluded lodge on Warnock Lake. For Seth Hawley, a restored plantation house in Charleston's White Point Gardens, complete with an unobstructed view of Charleston Harbor and Fort Sumter, a powerful reminder of his southern heritage.

The past month had been a nightmare for the governor. Instead of gaining ground on the President, Hawley had suffered a humiliating defeat in the primaries. With Claire Minton closing on him, the governor's political career was in jeopardy.

Hawley had received the phone call yesterday while licking his wounds at the governor's mansion in Columbia, an urgent request to meet with his backers in Charleston, an ominous sign in the midst of a campaign.

He recalled looking up at the bronze stars on the state house roof when his limousine pulled out of Columbia. Each gleaming star marked an artillery hit from Sherman's guns when the hated general shelled the venerable building on his march to Atlanta. A rather appropriate symbol for a governor under siege.

"They're here, Governor."

Hawley looked at the man standing at the door. "Thank you, John. I'll be down in a minute." He put down his pen and stared at the piece of paper lying in front of him.

It had taken only a few minutes to draft the speech, a simple one-page declaration that he was withdrawing his candidacy for the good of the nation and party. That the deteriorating Middle East war and economic recession had become too critical to risk defeat against the standing President.

> *Therefore, for the good of our country and its people, I am withdrawing my candidacy and asking my supporters to throw their full weight behind the next President of the United States…*

Hawley stared at the blank space he had left for his successor's name. He leaned back in the chair and looked at the sunlit harbor.

Would they pick Santene, a fellow gentleman of the south whose only flaw was his youth?

Hawley sighed. Santene was a good man, but his nomination would be a tragic mistake. The young senator was too green to deal with the crisis at hand. His indecisiveness would prolong the Middle East conflict to the detriment of the nation and its people.

Hawley stroked his chin. The only other legitimate candidate was Senator Kasden, a good choice except for one fatal flaw. Kasden was a loose cannon who could never accept defeat. If pressed to the wall by the media and war weary public, the hawkish senator might order an immediate withdrawal before launching missiles at every major city in Iran, Afghanistan, and Syria.

Hawley frowned while contemplating the bible on his desk. He stood up and slipped the paper in his jacket pocket. He would listen to their words and pull out the paper at the appropriate time. A few pats on the back for his unselfishness and it would be done. He would spend the rest of the year campaigning for their chosen candidate while completing his term as governor. After that, he would bid a fond farewell to the political arena and retire to private life. He smiled and stared at Fort Sumter. "And go fishing."

He was opening the study door when he glanced at the mirror above the fireplace. He smiled at the handsome face looking back at him. "Well, old man ... you gave it your best shot. Their loss, Mr. President. So be it." He stepped through the door and headed for the downstairs conference room.

The four men sat at a chestnut conference table with a breathtaking view of the harbor and fortress. The grandfather clock in the corner was chiming three when Hawley stepped into the room.

"Good afternoon, gentlemen." Hawley flashed a smile at the four men who rose from their chairs and stepped toward him for the customary handshakes.

After exchanging pleasantries, Hawley gestured for them to return to their chairs while taking his position at the head of the oval table. Everyone remained standing while the servants placed tall glasses of mint juleps on the table before withdrawing from the room.

Hawley waited until the double doors closed before snatching his mint julep and extending it to his guests. "To good health, good friends, and good liquor." He raised his glass in a toast and took a hearty sip.

Hawley put down his drink and gestured for his guests to be seated. He sat down and rested his hands on the table. "Well, what do we have?"

Lucas Mansted rose to his feet and looked Hawley in the eye. "I won't mince words, Seth. It doesn't look good. We're at twenty-four percent and dropping." He paused and scanned the others. "We thought it would be a good idea to put our heads together and come up with something."

Hawley smiled at his friend of twenty years. "Of course, Luke. Whatever you want." He watched his friend sit down. "It's been a hell of a month."

Sam Callup leaned toward him. "How do you feel, Seth?"

Hawley knew those words too well. He leaned back in his chair and stared at the most powerful oil man on earth. "I take it you're not pleased."

Callup shrugged. "It's business, Seth. The idea was to deflect public attention from our interests over there. If we could unseat the President with the right man, we could ensure an orderly withdrawal of our forces without compromising our position."

Hawley nodded while concealing his anger. *What a line of bull. All Callup wants is four more years of war to fatten his swollen pockets from the oil rigs he's replacing over there. Just keep blowing up those rigs and bringing in replacements. Hell of a way to make a profit.*

Cedric Marshall leaned forward and smiled. "Please understand what we mean, Seth. If the President wins the election, he'll be impeached within two years. That's not good for a country in the middle of a war. By replacing him, we buy time to stabilize things while we try to dig out of this recession."

Hawley nodded. *More bull. Marshall just wants to keep pumping arms, ammo, and equipment to the military. Need a good war for that. He doesn't give a damn about the recession or this country.*

Marshall eased back in his chair. The room fell silent as the three men looked down at the table, waiting for their words to sink in.

Hawley reached into his jacket pocket and pulled out the paper. He unfolded it and handed it to Bradley Forester who was seated on his left. Forester had spearheaded the public relations campaign from day one. He read the brief statement and frowned before passing it down the line.

Marshall was the last to read it. He nodded while heaving a deep, contrived sigh. "Well … if you think it best." He placed the paper on the table in front of Hawley.

"Wait."

Hawley was reaching for the paper when Forester spoke up. All eyes focused on the angry campaign manager.

Forester nodded at the paper. "You're forgetting something, gentlemen. If our friend withdraws, expect an immediate surge in Minton's popularity."

Marshall shrugged. "Hell, that won't last long. Once we throw our support behind Santene, we'll gobble her up and then some."

Hawley stared at Marshall. *My god, they're going to back Santene. The economy will collapse while they hoard the spoils of war.* He felt a trickle of perspiration on his neck. *Lord, that's what they planned for me. They push me into the presidency with promises that I'll end the war. Then business as usual while four years pass, twenty thousand more die, and the richest nation on earth becomes a third world economy.*

Hawley was jolted from his thoughts by Forester's sharp retort.

"You're wrong, Mr. Marshall."

Marshall glared at Forester. "How dare you. You work for us, remember?"

Forester rose to his feet. "That's right, and that's why you should listen."

The two men stared at each other before Mansted broke the silence. He leaned forward and looked at Forester. "Get to it, Brad."

Forester opened a folder lying on the table. He lifted out a paper and held it in the air. "These statistics are accurate, gentlemen. Minton's currently at eleven percent and dropping. If Seth withdraws, she'll shoot up to fifteen percent within a week."

Forester hesitated while eyeing the others. "Minton's team is very good. They won't pass up an opportunity to cash in on a favorable jump in the polls. She'll be on every talk show and media event possible, firing her salvos about the war and economy." He glanced at the paper. "I'm projecting her at eighteen percent within thirty days of Seth's withdrawal."

Marshall shrugged. "That's it?"

Forester put down the paper. "Not quite. My sources are on to something in her camp, but we're not sure what it is."

Marshall threw up his hands in frustration. "What the hell does that mean?"

Forester shook his head. "We think she has some kind of smoking gun. We're working on it, but until we know more, I urge you gentlemen to hold back on Seth's withdrawal.

Hawley couldn't take anymore. He stood up and glared at Forester. "You expect me to go through the motions while you search for this smoking gun? What if she has nothing? We could lose valuable weeks." He shook his head. "No, Brad. Let's finish this and bring in Santene."

Forester took a calming breath while eyeing his comrade of six months. "I know how you feel. It's not easy to walk away from the battle, much less faking it for a few weeks." Forester looked at the others. "If I'm wrong, I'll be happy to step aside and refund my fee."

Mansted raised his hand. "Now wait a minute, Brad. There's nothing personal about this. We don't want you stepping aside."

Forester sighed. "I don't think you gentlemen understand. If we lose and the President stays in office, it won't matter whether he's impeached. You'll still collect a healthy sum for the next two years. If we win, all the better." He jabbed his finger at the paper on the desk. "But what if I'm right about Minton's smoking gun?" He looked them in the eye. "She'll have thirty percent by November."

Hawley sank in his chair and stared at the three stunned faces. He looked at Forester while trying to digest his words. "Thirty?"

Forester nodded. "The nation's looking for real change, gentlemen. If Claire Minton takes thirty percent, they might get it."

Callup leaned forward. "Are you saying she could win?"

Forester slipped the paper in the folder. "Yes, and if she does, you gentlemen can forget your overseas oil profits, arms sales, and building contracts." He dropped in his chair. "We have trouble, gentlemen. More than you know."

CHAPTER 16

FIRST VOLLEY

Perry put down the *Los Angeles Times* and squinted at the sun setting over the Pacific. A hundred feet below him, a marimba band broke into a medley of tropical tunes for the beautiful people sprawled on the deck chairs beside the swimming pool.

The breeze carried a pleasant odor of barbecued beef and fish from the grill beside the pool. Through the marimba music, he could hear boisterous laughter coming from the patrons gathered at the outdoor bar.

He glanced at his watch. Almost eight. Time for the fireworks. He pushed off the lounge chair and took a last look at the darkening California sky before stepping through the balcony doors into his plush living room.

It was Wednesday, July 1st, and the media was pouring into the *Ritz Carlton* for Claire Minton's unexpected press conference. Unlike Minton's previous press conferences, no advanced briefing had been distributed to the media. The only clue to tonight's nationally televised press conference was Jess Wilkin's warning that his candidate was about to drop a blockbuster.

Perry sat on the couch and snatched the remote off the cocktail table. He leaned back on the silk cushions and gazed at the living room's vaulted ceiling.

Amazing how things had changed in two months. From a washed up reporter in tattered street clothes, he'd morphed into a high-class dude in a *Tommy Bahama* shirt, tropical slacks, and leather sandals.

He raised his wine glass to the television. "Hell, Ambrose, all you needed was a bloody angel." He cracked a smile. "Here's to you, Queen Minton." He gulped down the wine and listened to the mantle clock chime eight p.m.

They'd checked him into the *Ritz Carlton* with the usual warning that his bodyguards would only be a heartbeat away. No way were they going to let him out of their sight, not with Claire Minton's political career on the line.

In two months, Perry had been jerked from Manhattan's *Hotel Pierre* to Los Angeles' *Ritz Carlton*, and between them, to nine other swank hotels in the path of Claire Minton's relentless westward march. In that time, Perry had seen little of her except for an unexpected encounter after last night's fund raiser at the University of Arizona where his angel spewed out her message of hope to ten thousand roaring supporters.

He poured another glass of wine while recalling the stressed bodyguard inadvertently jamming him into Minton's limo as they pulled away from the mob scene outside the university's auditorium, an obvious error that probably cost the poor bloke his job.

Clearly displeased with Perry's unexpected intrusion, Minton gave him the evil eye when he introduced himself to the man seated beside her.

Perry wouldn't easily forget the man's piercing green eyes and pony-tailed white hair. The man appeared in his seventies with a handsome, tanned face that showed the wrinkles of hard times. He was a man of few words with a polite, *Pleased to meet you,* when they shook hands and an abrupt, *Have a good evening,* when they exited the limo at the hotel's security entrance.

When Perry asked the man's name, he was rewarded with a blank stare and blatant lie.

Smith … Jonathan Smith.

Perry looked down at his right hand while recalling the man's powerful grip. He remembered Minton's song and dance when he tried to corner her on the plane to California.

Interesting chap in the car last night.

Who?

The white haired bloke in the limo. The one who didn't talk much.

Oh, him. Yes, he's a quiet sort. You wouldn't know him. Works in the background. One of many.

You said his name was Smith?

Not important. See you in few days, Perry. You'll be staying at the Ritz Carlton. First class all the way. Enjoy.

Perry pressed the remote and watched the seventy inch television screen come alive with an attractive woman in a business suit and sunglasses hyping the latest foreign sports car. Not surprising she resembled Claire Minton with that short black hair and decisive tone.

Perry smiled as the woman climbed into the sports car and gave a parting wave accompanied by the words, "See you in November."

He broke out laughing as the car accelerated across the desert toward a line of sunlit mountains, the perfect segue for the press conference.

The camera focused on a blue-curtained stage with an empty lectern at the center. A large projection screen was neatly positioned beside the lectern. The only sound was the mumble of reporters huddled below the stage.

Perry's smile twisted into a sneer as he lifted his glass a second time. "Here's to you, Queen Minton. Let the bloody show begin."

****

The President looked across the desk at his chief of staff. "What does it mean, Jack? What the hell is she up to?"

Jack Wiley wasn't listening. His eyes were focused on the screen.

The President leaned toward him. "Jack?"

Wiley shook his head. "I don't like it. Something's coming."

The press room reverberated with whispers and clicking cameras as Claire Minton stepped through the curtains and took her position at the lectern. She wore her familiar black pin-stripe suit. The flashing smile was absent.

Minton eyed the reporters for a moment before raising her hands for silence. She waited until the room was still before speaking.

"I need to show you something that has come to my attention. It's a video that sums up the situation in Iran. It's a little dated, eight months to be exact. That's because the Pentagon and President have done everything in their power to keep it from you."

She turned toward a frozen picture on the four-by-six-foot projection screen. "The man on the left is Sergeant Waldo Hoffman. The man on the right is Corporal John Makely. The four men in the shadows are Privates Terell Kramer, Edgar Ramirez, Joey Matafuco, and Rafael Cambria."

She paused while eyeing the reporters. "The incident took place at 0655 hours on October 27th, eight months ago, in a bunker outside Tehran's Freedom Square. It was photographed by an embedded reporter who was subsequently kicked out of Iran."

She looked at the stunned reporters. "Yes … one of your own was kicked out for trying to get the truth to the American people. Well, it took some time, but here's his tragic video of those six men."

The President stared at the screen in disbelief. He collapsed in his chair while watching the horror of discharging M27's and dying men. Wiley poured a scotch and gulped it down. He rested his arm on the desk and watched the camera close on the blood spattered bodies and smoking M27's.

The President looked at his chief-of-staff with desperate eyes. "How, Jack? What the hell happened? You said we were covered?"

Wiley couldn't speak. He stared at the screen and listened to candidate Minton's shaking voice.

"I've been there, my fellow citizens. In the trenches and blood. I've felt the heat of the explosions. My ears still ring with the screams of dying men, women, and children."

She looked down. "It's hell, my fellow citizens. Hell on earth."

There was no sound except the whirring cameras. All eyes were focused on the shaken woman at the lectern.

"In war, there is always tragedy. Soldiers are sometimes killed by friendly fire." She pointed a trembling finger at the frozen screen. "But this is beyond that. An army revolting against its commander in chief. I know for a fact that dozens of similar incidents have occurred in Iran, Afghanistan, and Syria. And they're increasing."

Minton blinked away a tear. "In the name of god, please stop this war. I don't care what happens to me, but please bring our brave men and women home before it's too late."

She took a last look at the frozen picture. "For them, my fellow citizens. For our brothers and sisters … my comrades at arms."

Wiley watched her step away from the lectern while the camera zoomed on the frozen picture of dead men. He lowered his head and took a deep breath. "Mr. President, I need that three million now."

****

Sid Rubin was seated at the *Horticulture Bar* in downtown Atlanta when Minton spoke. He was lifting his third white wine when the video hit him between the eyes. He lowered his glass and stared at the television screen in shock.

He wasn't the only one. Fred Millingkamp sat beside him, his eyes staring at the screen, his body frozen. It wasn't possible. Nothing had been left to chance.

Millingkamp looked down at his trembling hands while recalling his meticulous handling of the Ambrose situation.

It was Millingkamp who recommended Josh Barden after they removed Perry Ambrose eight months ago. When Carlton and Rubin gave him the okay, Millingkamp took charge of sterilizing the mess from Perry's dismissal to the video's confiscation and handoff to the Pentagon. His final act was to purge the video from WNN's database while ensuring no copies had been made.

Rubin looked at Millingkamp with fire in his eyes. "What the hell went wrong?"

Millingkamp shook his head. "I don't know, Sid. Maybe the military missed a memory stick or CD on his person. They were pretty shook and Perry is damn shrewd."

Rubin plunked down thirty bucks and stood up, his eyes locked on Millingkamp. "We're in deep shit, Fred. We'll be lucky to have jobs tomorrow."

Millingkamp looked at him with desperate eyes. "Where are you going?"

"I better call Franklin. He'll want to know what happened."

Millingkamp couldn't speak. His brilliant twelve year career flashed through his mind. Francine and the kids. Their three million dollar home. The golf membership and sailboat, and all those fucking bills!

Rubin started to turn away and hesitated. "We should've killed the bastard." He walked out of the bar and left Millingkamp sitting on the stool, his eyes fixed on the television.

CHAPTER 17

HELL ON EARTH

General Malcolm Taylor burst out of his quarters into the dimly lit tunnel, accompanied by four Special Forces guards. It would take him and his escort two minutes to reach CENTCOM's command center despite their rapid pace.

Taylor adjusted his battle helmet and stared at the string of overhead lamps stretching down the tunnel. After spending two months in the renovated mountain complex, he was still awed by its size.

The complex had been given the code name *Atlantis* during last year's invasion. If the Iranians had nukes and missiles, they would surely be stored in the vast labyrinth of tunnels in the Elburz Mountains north of Tehran.

Using classified satellite technology, *Atlantis'* location had been pinpointed in the days preceding the invasion. The complex was taken in the first twenty-four hours of battle despite heavy resistance by the Iranian army. To their dismay, the coalition forces found no weapons of mass destruction, leading to rumors that *Atlantis* was a decoy designed to draw the invaders away from the true nuclear sites, which were nearing launch readiness.

Taylor had spent the past two months inside *Atlantis* under strict orders to remain there while the insurgents intensified their suicide attacks and ambushes in a desperate effort to break the coalition's will, and it appeared to be having some effect. At a recent briefing, the frustrated general boldly remarked that it seemed strange for an invading force to be holed up like rats while their enemy stalked them.

It was Thursday, July 2nd, and the news was not good. The first message had come in at 0524 hours, followed by three others at 0547, 0601, and 0614. Coordinated insurgent attacks were underway in Arak, Kermanshah, Isfahan, and Qom. Coalition forces were under heavy bombardment from weapons not previously encountered. The insurgents were attacking in numbers beyond anything anticipated, launching fanatic human wave thrusts into the coalition's so-called safe zones. Insurgent losses were heavy, but they didn't seem to care. With embedded reporters at the front lines, word would soon reach the global media that chaos had broken out in Iran.

Lieutenant General Morell snapped to attention when Taylor stormed into the communications center. Per protocol, the technicians remained seated at their consoles while maintaining contact with the field commanders.

Taylor returned Morell's salute and gestured for his number-two man to join him in one of the small offices adjacent to the cavernous room. Before closing the door, Taylor glared at the four video screens on the wall, three of them flashing airborne shots of the battles. He glanced at Morell. "What happened to screen four?"

Morell frowned. "One of their hand-helds took out the drone. We're sending another up, but it'll take twenty minutes before we re-establish video with Arak." He reached for a speaker on the table and pressed a button. The small room came alive with automatic weapons fire and the cries of desperate men.

Taylor sat down and stared at the speaker while listening to the crackling exchange between CENTCOM and Major Dorman at the Arak oil complex.

"Please repeat, Major. You're breaking up."

"We have incoming missiles. Looks like ground launched." The speaker echoed with explosions.

"Can you read me, Major?"

"I'm pulling back. Heavy explosions at the refineries. Their first wave of missiles took out our front line."

"We need coordinates, Major."

"They're launching the missiles from the southwest, two-four-zero degrees. Range unknown, but my guess is the Zagros Mountains."

"Zagros? That's fifty miles, Major."

"Guess so."

"Clear, Major. Will request air support. Can you hold."

"Everyone's falling back. Can't re-establish defensive perimeter. They're coming through the town in suicide waves. The more we kill, the more they come. I—"

Taylor clenched his fist and listened to the high-pitched whine coming from the speaker.

"Are you there, Major? Please advise."

The whine faded to static.

Morell looked at his commander. "Requesting Apache One, sir."

Taylor nodded, his eyes fixed on the speaker. He listened to Morell press the intercom button while giving the order to send in the *Apaches.*

Morell pushed back from the intercom. "Order given, sir."

Taylor frowned. "What about the other attacks?"

"We're holding so far, but these new missiles are a trump card." Morell shook his head. "Given their numbers and fire-power, the ghosts will overwhelm us without close air support."

Taylor nodded. "Put Apache Two, Three, and Four on full alert. We'll see what happens in Arak before sending them in."

"Yes, sir."

Taylor pushed out of his chair. "Thank you, Farley. Let me know when Apache One engages the enemy." He patted Morell's shoulder and left the room.

****

Doug Kinkaid was out cold when a sharp voice snapped his eyes open. He sat up and squinted at the sunlight streaming through the gun ports in the sandbags.

"Scramble Apache One! Scramble One!"

Kinkaid jumped to his feet and banged his head on the bunker roof. He let out a curse and peered through one of the ports. The chopper crews were rushing past the bunker in full battle gear. He could hear the blades whining as the loudspeaker crackled again.

"Scrambling One! Good hunting Apaches!"

"Holy shit." Kinkaid snatched his camera bag off the floor and ran out of the bunker into the blowing sand. After spending two nerve-wracking months in Tehran, the *Associated Press'* top reporter was finally going to see some action with the famed *Apache One* attack squadron.

Choppers One through *Five* were already rising from the desert floor, their blades kicking up the sand. Kinkaid stopped and took a video of the five lead choppers lifting into the morning sky. He caught a mouthful of blowing sand, but never flinched. He stuffed the camera in his bag and ran toward *Chopper 16*.

Kinkaid was climbing aboard when *16's* pilot broke out laughing while pointing a gloved hand at the disheveled reporter.

"Hey newsman, don't forget your pants!"

Kinkaid looked down at his bare legs. "Damn..." He ran back to his bunker and snatched his battle fatigues off the makeshift clothesline he'd strung last night, then stumbled across the sand toward the waiting chopper while stepping into the damp fatigues.

The second wave lifted off the sand at 0649, followed by the third. It would take fifteen minutes to reach Arak and every minute would be used to guide the *Apaches* into battle.

Kinkaid videoed the takeoffs before climbing into the seat in front of the pilot's command chair. From the nose seat, he would have an excellent view of the action. The only drawback was the stack of puke bags beside his foot. He glanced at the bags and frowned.

Chopper 16 would be used for strike evaluation. Its pilot, Captain Jacob Worley, had received special training at Langley, Virginia's classified reconnaissance school. His chopper would provide central command with vital information concerning insurgent weaponry and tactics. His video and audio transmissions would be relayed to central command via the drone circling Arak.

Worley's voice crackled in Kinkaid's helmet. *"Here we go, Mr. Kinkaid. All strapped in?"*

"All set, Captain." Kinkaid felt the G's press him against the leather seat as *Chopper 16* rose into the blue sky behind the third wave. He gave his camera bag a pat and asked the obvious question. "So, what's up?"

"Big firefight at the Arak refineries. The enemy's using new ground-to-ground missiles. We're going to take them out."

Kinkaid felt his stomach churn. "Can I take pictures?"

"Sure, but stay on your toes. They might have stingers and that means serious evasives."

Kinkaid knew what Worley meant. The *Apache* was known for its titanium armament, but its real strength lay in its extreme maneuverability. He patted the puke bags and stared at the smoke on the horizon. "That's Arak up ahead?"

"Yes, sir. Ten minutes to target. Get that camera ready. It's going to be quick."

Kinkaid stared at the three waves of choppers bobbing in front of him, their robot cannons firing test bursts. He was checking his camera when Worley's voice crackled in his ears. *"Tighten those straps, Mr. Kinkaid. We've got visuals of the enemy at ten thousand yards. First wave preparing to engage."*

Kinkaid raised his fist to acknowledge. He could see red plumes of smoke rising from Arak dead ahead. Below him, the desert churned with burning vehicles, retreating troops, and blowing sand. He leaned to his left and aimed his camera at the chaos. "Those fires below us … are they friend or foe?"

"They're ours, Mr. Kinkaid. Hang on, here we go."

Kinkaid watched the lead wave dive toward the flashes of gunfire. He could see flames billowing from the refineries. White bursts of smoke erupted from the desert floor. Then the screeching in his ears.

"Stingers! Incoming! Evasive!"

He felt the chopper pull sharply up as the first wave flared away from the target in an evasive starburst maneuver. For an instant, all appeared okay.

A tremendous blast shook *Chopper 16.* Kinkaid stared in horror at the two burning choppers plummeting to the ground. His ears rang from the high-pitched cries of men in battle.

"They took out three and five. Our Hellfire missiles got them good, but they're still firing their stingers."

"Fall back Chopper One. Second wave going in."

Kinkaid felt his gut wrench as *Chopper 16* leveled off and dropped into a power dive. He could hear Captain Worley's voice in his headset, but the words made no sense.

"They're using delayed fuses. Titanium noses on those warheads. Our armor's useless against that. Fire your ATG's and get the hell out!"

The *Apaches* flared with discharging *Hellfire* missiles. Kinkaid could see their robot guns blasting away at the insurgent positions. The sand exploded with impacting *Hellfires,* but the bursts of white smoke continued.

Wave two was veering off when three more choppers exploded in bursts of airborne flame. Kinkaid's chest strained against his harness as *Chopper 16* rolled to the right, executing a vicious one eighty. True to his mission, the shaken reporter continued shooting video of the downed choppers, retreating ground forces, and burning refineries.

CHAPTER 18

BENEATH THE PENTAGON

"**S**omething's come up, sir. We need you over here."

The President glanced at the desk clock. "How bad, Edwin?"

"Better we talk here, sir. We're sending a car for you, if that's alright."

The President felt his stomach churn. They hadn't summoned him to the Pentagon since the night before Operation Scorpion.

"Sir?"

"Give me fifteen minutes, Edwin. I'll meet your car at underground security."

"Yes, sir."

"Does Jack know?"

"We're phoning him now."

"Tell him to meet me at security."

"Yes, sir."

The President released the speaker button and stared at the portrait of George Washington above the fireplace. It was ten minutes past midnight and the world's most powerful man wasn't a happy camper. He pressed the speaker button and took a calming breath.

"*Yes, sir?*"

"Please tell my wife not to wait up for me. It looks like a long night in the oval office."

"*Yes, sir.*"

The President released the speaker button and stared at the photograph of his lovely wife and two daughters. He grimaced and pushed up from the chair.

When the President strode out of the oval office, he was intercepted by two secret service agents who accompanied him to the elevator for a quick descent to the west wing's underground garage. Jack Wiley joined him ten minutes later.

The President eyed his chief of staff and forced a tired smile. "Where the hell is your tie? You look like you just crawled out of bed."

Wiley frowned. "What's up?"

The President shook his head. "Don't know. They want to brief us there." He smiled at the military officer standing off to the side. "Nice evening."

"Yes, sir." Colonel Sizemore returned the smile while thinking of his wife and two sons asleep in their Bethesda home. He glanced at the titanium briefcase in his hand and said a prayer this was nothing more than a minor international incident that would quickly blow over. The briefcase weighed only five pounds, but if properly activated its computer would unleash more devastation than all the wars in human history.

The black limo picked them up at 1232 and sped across the Memorial Bridge toward Arlington, Virginia, and its five-sided fortress known as the Pentagon, symbol of the world's most formidable military power.

They were met by a cordon of Marines who escorted them to an elevator that descended three hundred feet to the Pentagon's global command center. It was 0052 hours on the morning of July 2nd.

Secretary of Defense, Edwin Hammel and Joint Chiefs of Staff Chairman, Augustus Cook were waiting for the President and Jack Wiley when they stepped off the elevator. Hammel stepped forward and extended his hand. "Sorry about this, sir."

The President shook Hammel's hand. "What's going on?"

"This way, sir." Hammel gestured toward the metal door at the end of the corridor where two Marines stood guard, their eyes focused on the four men approaching them.

The President resented the retinal scan, but no one entered global command without proper clearance. He took his turn at the scanner and followed the others through the opened metal door.

The massive communications amphitheater bristled with colored lights and flickering monitors. Twenty operators sat at twin decks of consoles, their eyes focused on the thirty foot projection screen in front of them. Their voices mingled with the warbling static coming from the speakers above their heads.

The President stepped on the rear viewing platform and stared at the projection screen. He recognized the image from his prior visits, a computerized map of Iran, its triangles, squares, and circles identifying troop and equipment deployments within the past twenty minutes. Most of the geometrics were inert, but four flashed bright red.

The President gripped the railing. "Looks like some activity in Arak and Qom."

"Yes, sir." Hammel stepped beside him and pointed at the other red flashes. "And in Kermanshah and Isfahan." He stared at the screen. "We're pulling back, Mr. President."

The President looked at him in disbelief. "We're what?"

Hammel frowned. "I don't know how they did it, but those madmen have gotten their hands on the most sophisticated field weapons ever devised."

"Weapons?"

Hammel pointed at the screen. "We sent sixteen Apaches into Arak and six were blown out of the sky before they reached effective target range. Before that, the insurgents hit our ground troops with firepower we can't match. The oil fields in Qom and Arak are infernos."

The President slumped against the railing. "What about our jets?"

"We had to wait for our forces to pull back. We're running sorties now."

"And?"

General Cook cut in. "We're clobbering them, but they've taken out four F-18's."

The President looked at Cook in shock.

Cook sighed. "Our defensive tactics and equipment are useless against those missiles. I have one report of a missile tracking our F-18 to fifty thousand before it caught him. The pilot threw his entire arsenal at it … chaff, evasives, lasers, but the damn thing kept coming until it took him out."

Wiley stepped between the three shaken men. "Maybe we should pick this up in a conference room. No sense disturbing the operators."

The President nodded at his chief of staff. He knew what Jack meant. If word got out that the finest army in history was retreating from suicidal fanatics armed with super weapons, all hell would break lose. The war would be finished and so would the President.

Hammel took the hint and gestured toward a nearby conference room. He waited for the others to take seats inside before closing the door and joining them. The only sound was the conditioned air rushing through the ceiling vents.

General Cook placed a blue binder on the table and opened it. He frowned while handing a photograph to the President. "This photo was cleared an hour ago. It was taken from gun cameras on our lead Apache. Those flashes are ground fire, but they're not the problem." He pointed to the photo. "It's those three contrails on the right."

The President squinted at the photo. "Rockets?"

"Yes, sir. They're XGA99's, the latest in ground-to-air technology. They make the stinger look Stone Age. Six times as fast, six times as lethal, and relentless in hunting their target."

Cook handed the next photograph to the President. "This is a photo of their incoming GG100 missiles. You can see the plumes of flame from their hits on the oil wells." He handed the President the last photo. "This was transmitted by an embedded Associated Press reporter before his chopper was shot down."

The President squinted at the name on the photo. "Kinkaid?"

"Yes, sir. His chopper was pulling back when it was hit by a '99. We lost him and the pilot." He pointed at the photo. "Those incoming contrails are GG100's."

The President studied the photo. "How many did we lose?"

Cook's face reddened. "They blew away four hundred eighty-seven Marines, sir. Our men never had a chance."

The President dropped the photo. "Four hundred eighty-seven?"

"Yes, sir. Two direct hits with tremendous explosive force." Cook looked down. "They never knew what hit them."

The door opened and Zach Kingston stepped into the room. He closed the door and took the vacant seat across from the stunned President.

Wiley rested his hand on the President's shoulder. "I told Zach to come, Mr. President. He's uncovered something."

The President nodded. He'd hated Kingston's guts from the moment Jack Wiley advised him that the FBI director must stay. Understandable, no President wants a cancer in his ranks, especially when the cancer is leftover from the prior administration, but Kingston knew too much to be treated harshly.

The President eased back in his chair. "Go ahead, Zach."

Kingston tucked his tie inside his suit jacket and pulled a red binder out of his attaché case. He placed it on the table and opened it, his eyes studying the exposed paper.

Kingston looked at the President. "We have a trace on the missiles."

The President stared at him. "Trace?"

Kingston nodded. "It appears they were smuggled to Iranian insurgents through arms merchants in Europe, India, and Africa."

"From?"

"The United States."

The President's eyes widened. "Here?"

"Yes, sir."

"You have proof?"

Kingston nodded. "Our field agents have images of the transactions. It took some time to pick up the money trail, but the evidence is conclusive." Kingston hesitated. "They hijacked our missiles."

The President looked him in the eye. "Do you know what you're saying?"

Kingston handed the President the paper. "Well-conceived and financed. From what we can determine, it was a multi-billion dollar operation using implants at our most secured facilities. By the time we knew what happened, the missiles had disappeared from three in-transit sites."

The President put down the paper. "In-transit?"

"Staging areas in Tel Aviv, Ankara, and Kuwait. We think the thefts occurred at those storage facilities within minutes of each other."

The President eyed the paper. "Just like that?"

Kingston nodded. "Their security badges were valid, sir. They were able to penetrate and corrupt our most sensitive personnel databases."

The President's head snapped up. "Now really, Zach. You expect me to believe that a bunch of profiteers compromised our command and control security?"

Kingston nodded. "It appears they trucked in dummy missiles, switched them with the real ones, and trucked the real ones away under the guise of normal transfer operations. They knew the exact times of guard turnovers and weak spots at the storage depots." He hesitated. "They even intercepted our video surveillance transmissions to mask the transfers."

The President glanced at the paper. "How many missiles?"

"Twenty-seven GG100's and fifty-three XGA99's."

The President's face reddened. "That's impossible, Zach. Those missiles don't exist."

"Sir?"

The President leaned toward him, his brown eyes aflame. "Those missiles are still on the drawing board. At best, we have a dozen prototypes in New Mexico. No way could they get that many."

"I'm afraid there is, sir."

The President turned to Hammel who was staring at him with sullen eyes.

Hammel sank in his chair. "Sir, the prototypes performed so well, we authorized manufacture of one hundred each."

"You what?"

Hammel opened his hands in a pleading gesture. "They were ready, sir. We could gain the high ground."

The President stared at him in disbelief. "What are you saying, Edwin? No one notified me? No money was authorized?"

Hammel looked down. "We borrowed it, sir."

"Borrowed?"

"From the Star Wars program."

"Star wars? Hell, that money's allocated for defensive satellite prototypes."

Hammel sighed. "We borrowed from the advanced research phase, sir. There's no budget to track against because the ARP spans all test firing programs." He looked the President in the eye. "Sir, that money's been flowing into ARP's black hole for thirty-five years with no conclusive result."

The President clenched his fist. "You diverted it to the missiles?"

Hammel nodded. "Seemed like a good idea. Better to put the money on a winner."

"How much money?"

Hammel glanced at General Cook. "Ninety billion."

The President collapsed in his chair while trying to digest Hammel's words. He was about to unleash a tirade when Jack Wiley cut him off.

"Is that it, Zach?"

Kingston looked at Wiley with puzzled eyes.

"Thank you, Zach." Wiley nodded at the door and watched Kingston close his attaché case.

Kingston stood up and looked down at the shaken President. "I'm sorry, sir. I figured you'd want to know." He waited for the President's faint nod before leaving the room.

The President glared at Hammel and Cook. "There's a lot I want to say but this isn't the time. What the hell should we do?"

Cook leaned forward and rested his arms on the table. "Sir, I've consulted with the joint chiefs and we've concluded our best shot is to use field nukes."

"The President's face turned purple. "Are you insane? The Russians will freak out. The media will fry us. We'll be damned in history." He slammed his fist on the table. "No, General, under no circumstances."

Cook nodded. "Then I recommend we pull back to Tehran and open negotiations with Isis and Al Qaeda."

The President stood up, his body trembling. Wiley tried to grasp his arm but the President swiped his hand away. "Get out!"

Cook snatched the photos off the table and rose from his chair. He was nearly out of the room when he spun around and locked his black eyes on the President. "When you politicians start a war, there's no turning back. You should know that by now. We're not chess pieces, Mr. President. We're the finest army that ever walked the earth. You'll have my resignation within the hour."

"Just a minute, General!"

Cook ignored him and stormed out of the room.

Hammel leaned forward. "Mr. President, I'm sorry for—"

"Get out, Edwin!" The President watched his secretary of defense push up from the table and stagger out of the room. He sank into his chair and stared at the opened door.

Wiley leaned toward him. "You okay?"

The President lowered his head. "I'm history, Jack. The Judases finished me."

Wiley patted his wrist. "Not yet, old chum."

The President didn't respond.

Wiley stood up and gestured to the door. "Let's get out of here. I need some fresh air."

The two men said nothing on the ride back to the White House. A light drizzle was falling and the temperature had dropped considerably. They were approaching the west security gate when Wiley broke the silence. "I'll be out of touch for a few days."

"What?"

Wiley looked his friend in the eye. "It's time to pull our trump card."

"Trump?"

"The three million thing."

The President frowned. "No, dammit. You're too old to be running down dark alleys."

"I'll be fine."

"No!" The President pointed a finger at him. "I mean it, Jack. Let someone else handle it."

Wiley sighed. "Wish I could, but this one's too important to pawn off."

The President withdrew his finger. After all their years together, he knew when his friend was dead-set on something. He looked away and tried a different approach. "Hell, let Kingston handle it. He likes that sort of thing."

Wiley forced a smile. "Sorry, old chum. You can't rely on slugs like Kingston or Hammel. Like it or not, you need someone you can trust." He raised his arms in jest. "Oh shit, that's me."

The President fell back in the seat, his eyes glistening. "This is a bad time, Jack. You're all I have. If anything happens to you—"

Wiley patted his shoulder. "I'll call you on Monday morning with good news."

"That's all you're going to tell me?"

Wiley nodded. "If anyone asks about me, I'm visiting a sick friend."

The President sighed and lowered his head. "I'm tired, Jack. Damn tired."

"Yes, sir. Get some sleep, Mr. President."

They parted company in the west wing's underground garage. The President shook Wiley's hand and headed for the elevator and a warm bed with the woman he loved.

Wiley waited for his friend of thirty years to disappear into the elevator before climbing back into the limo with his cell phone. It took a few seconds for the secured line to kick in. He recognized Kingston's strained voice.

"*That you, Jack?*"

"Who else?"

Kingston breathed a sigh of relief. "*You had me off balance in there. I thought something had gone wrong.*"

Wiley glanced at his watch. "What time does the plane leave?"

"*Five sharp from Dulles. Ask for Charter nine-ninety-nine. One of our men will escort you to the plane.*"

Wiley frowned while recalling the President's warning.

"*You there, Jack?*"

"Yeah, see you on the plane." Wiley pressed the off button and slipped the phone in his jacket pocket.

****

"What time is it?"

The President embraced his wife and whispered in her ear. "Time for the most powerful man on earth to get lucky."

She patted his arm. "In the morning, sweetheart. You need rest."

"Hell I do." He pressed against her and made his intentions known.

"My, my, darling. Did you take one of those Viagras?"

"The whole bottle." He kissed her passionately on the neck and felt her turn toward him. It was 0411 and the President of the United States was a happy camper.

CHAPTER 19

ACCELERATION

The *Gulfstream* took off from Burbank Airport at 8:45 on Thursday morning. Perry's bodyguard sat across the aisle, his face buried in a newspaper. They hadn't spoken since leaving the *Ritz Carlton*.

Perry stared the shoreline fading beneath the haze. It didn't take a rocket scientist to know their destination. It would be his second visit to Lake Warnock. Nice time of the year with all those birds, sunflowers, and rustling trees. Add the rippling water and it was the perfect spot for a little chat with his favorite person.

He felt a chill. The past two months had been a joy ride, but last night's press conference changed all that. From now on, Minton would squeeze him like a tube of toothpaste until she had what she wanted.

His chill became a shiver. For two months, the second video had been his bargaining chip. It was more than the three million dollars. The video had guaranteed his safety. When he handed her those interviews with Kramer, Matafuco, Cambria, and Ramirez, he would lose that bargaining chip.

He felt his stomach churn. *Then what old chum?* What does a woman like Claire Minton do with someone she can't trust? Maybe nothing. Maybe just shake his hand and wish him well.

His fingers dug into the armrest. *What the bloody hell are you smoking? When you turn over those interviews, you're toast, Ambrose. Toast!*

"Toast?"

Perry nearly jumped out of his seat. He turned to the bodyguard who was extending a plate of buttered toast and cup of coffee.

The bodyguard gave him the evil eye. "You okay?"

Perry nodded. "Just a little hung over."

"Sure about that?"

Perry snatched the toast and coffee. "I'm fine. Where are we going?"

The bodyguard shrugged. "Ms. Minton is anxious to see you. Sounds like you have some unfinished business."

Perry watched the bodyguard drift off to sleep. He took a sip of coffee and stared at the toast.

The plane broke through the clouds at one p.m., Lawrence time, revealing a sea of golden wheat. A silo came into view and above it a windsock flapping on a pole. The plane flew past the silo and rolled into a steep left bank as it prepared to land.

Perry took a calming breath while recalling the photograph he'd seen at Purdue's library, and he suddenly knew what must be done. Whatever it took, however he pulled it off, he must break away from them long enough to finish what he had started two months ago.

He was snapped from his thoughts by a poke in the arm.

"Fasten your belt. We're landing."

Perry nodded and clipped his buckle.

The bodyguard glared at him. "Sure you're okay?"

"Yeah."

"No tricks, right?"

Perry nodded at the chisel-chinned hog sitting across from him. He leaned toward the window and looked down at the wheat fields while recalling the last image he saw on that library computer screen, two months ago.

The young face could be her. Impossible to know for sure, but it could be her.

He'd spent his final minutes studying photos of *Cadmore* girls who had found new homes through the institution's strict adoption procedures.

The young face flashed in his mind. Until that photo, his earliest look at Claire Minton was the 1991 Gulf War photo. The blue eyes looked the same, piercing and cold. And that jet black hair, except it was longer in the fourteen-year-old's photo. And there was the other problem. The caption below the photo read "Charlene MacAfee."

The girl had been adopted by the Jordans of Abilene, Kansas, a god-fearing family that would provide a good home for Charlene. Plenty of money too. The article described Matthew Jordan as a mechanic who had built a successful trucking business that carried grain to every farm state in the Midwest and Southwest.

Perry was jarred from his thoughts by a sharp jolt and screech of rubber as the *Gulfstream* touched down on the dirt airstrip. A quick application of brakes and the sleek jet rolled to a stop amidst the rolling wheat.

"Ready?"

Perry nodded at the bodyguard and pushed out of his seat.

The ride to Lake Warnock took forty-five minutes. She was waiting for him at the lodge's front door when their black SUV crunched to a stop on the cinder driveway.

She walked to the car and peered through the passenger window, her face showing the strain of the past few days. "I'm having lunch. Want to join me?"

Perry nodded and slid off the car's rear seat. It was cool for this time of year with a brisk southwest breeze blowing in his face. The sky was overcast with the threat of rain. He followed her into the lodge while wondering if it would storm. Nothing like a little lightning and thunder to spice the moment.

She wore a yellow jersey and jeans. No makeup, but she didn't need any. Claire Minton was an attractive woman who would melt most men with a glance of her blue eyes. Only problem was this black widow was best kept at arm's length.

They sat at a small table on the covered deck behind the lodge. She took a bite of her tuna sandwich and sipped some iced tea. "Something wrong?"

"What?"

She nodded at his plate. "I thought you'd be hungry."

"Oh, sorry." Perry snatched his tuna sandwich and took a healthy bite.

She leaned back in her chair. "I take it you saw the press conference?"

He nodded.

"Well?"

He listened to a rumble of thunder. "What I think isn't important."

She smiled. "I'd like your thoughts."

Perry shrugged. "It was well done."

Her smile faded. "That's all you have to say?"

Perry shrugged and bit into his sandwich.

She leaned toward him. "I'm at twenty-one percent."

Perry nodded and sipped his tea.

She leaned closer. "I couldn't have done it without you."

He looked her in the eye. "Good tuna."

She frowned and collapsed in her chair. The downpour had begun.

They sat facing each other with the rain spilling off the roof. Claire finally broke the silence. She sighed and looked at the blowing trees.

"I love the rain. So clean and fresh. Makes me feel good inside. Reminds me of the farm when my dad and brother rushed to bring in the cows." She looked him in the eye. "I can almost smell the hot apple pie cooking in the oven, and hear my mom calling us for dinner."

Perry smiled. "Sounds like you had a better childhood than me."

She stared at him with those blue eyes. "Tell me."

Perry shrugged. "Not much to tell. My dad was a Welsh coal miner who saved enough quid to open a small saloon in Cardiff." He sipped his iced tea. "The old guy was a real fighter. His dream was to accumulate enough quid to open a pub in London, but he died before he could pull it off."

"What about your mom?"

Perry put down his glass. "She died when I was four. Bloody cancer killed her, along with the polluted air."

"Do you remember her?"

"Some."

She sighed and looked down at the table. "It's hard being a child. We're so vulnerable."

The sky flashed with lightning followed by a clap of thunder. She gestured toward the sliding glass door leading to the living room. "We better go inside before we get soaked."

Perry nodded and followed her into the lodge. So much for tender moments.

She led him into her study and closed the door. Perry recognized Jess Wilkin staring at the rain through the study's bay window.

Wilkin walked over to Perry and shook his hand. "How's the arm?"

Perry glanced at his left arm. "Still there."

Wilkin smiled and sat in one of the two leather chairs facing the desk.

Claire gestured for Perry to sit in the other chair. She waited until he was down before stepping behind the desk and sinking into its high-back leather chair.

Perry smiled. "Quite presidential."

Wilkin ignored his crack. "Your video really shook them, Perry." He pulled a paper out of his jacket pocket and handed it to Perry. "That's my best guess at our possibilities going into the September debate."

Perry unfolded the paper and stared at it in disbelief. "Thirty percent?"

Wilkin nodded. "Yes, but it depends on you."

Perry looked down at the paper.

Claire leaned forward. "We need those interviews, Perry. They're going to hit us hard. They can't let us win. Too many powerful interests involved. They'll do anything to stop us."

Wilkin jumped in. "They're already formulating a scheme to discredit your video. We expect the first salvo before the week is over." He leaned toward Perry. "That's why we need those interviews now."

Perry frowned. "That's not what we agreed."

Wilkin threw up his hands. "What's the difference? You're going to get paid. We just want to move up the exchange."

"I need time."

Wilkin glared at him. "You trying to pull out?"

"No, but we have an agreement."

Wilkin's eyes flickered. "You still don't get it. We're talking survival here. We need that second video to counterpunch their attack. If we can air the first troop interview this week, we'll stretch the others over the next few months to gain momentum for the debate. If my projection is right, Claire will walk on stage with twenty-nine percent against Hawley's thirty and the President's thirty-four."

Perry held up the paper. "What about the other seven percent?"

Wilkin smirked. "That's the ball game, isn't it? The Golden Fleece. The mother lode. If Claire can snatch that seven percent in the debate, it's over." His eyes lit up. "We'll win."

Perry stared at him. "Win?"

Wilkin nodded.

Perry looked at Claire. "You didn't tell me that."

Her blue eyes burned into him. "I'm going as far as I can."

Perry collapsed in the chair. "Are you crazy? That's the worst thing that could happen. Pressuring them for deals is one thing, but winning will destroy everything you're trying to accomplish."

She gave him a puzzled look. "Sorry, Perry. You just lost me."

He shook the paper. "If you win, the government will be paralyzed at the worst possible time. The bloody war will become our worst nightmare in a hundred sixty years. They'll impeach you. Run you out on a bloody rail." He looked her in the eye. "They're too powerful, Claire. They'll do anything to protect their wealth." He placed the paper on the desk. "You can't beat them."

She looked down at the paper. "I need your help, Perry. I never expected we would come this close, but your video changed that." She nodded at the briefcase on the desk. "We have your second million in cold hard cash, but I need those interviews now."

Perry looked at the briefcase and felt a knot in the pit of his stomach. He had just run out of time. Nothing he could say would change that.

He sighed and looked her in the eye. "I can get you the video, but I need to do it alone." He watched them glance at each other.

She shook her head. "You know I can't do that. We almost lost you two months ago." She leaned toward him. "You said it yourself. There are powerful interests involved. If they take you out, they'll take me out too."

Perry glanced at the briefcase. "I need to do it alone."

Wilkin folded his arms. "Alone where?"

"Chicago."

"Where in Chicago?"

Perry hesitated. "That's my business."

Wilkin scowled at him. "Sorry, Mr. Ambrose. It's our business too. We're in this together and we can't let you out of our sight."

Perry leaned back in the chair. There was no sound except the rain spattering on the window. The three of them stared at each other like statues.

Claire broke the silence. "What if we meet you halfway? Give us a location in Chicago and we'll stay at arm's length. That way, you'll have your time alone and we'll know where you are."

Perry shook his head. "I don't like it."

Minton sensed an opening. "I'm sorry, Perry. That's the best I can do." She pushed out of her chair and walked to the window.

She folded her arms and stared at the lake. "The sun's breaking through."

Perry glanced at the window. "So it is."

She lowered her head. "They almost killed you. We saved your life and offered you a better one. Isn't that worth something?"

"That's not fair."

She chuckled. "I'm the dragon lady, remember? Anything goes."

"You're bloody insane."

"Sorry, it's what I do best."

Perry uttered a painful sigh and pushed out of his chair. "I need to think it over."

Wilkin glared at Minton. "There has to be another way. Chicago's a big city. Tough to stake anything out."

Minton smiled at him. "It'll be okay. We've come too far to mistrust each other." She glanced at Perry. "Right?"

Perry shook his head and walked toward the door followed by Minton's unhappy campaign manager. They were almost out of the room when she called out to him.

"Perry?"

He hesitated.

"Thanks for believing in me." She stared at the lake and listened to the door close.

"You *are* insane."

She turned toward the white-haired man standing beside the desk. He'd spent the last twenty minutes listening to their conversation from the small conference room behind the study. His frown said it all.

She watched him lean against the desk, his hand toying with the letter opener. She smiled and nodded at the jade knife. "Going to use that on me?"

"Not funny, Claire. We've come too far for childish jokes and misplaced trust."

She shook her head and eased beside him. "It'll be okay. If it weren't for Mr. Ambrose, I'd be out of the race."

His eyes flickered. "That's not the point, Missy. We can't lose sight of our goal. Your reporter is nothing but a tool, and a broken one at that."

She leaned against him and rested her head on his chest. "You smell good. New cologne?"

He sighed. "Bought it in Italy. Supposed to drive the ladies wild."

She gave him a hug. "It works."

He backed away and looked into her blue eyes. "No games, Missy."

She smiled the smile he loved so much. "You once told me the dumbest woman in the world can outsmart the smartest man."

He shook his head. "This is different. There's too much at stake to trust a loser like him."

She patted his arm. "I can handle him. After all, he's about to give us the presidency. Don't want to upset the applecart."

"You seem pretty sure of yourself."

She nodded. "Shouldn't I be? You taught me everything I know."

He looked down while trying to avoid those piercing blue eyes.

"Come, my darling. Let me have some fun."

His voice softened. "I'll be damned. You are the dragon lady."

"Not for you."

He took her in his arms and held her close. "You're the most important thing in my life, Claire. The gods sent you to me. You're going to make us proud, Missy. Don't get hurt now."

She reached up and kissed him on the cheek. "We'll be fine. Everything will be fine."

They clung to each other and listened to the clock ticking on the desk. His voice was barely audible.

"Okay…"

He waited for her to leave the room before snatching the cell phone out of his pocket. The damn thing had been vibrating for thirty seconds, but the moment was too important to lose on a phone call.

He flipped the phone open and placed it against his ear. "Go ahead."

"We've got trouble."

"Trouble?"

"Clyde's blown the whistle."

His eyes widened. "Clyde?"

"Confirmed. He's meeting with the President's contact today. Gonna trade everything for big bucks."

He stood speechless, his eyes gazing at the window.

The voice crackled in his ear. *"I know you two are close, but—"*

"Hold it, Charlie. This has to be a mistake."

"No mistake. We've got Clyde on tape with his finger in the cookie jar. He's in contact with the FBI."

He looked at the phone in disbelief. "How can that be? He's one of us. We've been through hell together."

The caller hesitated. *"We need to take care of it."*

He leaned against the wall. "I'll talk to him."

"Can't do that. It's too dangerous."

"Dammit, Charlie."

"*I know, it shook me too, but that's the way it is.*"

He gripped the phone. "Find another way."

The caller hesitated. "*You know there isn't one. You wrote the rules, remember? Without loyalty, we're finished.*"

He lowered his head, unable to speak.

"*You should know that others are involved. Pretty high up from what I can tell. I'll try to be surgical, but we might have collateral damage.*"

"How high?"

"*Chief of staff.*"

"What?"

I guess they're pretty desperate."

He glared at the lake.

The voice crackled. "*Matt?*"

"Yeah?"

"*Want me to handle it?*"

He hesitated. "My god, Charlie."

"*I'll be in touch.*"

"Charlie?"

"*Yeah?*"

"For god's sake..." The phone clicked. He slipped it in his pocket and staggered to the window.

The sun was breaking through the clouds, its beams striking the lake, but he wasn't looking at the view. He was staring at his reflection in the window. The tanned face and green eyes. The white hair streaming onto his shoulders. The same face Perry saw that night in the limo.

CHAPTER 20

COLLATERAL DAMAGE

The *Dassault* lifted off Dulles' charter runway at 5:14 on Thursday morning, July 2nd. With the lights of DC fading into the haze, the sleek jet rolled into a steep left bank toward its northwest heading.

The plane's two passengers were oblivious to the takeoff. They sat beside each other; their eyes trained on the blue folder spread across their snack tables.

Wiley stroked his forehead while studying the photograph in the folder. "That's him?"

Kingston nodded. "We've had him under twenty-four hour surveillance since our first contact three months ago."

Wiley frowned. "Expensive."

"But worth it." Kingston tapped the photo. "He's the one we've been waiting for, Jack. The smoking gun. If I'm right, he'll give your boss four more years."

"Go on."

"When Burble contacted us last month, he was having second thoughts, but now he's opened the vault." Kingston flipped the page and watched Wiley squint at a second photograph of three men clad in hunting jackets with their shotguns raised to the sky.

Kingston pointed at the man on the right. "That's Burble."

Wiley squinted at the photo. "It doesn't look like him."

"It's him. That photo was taken eighteen years ago in a forest near Flint, Michigan. Shave off the beard, thin the hair, and its Clyde Burble."

Wiley gave him a skeptical look. "Who are the other guys?"

"It's in the narrative." Kingston leaned back and watched Wiley read the text below the photo.

Wiley sighed. "What the hell's a red leg?"

Kingston smiled. "It goes back to the Civil War. A bunch of fanatics that ravaged Kansas with Quantrill. They got the nickname from their red leggings."

"Bandits?"

"More like war lords. They wanted to build their kingdom in Kansas."

Wiley shrugged. "Never heard of them."

"They faded away after the war, but sick causes have a way of resurfacing if the conditions are right."

Wiley nodded at the photo. "That's all you have?"

"There's more." Kingston flipped the page to the last two photos. He watched Wiley read the supporting text. The only sound was the hum of the engines.

Wiley closed the folder and leaned back in his seat. "I get the drift, but it's pretty thin." He looked out the window. "I need more to run with something like this."

Kingston slipped the folder into his attaché case. "I told Burble we're coming in good faith with a hundred thousand in unmarked bills. He understands any further reward will depend on what he gives us."

Wiley shook his head. "He sounds like a real slime."

"Aren't we all."

Wiley closed his eyes while recalling the day he told the President they must keep the dirt bag seated beside him. He could still hear the President's stinging words when he broke the news.

Get rid of him, Jack. He's a Judas goat. He'll bring us down. Cut the cord, dammit. We don't want that Judas at our throats. Hell, if you want I'll fire him myself...

Kingston leaned toward him. "You okay?"

Wiley nodded. "Just tired. Think I'll catch some sleep." He turned away from Kingston while cursing himself for chasing phantoms.

The *Dassault* touched down on a private strip near Grand Rapids at 7:21, seconds before a cloudburst swept over the runway. Its two passengers fled the aircraft and hopped aboard an FBI-issue van, which sped away amidst a clap of thunder.

Wiley leaned toward the rain-spattered window and peered at the river flashing through the trees. "I haven't seen that white water since we drove through here four years ago."

"Campaign stop?"

Wiley nodded.

Kingston stared at the river. "Can I ask you something?"

"Yeah?"

"How long do I have?"

"Long?"

Kingston sighed. "C'mon, Jack. Let's level with each other. The only reason I still have my job is because you're not sure what I have."

Wiley raised his hand. "This isn't a good time. Let's pick it up when we get back."

Kingston's face reddened. "Let's do it now."

"Just a damn minute!"

"Now."

Wiley stared at him. "You serious?"

"Deadly."

Wiley heaved a sigh.

Kingston looked him in the eye. "If I give you what you want, you owe me."

"Like?"

"An honorable resignation."

Wiley stared at him. Things were looking up. If the phantom called Burble turned out to be a phony, he could still salvage the wasted trip by bringing good news to his boss. Zach Kingston was ready to make a deal. A little phone call to the right people and ol' Zach would become a lobbyist for the Mid East reconstruction cartels, and the President's Judas goat would be out of the way.

Kingston leaned toward him. "Jack?"

Wiley nodded. "I'll consider it. Let's talk on the flight back." He watched Kingston ease back in his seat.

Their van pulled into Grand Rapids at 8:23 and headed south on Division Street. It only took a few minutes to reach the *Grand Rapids Inn*. A quick ride up the elevator and they were standing at room "241".

Kingston rapped on the door. The voice on the other side was barely audible.

"Yeah?"

"We're here."

The man's voice sharpened. "Back off so I can see you."

Kingston stepped back from the peephole and gestured for Wiley to do the same.

"Who's your friend?"

Kingston shrugged. "The man you want to see."

The chain lock disengaged followed by a deadbolt and what sounded like a chair being dragged away from the door. The door opened revealing a nervous, twitching face. A little vague with the unshaven beard, but it was him.

Burble squinted at Wiley. "You're the President's guy? The chief of whatever?"

Wiley forced a smile. "I'm him."

Burble looked at the black briefcase under Kingston's arm. "You got it?"

Kingston patted the briefcase.

"Well, let's get to it." Burble swung the door open and gestured for them to sit at the small table beside the bed.

It only took a second for Wiley to smell the liquor on Burble's breath. He glanced at the half-consumed bottle of gin on the table and sat across from Kingston.

Burble closed the door and engaged the locks before jamming a chair under the knob. He backed away from the door and turned to his two seated guests, his hands rubbing his soiled flannel shirt. "You got us covered?"

Kingston nodded. "Two agents at the stairs and elevator."

Burble frowned. "That's all?"

"Two is plenty, Mr. Burble."

Burble looked down at the gin. "You gents want a shot?"

Wiley shrugged. "It's a little early, but what the hell."

"Now you're talkin.'" Burble cracked a smile and snatched a plastic glass from the top of the TV. He poured Wiley a shot and extended the glass. "Sorry about the ice. I like it warm myself."

Wiley took the glass and swigged it down. It burned like hell, but he wasn't going to show it.

Burble extended the bottle to Kingston who waved it away. He gave Kingston a dirty look and extended the bottle to Wiley. "Another?"

Wiley slid the glass toward him.

Burble poured him a healthy shot and backed away. "You're not what I expected."

"No?"

Burble swigged the bottle and wiped his mouth with his flannel sleeve. "You're human." He put the bottle on the table and looked at Wiley. "What's your roots?"

Wiley slugged down the gin. "Tampa, born and raised."

Burble grinned. "Ah, a gator. Tough boys down there." He snatched the bottle and took another swig. "You from the swamps?"

Wiley shook his head. "I left Tampa when I was a kid. My dad was in the Air Force so we moved around a lot.

Burble extended the bottle but Wiley raised his hand. "Let's talk."

Burble pulled back the bottle and placed it on the table. "Yeah, might as well." He sat in the chair between them, his black eyes trained on Wiley.

Wiley pulled out a notepad and flipped it open. "What do you have?"

Burble tapped his fingers against the bottle. "Ever visited Lawrence?"

Wiley shrugged. "On the campaign trail."

"Like it?"

Wiley nodded. "People seemed friendly. Nice town from what I recall."

Burble took another swig. "You don't know Lawrence." He scratched his stubbled chin and looked at Kingston. "Let's see the money."

Kingston popped open the briefcase and tilted it so Burble could see the cash. "One hundred thousand in untraceable bills." He slid the briefcase across the table.

Burble eyed the money for a moment, then closed the bag and placed it on the floor. He took a swig of gin and stared at the empty bottle.

Wiley leaned toward him. "I've come a long way, Mr. Burble. I don't have much time."

Burble pushed back from the table and looked at Wiley with those black eyes. "Know anythin' about militias?"

Wiley hesitated while recalling the text in the folder. "You mean, red legs?"

Burble smiled. "Done some research, eh? Hell, they're only a small cut of the pie."

Wiley nodded. "And the other cuts?"

Burble's face twisted in a sneer. He lifted his hand and started counting his gnarled fingers. "Well, let's see. We got the Michigan boys, the Massachusetts boys, the Maryland boys, the Utah boys, the Arizona boys, the Ohio boys, the Arkansas boys, the Florida boys, the—"

Kingston pointed a harsh finger at him. "Get to it."

Burble snapped his head toward Kingston, his eyes flashing. "This ain't easy, big shot. Those men in the picture are my friends. We've been through hell together. Lost our farms, our businesses, our jobs, even our families because of you government boys and your corporate bosses." He sank in the chair and stared at the bottle. "It's not easy to back-shoot your friends."

Wiley leaned toward him. "We're listening."

Burble looked down at the empty bottle. "Matt and Charlie are my buds. I love them more than anythin', 'cept—"

Wiley leaned closer. "Yes?"

"They're killin' our boys."

"Our boys?"

"Our troops. We're losin' so damn many in that damn war." He looked at Wiley with pleading eyes. "I won't be part of that."

Wiley nodded. "Go ahead, Mr. Burble."

Burble grasped the empty bottle and nodded at the closet door. "Get us another gin."

Wiley almost fainted when he slid open the closet door and saw the twenty unopened bottles on the shelf. He snatched a bottle and poured Burble a stiff one.

Kingston leaned toward Burble. "Tell Mr. Wiley how they're killing our boys."

Burble guzzled the gin and squinted at Wiley. "Matt's got lots of money. More than most. He and Charlie are tight with the other militias. They use the internet to talk. Lots of code and all that." He poured another shot and swigged it down. "Lots of money in the militias. Lots of powerful folk who want to return to the old ways so we can get back our farms and take care of our families…" His face twisted in a scowl. "… and throw out the scum that's invaded our borders."

Wiley leaned toward him. "What about our troops?"

Burble pushed back in the chair, making it creak. "What I'm gonna tell you is my death warrant."

Wiley stared at him.

"I want witness protection."

Wiley nodded. "You'll have it along with the money, but we need to know everything."

Burble looked down at his trembling hands. "Matt and Charlie set up the missile thing."

Wiley froze. "Missile?"

"The hundreds and ninety-nines. They set the whole thing up with their rich buds in the other militias." Burble raised his hand. "Not all of them, mind you. Most of the militias would never go along with it, but they didn't know."

Wiley stared at him. "How do you know?"

"Cause I was the contact man with the arms guy from London."

"London?"

Burble nodded. "I gave the London guy a bunch of coded papers and he gave me another bunch to take back to Matt and Charlie. Couldn't read the damn things. Looked like chicken scratches." He glanced at Kingston. "I guess you guys decoded them."

Wiley glanced at Kingston who nodded. "You gave Mr. Kingston copies?"

Burble took a swig. "Guess I did."

Wiley took a calming breath. "Who set it up?"

Burble shrugged. "Don't know, but the London guy handled the computer stuff."

Wiley's eyes lit up. "The personnel files?"

"Yeah."

Wiley shook his head. "Those files are top secret. They're unbreakable."

Burble smiled. "Lots of militia in the government. Some have real good jobs, even in your capital."

Wiley couldn't believe his ears. He tried to stay calm while forcing out the words. "The defense department?"

Burble's smile widened. "You'd be surprised."

Kingston placed his pocket recorder on the table. "Go on, Mr. Burble. We need names and dates."

They spent the next hour listening to Burble spill his guts about bitter people and their crusade to right the wrongs done to the good folks that built this nation. He talked about the desperation that rekindled the militias after Ruby Ridge, Waco, Oklahoma City, and the broken borders. He ranted about lost jobs, lost farms, and lost self-respect. All because the global corporate maggots had taken over the nation.

In everything Burble said, the common thread was a fierce commitment to bring down the corrupt government that had betrayed its people, a government ruled by global profiteers whose only goals were money and power.

At 10:44, Burble pushed back from the table and stared at the two shaken men. "What's wrong, gents? Cat got your tongue?"

Wiley sighed. "You can prove all this?"

"For the right price."

Kingston checked his pocket recorder. Still a few minutes left. He placed the recorder on the table and looked at Burble. "What about Claire Minton?"

Burble's eyes lit up. "Oh yeah, can't forget ol' Claire." He poured a shot and guzzled it down. "You got the pictures I gave you?"

Kingston reached into his attaché case and lifted out the blue folder. He opened it and placed it in front of Burble.

Burble flipped to the last page and pointed to the photo of Matthew Jordan. "Matt and I were real close with Claire's mom and dad. We took it hard when Pete and Connie killed themselves." He stared at the photo. "We offered to take Claire in, bein' she was only twelve, but her brother, Bobby, said he would care for her."

Burble pushed the folder away. "Then Bobby died from an overdose and the judge sent Claire to that home."

Kingston interrupted. "Cadmore?"

Burble nodded. "Yup, but ol' Matt had other plans for Claire. No way was our friend's daughter gonna rot in that place while them perverts tried to defloriate her."

Wiley leaned forward. "He adopted her?"

Burble nodded. "Matt paid off the headmaster and covered the whole thing up."

Wiley gave him a puzzled look. "Why cover it?"

"Matt had big plans for Claire. He couldn't let anyone know about the adoption cause it would ruin everythin'."

"Ruin?"

Burble shrugged. "Because of Matt's roots, bein' a red leg and all that. Can't have a future presidential candidate carryin' that baggage. Make her look like one of them radicals."

Wiley's eyes widened. "Jordan's in the militia?"

Burble smiled. "Matt's the top dog in Kansas. That's why he's so connected with the top dogs in the other militias." He shook his head. "You know, after this missile thing, I think Matt's gonna be top dog of all the militias."

Wiley started to speak but Kingston cut him off. "Tell Mr. Wiley how they covered it."

Burble shrugged. "The headmaster switched Claire's photo and records with another Cadmore girl named Charlene MacAfee. That way, the records showed Claire was still in the home. Made it look like Matt's family adopted Charlene."

Wiley stared at him in disbelief. "But someone must have noticed? Said something?"

Burble shook his head. "That's not the way Matt set it up. After he took out Claire, no one ever saw Charlene cause the home never put her up for adoption."

Wiley stared at him.

"Matt bribed the headmaster to keep Charlene at the home permanently."

Wiley glanced at his notes. "But there must have been attempts to adopt Claire Minton? The headmaster would have to present MacAfee in her place?"

Burble shrugged. "Not that complicated. The headmaster always had an excuse to keep Charlene out of sight when a family wanted to meet Claire, and that didn't happen but once or twice." Burble looked at the bottle. "Poor little Charlene rotted in that home until the good lord put her out of her misery forty years ago."

Kingston sighed. "In the fire?"

Wiley looked at Kingston. "Fire?"

Kingston nodded. "Charlene MacAfee was one of four girls killed along with the headmaster."

Burble took a swig of gin. "God rest their souls."

Wiley glared at Burble. "This is crazy. How did they explain Minton not dying?"

Burble shrugged. "Cadmore burned to the ground one week after Claire's graduation from her four year stay."

"But she wasn't there?"

Burble smiled. "Matt bribed the headmaster to fake Claire's graduation photo. He made sure it appeared in the Lawrence and Kansas City papers. Claire was eighteen by then. She'd lived with Matt's people four years."

Wiley leaned toward him. "What do you mean, his people?"

Burble shrugged. "Claire couldn't stay with Matt's family. That would blow the whole thing." He burped and poured a shot of gin. "So ol' Claire spent four years in a red leg commune near Lake Warnock. When people asked about Charlene, Matt told them she was in a private school in California."

The room fell silent while the two men stared at the drunk seated between them.

Wiley glanced at his watch while trying to digest Burble's words, and it hit him. He clenched his fist and asked Burble the hard question. "Was the fire set?"

Burble slugged down his gin. "Matt never meant for the other three girls to die. They were supposed to be on a field trip, but the damn thing got cancelled at the last minute." He put down his glass and lowered his head. "Poor souls. Poor damn souls…"

Wiley's eyes flared with anger. "He killed them?"

Burble sighed. "There's an old saying you might know. Sacrifice few to save many."

"My god."

"Yup, that wasn't a proud moment for the red legs, but it had to be done. Without Charlene and those records, there was no way to uncover Matt's little scheme." Burble shrugged. "After all, here we are forty years later tryin' to dig up the past."

Wiley fought a surge of nausea. He poured a shot of gin and gulped it down. He wanted to throttle the slime seated beside him, but it wasn't to be.

"Like my gin, eh? Go ahead, drink all you want. I'm gonna buy a mountain of bottles with all that money."

Wiley took a deep breath and flipped through his scribbled notes. The only sound was Burble tapping his fingers against the bottle.

Wiley leaned back in his chair and folded his arms. "Okay, we have Claire Minton living in a commune four years after being bailed out of an orphanage by one Matthew Jordan." He locked his brown eyes on Burble. "My problem is motive. I can understand a friend trying to save his dead friend's daughter, but that's no reason to cover it up and kill the witnesses."

Burble rubbed the back of his neck. "I told you, Matt's real smart. I think he saw Claire as our avengin' angel. Through her, he could get even with the pigs that took away our farms and jobs, and killed her family."

Wiley gave him a puzzled look. "But they didn't kill anyone? Her family committed suicide?"

Burbled glared at him. "There's lots of ways to kill people. Them corporate pigs might as well have put a gun to the family's heads when they took away the Minton farm."

Wiley looked down at his notes. "Sorry, I'm having trouble believing Claire Minton is a brainwashed candidate for President of the United States."

Burble's eyes flickered. "Brainwashed? Hell, you still don't get it. You and your corporate pig bosses have hurt lots of good people. People like Claire's family. She doesn't need brainwashin'. You've given her plenty of reason to hate you. You and your scum leaders who've sold us out for thirty pieces of silver."

Kingston pointed a finger at Burble, but the enraged red leg swiped it away. His black eyes locked on Wiley. "Now listen close cause I'm not gonna repeat myself. Claire Minton is our chosen one. She's been trained for this from the time Matt freed her from that home. You think she sat in some hippy commune smokin' joints for four years? Hell no, she got the best schoolin' and military trainin' possible. Matt brought in the best teachers to make sure she came out of that commune ready to begin her long road to the presidency."

Wiley shook his head. "You expect me to believe this genius friend of yours planned Claire Minton's run for the presidency when she was only fourteen?"

Kingston poured a stiff one and extended it to Burble, but Burble pushed his hand away. He leaned toward Wiley, his black eyes on fire. "She did two stints in the army and came out a war hero. Between tours, she graduated from Kansas University and attended the War College. She's a warrior with a superior mind who hasn't forgotten her roots, and she's on her way to the White House to throw your scum suckin' boss out the window."

Wiley glared at him. "If you're telling the truth, she's no different than the rest of us. Another puppet on a string."

Kingston raised his hand for calm, but it was too late. Burble rose from his chair, his fists clenched. "Get this straight, big shot. You and your liberal scum can't stop her. If you don't get that by now, you're dumber than I thought. I'm your only hope, big shot, so get me the rest of that money or the deal is off!"

Wiley kept his cool while absorbing Burble's tirade. The man standing in front of him was a raving alcoholic on the verge of a breakdown, a brainwashed backwoods creature whose limited mind had fallen prey to a bunch of cultists. He might be telling the truth, but the whole thing was probably a hallucination. He started to speak, but Kingston's outburst stopped him.

"That's it, dammit!" Kingston swept the folder off the table and jammed it in his attaché case. He reached for the briefcase but Burble snatched it away.

Burble looked at Kingston in shock. "What you doin'?"

"The deal's off. You don't talk to us that way. We're all you've got." Kingston pointed at the briefcase. "Now hand it over or I'll have my men take it from you."

Burble raised his hands for calm. "Hey, I didn't mean nothin'. Just a friendly exchange, right Mr. Wiley?"

Wiley caught on. Time for a little game of good cop, bad cop. He frowned and looked at Kingston. "Is anything he said new?"

Kingston shook his head. "Some, but I already had most of it."

Wiley looked at Burble who was shaking in his boots. "Sorry, Mr. Burble. I thought you had more. The connection with the militia helps, but it isn't worth what we're offering."

Kingston lunged at Burble and ripped the briefcase out of his hands. "Let's get out of here, Jack. Sorry for wasting our time." He turned for the door and listened to Burble spill his guts.

"No, wait! There's more. A lot more. Just give me a chance to find out the details."

Wiley started toward the door and hesitated. "Details of what?"

Burble clutched his head and slumped against the wall. "Matt's desperate. He'll do anythin' to help her win. She's like a daughter to him."

"That's all you have?"

"They're gonna do somethin' big. I'll know by Saturday. Just give me until then and I'll make it worth your while."

"Why should we trust you?"

Burble looked at Wiley with pleading eyes. "I already told you enough to put me in a grave. You're all I've got! Why would I lie to you now? Please, Mr. Wiley. Just two more days and you'll have what you want."

The next ten minutes were a blur. The two stunned men resumed their seats and listened to Burble's feeble attempt to prove the words spewing out of his mouth. Burble kept babbling about a July 4th meeting that was to take place on a farm near Dubuque, Iowa. A clan meeting of sorts to be attended by the heads of six militias, all of whom were involved in the Minton plot.

It sounded like a bad movie script with Burble promising to give names and dates after the meeting. Probably nothing but a lunatic's act of desperation to claim the three million, but his claim was too serious to ignore.

Wiley waited until Burble collapsed in his chair, his hand grasping the empty bottle. He leaned toward Burble and spoke in a subdued voice. "Two days?"

"Saturday, I'll know by then."

Wiley glanced at Kingston. "You know how to reach Mr. Burble?"

Kingston nodded.

Wiley stood up. "Give Mr. Burble his briefcase."

"But Jack—"

"Give it to him." Wiley looked down at Burble. "You won't let me down?"

Burble raised his right hand. "I swear. I'll have everythin' by Saturday."

Wiley nodded to Kingston. He watched the FBI director place the briefcase on the table. "Good day, Mr. Burble. Talk to you then."

They were joined at the elevator by the two agents who escorted them to the waiting van. No words were spoken as they climbed aboard. The rain had stopped, but a dank fog blanketed downtown Grand Rapids.

The van was headed south toward the airstrip when Kingston broke the silence. "Well?"

Wiley rested his head against the seat and stared at the fog-shrouded trees. "If he's telling the truth, we're in big trouble. Last thing we need is a confrontation with our state militias."

Kingston nodded. "We'll watch him like a hawk. If he heads for Iowa, we'll track him there and set up a raid."

Wiley sighed. "I wonder how much Minton knows."

Kingston shrugged. "I've had three sessions with Burble. He insists Minton doesn't know about the dirty stuff ... that Jordan wants to keep her clear of all that."

Wiley cracked a smile. "If we can nail a bunch of subversive militia heads, and one of them is Claire Minton's adopted father, it won't matter what she knows. We'll crush her on guilt by association." He glanced at his watch. "I better let the boss know." He yanked out his cell phone and flipped it open.

"Shouldn't you wait for a face-to-face?"

Wiley shook his head. "This thing's too hot." He started to punch the President's access code and paused. "You did well, Zach. You'll get what you want."

Kingston nodded. "I just wish we'd nailed the damn reporter. He hurt us plenty and it's my fault."

"Too late to worry about him. If Burble's telling the truth, we'll smother Minton's Iran exposé with news about a domestic terror plot that rivals Oklahoma City and Nine-Eleven. We'll link her to Jordan and pick off two birds with one stone."

Kingston hesitated. "I wouldn't mind seeing this through, if it's okay. Give me a chance to go out in style."

Wiley nodded. "You might have something, Director Kingston. Let's talk it over when we get back." He punched the security code and placed the phone against his ear.

****

The President was in the midst of a shouting match with Dalton Kramer, his secretary of state, when his cell phone went off with an annoying ring. He knew it was important because few people knew that secured number.

The President snatched the phone out of his jacket pocket and raised his hand for silence. "Go ahead."

"I have news."

"Hang on." The President lowered the phone and forced an impatient smile. "You have some good points, Dalton. I know it's been rough, but I have an urgent call. Can we pick this up in a bit?"

Kramer heaved an angry sigh and rose from his chair. "We need to get closure on this, sir. My plane leaves at four."

"Of course. Tell Alice I asked you to wait. We'll pick it up in a few minutes." He watched his incensed secretary of state storm out of the oval office.

The President placed the phone to his ear. "Sorry about that. Had a little scuffle with Dalton."

"Africa?"

The President smiled. "He wants to give away the farm. We just don't have that kind of money these days."

Wiley hesitated. *"We met with our three million dollar man."*

The President rested his elbows on the desk. "Productive?"

"I guess you could say that. You sitting down?"

"Go ahead, Jack."

"I struck the mother lode on Minton, but there's something more important that came up. We're going to—"

"Yes?" The President waited for a response but only got a high-pitched whine. He squinted at the cell phone's display. The graphic symbols were gone, replaced by three words—

OUT OF SERVICE

He scrolled to Wiley's security access code and punched it, but the connection could not be re-established. He tried again but four words kept flashing on the display—

PHONE OUT OF SERVICE

"Damn dead zones. What good are you!" He glared at the phone and jammed it in his pocket. His chief of staff's important news would have to wait.

But the news would never come because Jack Wiley was dead along with FBI Director, Zach Kingston, and the two agents who were riding with them.

The rocket propelled grenades were fired from the trees at opposing sides of the road as the van raced by. The timing was perfect, triggered by a call from the Volkswagen trailing the van at two hundred yards.

The VW skidded to a stop when the grenades struck, its driver studying the inferno. The driver glanced at his rear view mirror and saw a car approaching from the rear. No time for analysis. He placed the walkie-talkie to his mouth and shouted, "Finish it!"

Six seconds later, two more RPG's struck the burning van from opposite sides of the road, scattering flaming debris into the fog-shrouded trees.

When news of the disaster reached the President, he withdrew to his office, his eyes locked on the photo taken after his election victory four years ago, a simple study of two men, their arms wrapped around each other, their faces beaming like children.

The President had lost his closest friend and confidant. Without Jack Wiley, the President would stagger through the next four months while his opponents pulled ahead. Everything he had fought for would be lost to the jackals closing on the White House.

The news became more devastating when FBI officials confirmed that Wiley's van had been struck by at least three RPG's fired from close range.

But that news would not come out. Instead, the area was secured and cleansed while carefully worded press releases described the tragic accident that had occurred on a lonely, fog-shrouded road outside Grand Rapids where Jack Wiley and Zach Kingston had escaped for a brief fishing trip after returning from a top security briefing at NORAD.

And while the President directed the nation's massive security infrastructure to pursue all leads in a futile effort to hunt down the assassins, FBI lab experts probed the debris for some clue to the brutal ambush, but all they found was a melted lump of plastic that was once a digital recorder.

****

Thirty minutes after his visitors left, Clyde Burble was awakened from his stupor by a jarring shake that snapped his eyes open. He squinted at the blurred face peering down at him. "Charlie?"

"How's it going, Clyde?"

"What are you doin' here?" Burble glanced at the door. "How did you get in?"

"Gotta watch that chair, Clyde. Won't work unless you push it under the knob real tight."

"But the door was locked?"

"Come on, Clyde, gimme some credit." Mootley jammed the nine-millimeter against Burble's forehead and pressed him down on the pillow. "Sorry, Clyde. Can't let you walk away."

"No, Charlie! I can explain! It's not like—"

The first round blew off the back of Burble's head. The second and third were to each ear. The fourth and fifth to each eye. The sixth through the mouth.

Mootley backed away from the pulp that was once Clyde Burble's head. He snatched the briefcase off the floor and headed for the door. A quick glance at the room and he was gone, muttering the nine words symbolized by the body lying on the blood-soaked bed—

"Hear no evil, see no evil, speak no evil…"

CHAPTER 21

THE VOICE

Perry sat up and glared at the darkness. The illuminated clock on the nightstand read 1:42. Everything was still. He rubbed his forehead while recalling the iced tea he'd sipped on the deck with candidate Minton twelve hours earlier. Then the sudden rush of fatigue after their meeting.

Yes, that had to be it. Nothing like a tall glass of iced tea spiked with a powerful sedative to ensure he remained at Lake Warnock until his early morning flight.

"Blast." He crawled off the bed and staggered to the window. He could see the lake through the trees, its black water sparkling in the moonlight. It was a beautiful night in western Kansas, except for one thing. His time had run out.

In a few hours, Minton's private jet would fly him to Chicago where a waiting car would take him to his destination. When he stepped out of that car, he would be allowed four hours to produce the video interviews with Kramer, Ramirez, Matafuco, and Cambria — and he would lose his bargaining chip.

He rested his hands on the sill and stared at the lake. A bead of sweat trickled into his eye, making him wince. He brushed it away and cursed the day he stumbled into that gutted Tehran house.

He was snapped from his thoughts by a muffled voice. He turned around and squinted at the shadows. The voice seemed to be coming from inside the room.

He looked down at the bed and noticed an air vent on the floor. Unless he was sleeping with a ghost, that had to be the answer. He dropped on the floor and pressed his ear against the opening.

It sounded like a man's voice, but he couldn't make it out. He sat up and leaned against the bed. Someone was staying up late at Lake Warnock.

The pen, Ambrose! Get the pen! He scrambled across the wood floor to his bag and dug through his clothes until his fingers grasped the fountain pen, a little gift from his stint with Mr. Caliento.

He yanked out the pen and crawled back to the vent. It only took a second to activate the pen's micro-digital recorder. He placed the pen against the vent and listened to the voice.

A minute later, he heard someone walk across a creaking floor. The door opened and closed. Then nothing.

He snatched the pen off the floor and played its muffled recording. The voice was indiscernible.

CHAPTER 22

CHICAGO

It was still dark when Perry climbed into the sedan with his two-man escort. He didn't know their names, but he'd given the bull-necked guy the moniker "Toast" because he always had a slice of toast in his hand.

No exception this morning. Toast jammed the last morsel in his mouth and brushed the crumbs off his suit. He opened the rear door and gestured for Perry to get in. Seconds later, they were crunching down the cinder road on their way to the airstrip.

Perry caught a final glimpse of the lodge fading into the moonlit trees. He dropped back in his seat and stared at Toast. "No sendoff from candidate Minton?"

Toast ignored him.

Perry leaned forward. "How are we going to do this?"

Toast shrugged. "We'll talk when we get there."

Perry slid his hand under his jacket and grasped the fountain pen. The next twelve hours would be the most important of his life.

The *Gulfstream* touched down at Midway Airport at 12:10. It was drizzling in Chicago with thunderstorms in the forecast.

Perry stepped down the plane's exit ramp, accompanied by his bull-necked bodyguard. They walked toward a gray-suited man standing beside a black sedan at the security fence. Perry glanced at Toast and managed a smile. "Impressive, it takes a lot of clout to park your car on a commercial tarmac."

Toast ignored him and said something to the gray-suited man before turning back to the plane.

Perry watched Toast climb aboard the *Gulfstream*. "Where's he going?"

The gray-suited man gripped his arm. "Not important, Mr. Ambrose. The big question is where you're going."

Perry frowned. "Mercantile Bank, Twenty-one-eighty, North Lake Shore Drive."

"Get in." The gray-suited man watched Perry climb into the sedan's back seat before slamming the door and climbing into the front seat beside the driver.

They pulled up to the bank at 1:11. It had begun to rain and people were opening umbrellas on North Lake Shore Drive.

The gray-suited man stepped out of the car and opened Perry's door. He leaned toward him and spoke in a harsh tone. "You have until five. That's when the bank closes. If we don't see you on those steps at five, we're coming after you and it won't be pretty … clear?"

Perry managed a feeble nod.

Gray-suit backed away from the door. "Then get out, the clock's ticking." He watched Perry climb out of the car and head for the crosswalk.

When Perry reached the bank's entrance, gray-suit climbed back in the car and looked down at the small screen on the console. "That's him?"

The driver nodded at the screen's flashing red blip while snatching a mike from its holder. "Car one to two and three. He's entering the bank. You got him?"

"*Affirmative two.*"

"*Affirmative three.*"

"Ten-four." The driver snapped the mike into its holder and looked across the street in time to catch a glimpse of Perry pushing through the bank's glass entrance doors.

CHAPTER 23

REVELATION

The bank's main lobby wasn't very busy with lunch hour over and everyone back to work. Perry sat across from an attractive young lady at one of the front desks while waiting for her to complete her phone conversation.

She hung up the phone and smiled. "Yes, sir? What can I do for you?"

"Perry Ambrose. I'd like to check my safe deposit box, but I need to show you some ID to claim my duplicate key."

"We're holding the key for you?"

Perry nodded. "I can't trust myself with it." He tapped his head. "Memory problems and all that."

"Certainly, Mr. Ambrose. You have other accounts with us?"

"Just one." Perry handed her his driver's license and watched her eyes light up when she accessed his account on the computer.

It only took a minute to validate his identity. A quick fingerprint check, retinal scan, and signature verification, all via computer, and it was done. She stood up and gestured toward the vault at the rear of the bank. "This way, Mr. Ambrose."

Perry stood up and leaned toward her. "Perhaps you can help me. I didn't want to carry my laptop over here. Do you have one I can borrow?"

She smiled. "Of course. I'll set you up after we get your box. Do you want internet access?"

"That would be very helpful. Can you manage a CD?"

"Certainly."

"And if possible, a USB-X3 cable?"

Her smile faded. "I'll see what I can do."

Perry followed her toward the vault while recalling her widened eyes when she saw his one million dollar balance.

After removing safe deposit box #3334 from its slot, the young lady escorted Perry to a private viewing room in the vault. Ten minutes later, she reappeared with the laptop, CD, and USB-X3 cable.

"Just take a second to set you up." She placed the laptop on the table and popped it open. She was scratching her blond hair when Perry smiled and took the USB-X3 cable from her hand. "I can do this. Thank you so much, Ms.—"

"Jean Nelson, Mr. Ambrose." She turned on the laptop and backed away. "Julie will be at the vault entrance. Just give her a wave when you're done."

Perry nodded. "I'll be quite awhile."

Her smile returned. "No problem, Mr. Ambrose. We're open until five." She closed the door and left him standing at the viewing table.

He sat down, his eyes focused on the metal box. He knew they had him wired, probably a micro-transmitter sewn into his clothes. One wrong move and they'd be on him like a pack of wolves.

He glanced at his watch. One thirty-two. Just three and a half hours to pull off a miracle. He frowned and lifted the box's metal cover, exposing the CD.

The CD had lain in that box since he placed it there last November. Its two clones lay in similar boxes at *Hoosier National Bank* and *The Bank of Atlanta*.

He lifted the CD out of the box and slipped off its protective sleeve. It only took a few seconds to insert it in the laptop and activate the recording.

He stared at their camouflaged faces and listened to their shaking voices. They were good men who had come from the streets of America to fight a ruthless enemy in a far-off land. There were so many of them, soldiers trying to retain their sanity while an uncaring nation looked the other way.

Terell Kramer impressed him most, so hopeful in the midst of his living hell. All Terell wanted was to survive another six months so he could collect his hazardous duty pay and return to his home in South Central.

Perry froze the video when Terell held up his mother's photo. He would never forget the woman's face or the face of her son and the other three men. They were burned into him like the star shells exploding in Tehran's night sky.

He popped out the CD and returned it to its paper sleeve. It was 1:45 in Chicago.

"God, I'm screwed."

He slumped in the chair and stared at the screen. He'd never felt so alone. He had stepped into a political war and his time had run out. He had no weapons except the black laptop and CD.

The photograph, idiot! Start with that!

He was working on instinct now, the same instinct that once made him a promising investigative reporter with the *Hartford*

Courant, Chicago Tribune, and *WNN.* The mistakes he'd made along the way no longer mattered. It was survival now, and the clock was ticking.

He connected to the internet and repeated the Cadmore search he'd done at Purdue's library a month ago. The Charlene MacAfee adoption photo flashed on the screen.

He scanned the article below the photo until his eyes focused on one word—

Jordan

Matthew Jordan was a prominent figure in Kansas, a self-made billionaire who had built a successful agricultural trucking business throughout the Midwest and Southwest.

Perry leaned back in the chair and stared at the handsome man standing behind Charlene, his hands resting on her shoulders. There was something familiar about Jordan's strong, tanned face. Maybe the firm jaw and piercing green eyes. Maybe the confident smile and blond, swept-back hair. Whatever it was, it tugged at him like a magnet.

He keyed a search for "Matthew Jordan" and stared at the screen. Nothing.

He altered the search to "Jordan" and waited.

Still nothing.

Think, dammit. It's two-fifteen.

He re-read the article below the photograph. *Trucking. Jordan Trucking. Try it.* He keyed "Jordan Trucking" and waited.

The search screen displayed seven articles spanning forty-four years. He disregarded the first one because it dealt with Charlene MacAfee's adoption in 1976, the article he'd already read.

The next three articles described Matthew Jordan's phenomenal rise to power as head of *Jordan Trucking.* The articles emphasized Jordan's close relationship with the farmers of Kansas, Nebraska, Missouri, and Iowa as his business spread across the Midwest. It was more than his personality or humble roots. There was something deeper only a reporter could sense.

Perry scanned the fifth article covering *Jordan Trucking's* expansion to the southwestern states in 1982. Nothing there but a bunch of financial projections and corporate jargon. He jumped to the sixth article and waited for the screen to bring it up.

He leaned forward and stared at the *Kansas City Star* headline dated February 14, 1991—

Jordan Linked to Militia

He started reading the article and hesitated. *Careful, chum. Lots of spin here. Looks like an old-fashioned political attack. Must take everything with a grain of salt. Don't jump to conclusions.* He scrolled down the page and continued reading.

If the article was accurate, Charlene MacAfee's foster father wasn't quite the role model he appeared. The two page article was part of an exposé launched by the *Kansas City Star* to probe the increasingly powerful Kansas militia movement.

The article focused on Jordan's extensive financial empire and his deep ties with a fringe group called the "red legs", a name that hadn't been heard since the Civil War.

The article mentioned Jordan's friend, Charles Mootley, a mechanic who had built a lucrative farm equipment business in tandem with Jordan's successful trucking venture. It described Mootley as a fanatic bent on fomenting another civil war to right the wrongs done by the liberals that ruled America. To drive its point home, the article quoted excerpts from Mootley's impassioned speeches to the distraught farmers of Kansas.

Also mentioned was Jordan's closest friend, Clyde Burble, a dispossessed farmer and member of the red legs, a zealot whose cries for revolution and white supremacy echoed throughout the Midwestern states.

The article focused on Jordan's crusade for a militia-backed third party to challenge the state's Republican and Democrat controlled legislature. References were made to Jordan's speech at a recent gathering of six state militias in which he shook his fist at the sky and shouted a clarion call to arms—

"Damn the hypocrites and Judas goats that pervert this crippled nation! They are too far corrupted for salvation. There is only one hope for the men, women, and children that built our land. We must take it back! We must do whatever necessary to drive the perverted gay, colored, and communist liberals from our government. We must beat our plowshares into weapons. We must come together as one national militia and march against the heathens and their pig masters. The call is given my brethren. March with me!"

Perry stared at the words. A bit over the top, but they did strike home. He frowned while recalling Claire Minton's fiery speech at the University of Kansas. The speeches were similar in their stinging tone and common touch that seemed to resonate with the masses.

He selected the final article dated July 4, 1999, and began reading—

Kansas Billionaire
Welcomes Candidate Minton to the Fight

Matthew Jordan, Abilene's self-made billionaire embraces Claire Minton after endorsing her candidacy for the upcoming state elections. In his brief but powerful speech, Jordan declared that Claire Minton offered a fresh new face to the forgotten farmers of Kansas because of her own bitter history at the hands of her corporate oppressors. Jordan pulled no punches when questioned about Minton's third party candidacy.

"We're at a crossroads and our only hope is to build a grassroots third party movement across the land. With legislators like Claire Minton, we can steer our great ship out of the dangerous waters our corrupt leaders have placed it in. I will therefore throw my full support behind Claire and the other four candidates representing the good people of Kansas."

When grilled by the press regarding his alleged ties with the Quantrill and red leg militias, Jordan dodged their questions with the same hyperbole that had propelled him to power in Kansas politics.

"I won't lower myself to responding to your trick questions, but mark me well. This nation was created and defended by citizen militia who took up arms at Lexington and Concord, and died in the subzero cold of Valley Forge. Men, women, and children who refused to bend to their oppressors."

"I ask you, ladies and gentlemen of the press … are the vermin that rule us today any better than our British masters two hundred and twenty-three years ago? Are we free of undue taxation? Can we freely speak without fear of retribution? Are our homes safe from unlawful entry? Can a man or woman dream of a better life, or have we become a broken, disillusioned people?"

"I swear before God, we must turn the tide. Our one chance is a fresh, new party that will rally the forgotten ones to its side. The Heartlanders are that party, and Claire Minton, Frank Borner, Marve Clansbury, Chad Pimsley, and Zachary Taylor Woodruff are the minutemen that will launch the new revolution!"

Perry stared at the screen in disbelief. It wasn't the article that floored him, but the photograph of Jordan embracing Claire Minton in front of the screaming throng of farmers and blue-collar workers. In another instant, that photo would have been meaningless because it would have missed Jordan whispering in her ear while he held her tightly against him.

Yes, old chum. This was more than a kind embrace between political allies. This was love — deep, passionate love.

Perry switched to the forty-year-old photograph of Charlene MacAfee. He switched back to the photo of Jordan and Minton embracing. He switched them again — and again.

Yes, it was her. Whatever fate had befallen Charlene MacAfee, the young girl in the forty-year-old photograph was Claire Minton, and the man standing behind her was the same man embracing Claire Minton in front of the farmers — her stepfather and lover, Matthew Jordan.

He collapsed in the chair. *Careful chum, this is the biggest decision of your life. If you're wrong, you'll walk out of here into hell. No mistakes, Ambrose. Not this time.*

He squinted at Jordan's face. Something was tugging at him like a vague memory. He'd seen that face before, but where and when?

He leaned toward the screen and studied the yellow-gray hair streaming past Jordan's ears. The article was dated twenty-one years ago. By now, that hair could be white.

His eyes widened. "Blast … hello, Mr. Smith."

He downloaded the seven articles and re-read them until a soft voice snapped him out of his trance.

"The bank will close in thirty minutes. If you need assistance in completing your business, please contact one of our help desks in the main lobby."

He glanced at his watch. Four thirty. He'd lost track of time. He rubbed his forehead and tried to clear his head.

The pen, Ambrose. Don't quit now, you're on a roll. Pinch yourself or something, but snap out of this bloody trance.

He pulled the pen out of his shirt pocket and unscrewed the cap, exposing the micro-recorder and USB-X3 download port.

Through the fog, he managed to connect the cable to the pen and laptop's USB receptor port. He activated the laptop's voice digitization software and downloaded the recording into the computer's memory. Then came the attempt to extract the man's voice from the muffled recording.

He watched the oscillations flow across the screen as the software diagnosed each pulse in an attempt to filter out unwanted noise. It took five minutes to cleanse the recording. It was 4:35 in Chicago.

He wiped away a bead of sweat and clicked the play icon. The voice was thin, but audible—

"What about Clyde's sister? Someone should talk to her? … I don't care about secrecy. She had nothing to do with this mess.

She'll need financial help. I'll call her first thing. The Michigan papers will have his death smeared all over their front pages by then ... What? ... Oh, yeah, almost forgot. With all the other news, he'll barely make the obit page ... What about the pow-wow? Still on for July fourth? ... How many groups? ... Got Michigan and California? ... Well, that's good. They won't be happy when I hit them for the dinero, but it has to be done ... Why? More missiles dammit! Not easy since the last time. They've really tightened security at those bases. If we can get those camel jockeys a hundred of the new Chinese RPG's, the damn war will be over in a week. Just one more deal and we'll be done with this Mideast crap ... Cool it with the questions, Charlie. I'll call you tomorrow at five ... No, I'll still be here. I'm not sure how Claire will handle the news ... Are you nuts? She doesn't know a damn thing and we're going to keep it that way ... No, dammit! Get this straight, Charlie. Under no circumstances is she to know we had anything to do with it ... I'd better go. I'm dog tired and I have to review Claire's condolence speech with Jess ... Hell, how do you think I feel? Not easy whacking your best friend. At least I have some consolation knowing that sonofabitch in DC no longer has a chief of staff and FBI director. What the hell did you use, one of those chink RPG's? Hell, nothing left but melted metal ... Yeah, yeah, I'll talk to you tomorrow..."

Perry's face blanched while the words rang in his ears. Chief of staff? FBI director? Clyde? Charlie? He sank in the chair, his eyes trained on the screen.

Play it again, Ambrose. He reached for the play button, but was interrupted by the soft voice on the PA system—

"The bank will close in fifteen minutes. If you need assistance in completing your business, please contact one of our help desks in the main lobby."

"Think, dammit!" He gritted his teeth and inserted the blank CD into the PC. It only took a few seconds to download the voice recording, articles, and Tehran interviews. Then another three minutes to type the most important letter of his life.

Julie Logan was clearing her desk at the vault entrance when Perry burst out of the viewing room. She gave him a polite wave and watched him rush toward her.

"Anything wrong, Mr. Ambrose?"

He waved his hand impatiently. "I need a blank CD and two envelopes."

Startled by his abruptness, she maintained her calm while pulling a CD from her desk drawer and handing it to him.

"The envelopes?"

"Yes, sir. No problem." She reached into the drawer and handed him two legal envelopes.

He waved them aside. "Reinforced."

"Yes, sir, but please hurry. We're closing in fifteen minutes." She lifted two reinforced mailing envelopes out of the drawer and watched him snatch them out of her hand. "Really, Mr. Ambrose. There's no need to be rude."

He didn't hear her. He ran into the viewing room with the CD and envelopes dangling from his hand.

It only took a minute to create a second CD copy of the voice recording, articles, and Tehran interviews, this one including the letter he'd just typed. He inserted a copied CD into each envelope and sealed it. He was slipping the first envelope into his jacket pocket when the soft voice crackled on the bank's PA system—

"The bank will close in five minutes. If you need assistance in completing your business, please contact one of our help desks."

He glared at the second envelope lying on the table. *One shot, Ambrose. You're out of time.* He inserted the original CD into the

PC and fast forwarded it to the instant Terell Kramer held up his mother's photo and spoke the words that would determine Perry's fate—

"I just want to get back to my mom in South Central."

"You live in the hood?"

"Yes, sir. Fifteen-three-sixty-five, Harmony Road. That's my home and here's my mom's picture so she'll know I carry it with me."

"I'll see she gets the message."

"Thank you, sir. Could you do something else for me?"

"If I can."

"In case anything happens to me, maybe you can look her up?"

"Of course, son. Of course I will."

Perry clicked the stop icon and put down the pen. He took a deep breath and gazed at the address he had scribbled on the envelope.

"Mr. Ambrose?"

He jumped out of his chair and stared at Julie Logan who was standing at the opened door with an impatient look on her face.

"Sorry to disturb you, Mr. Ambrose. We're closing."

Perry popped out the original CD and inserted it in its paper sleeve. He placed the CD in the safe deposit box and stood up. "Can I mail something?"

"Sure, Mr. Ambrose. I'll take care of it."

He snatched the second envelope off the table and handed it to her. "It needs postage, but I can pay you."

She smiled. "No problem, Mr. Ambrose. I can afford a stamp for one of our top customers."

He nodded at the envelope. "I'm not sure of the zip."

"No problem, I'll look it up." She watched him pick up the safe deposit box and walk through the door.

The clock above the entrance was chiming five when Perry stepped out of the vault into the main lobby. He leaned against a counter and wiped the sweat off his forehead.

"Are you alright, sir?"

Perry looked at the guard who was staring at him with concerned eyes. "Just a little tired. Could I sit down for a minute to call my office? I'm supposed to be there for a meeting and I need a ride back."

The guard patted his shoulder and nodded at the vacated desks. "Take your pick. I can get you a doctor if you'd like."

Perry shook his head. "I'm fine. It's this new blood pressure medication. I'm still getting used to it."

The guard smiled. "Understood. Take as long as you need. I'll get you some water." He watched Perry walk to the first desk and plunk down in the chair.

Perry didn't need to look up Terell's cell phone number. It had been etched in his brain since that desperate call from Terell two months ago. He punched the eleven digits and waited for the ring.

"Hello?"

He was startled by the woman's voice. "Yes, I'm trying to reach Terell Kramer."

Her voice sharpened. *"Who is this?"*

"I'm an old friend from the service. I just got back and would like to speak with Terell."

She hesitated. *"You don't know?"*

"Know?"

Her voice broke. *"My Terell's dead. They killed my boy."*

Perry felt the phone drop away from his ear. He collapsed in the chair and fought for words. "You're Terell's mother?"

"Yes."

He lifted the phone and spoke softly. "I'm very sorry, Mrs. Kramer. I'm so sorry."

She fought a sob. *"You were in the war with Terell?"*

Perry took a deep breath and spilled his guts. "I'm a reporter, Mrs. Kramer. I just mailed you a recording of my video interview with Terell and his three comrades. You should receive it in a few days."

"Reporter? You mean in Iran?

"Yes ma'am."

Her voice rose. *"Why were you talking to my boy?"*

Perry glanced at the clock above the entrance. If he had anything left, he must use it now. He forced out the words. "Mrs. Kramer, how did your son die?"

She sobbed. *"Gang bangers shot him dead. He was just taking a walk to see his friends. They gunned him down in cold blood."*

"Did they get the people that did it?"

"They're still looking."

Perry clenched his fist. No turning back now. He was down to his last card and it was time to play it.

Her voice crackled in his ear. *"Who are you?"*

"Ambrose, Mrs. Kramer. Perry Ambrose."

"You English?"

"Yes, ma'am."

"Why do you care about Terell?"

Perry took a deep breath and played his card. "Mrs. Kramer, I'm going to tell you something you won't believe. All I ask is you give me a chance. When the recording comes, play it and you'll know I'm telling the truth."

"I don't know what you're saying. I don't want to hear anymore."

Perry gripped the phone. "For god's sake, don't hang up! Please, Mrs. Kramer, you're all I have!" He blinked away a tear and listened to the silence. "Mrs. Kramer?"

"I'm here."

"I know who killed your son."

She gasped. *"My Lord, what are you saying?"*

"Your son saw too much, Mrs. Kramer. He saw our soldiers turn on their commanders. He saw the beginning of the end in a war we can't win. The people that put us there are afraid of the truth, so they kill the witnesses."

"And that's what they're trying to do to you?"

Perry couldn't hold on any longer. He lowered his head and broke down.

"What's wrong, Mr. Ambrose?"

"Oh, Mrs. Kramer. I'm so sorry…"

"What do you want?"

He took a deep breath and clenched his fists. "Do you have a pencil and paper?"

"Yes."

"You should receive the envelope by Wednesday. If you don't hear from me by next Friday, please mail the CD to Harvey Weissman at The Chicago Tribune, 435 North Michigan Avenue, Chicago, Illinois. I don't know the zip, but you can look it up."

"Why should I do that?"

Perry forced out the words. "Because I'll be dead and you'll be striking back at the people who killed your son and our boys over there."

"Why should I believe you? This isn't your country. We took it from you English."

Perry cracked a smile through his tears. "That you did, Mrs. Kramer. That you did."

"Then why should I believe you?"

Perry was about to speak when he heard a rap on the bank's entrance door. Gray-suit was standing on the other side, peering at him through the glass.

"Mr. Ambrose?"

"I'm sorry, Mrs. Kramer. I have to go."

"You didn't answer my question."

"You'll know when you see the CD. Goodbye, Mrs. Kramer. I'll say a prayer for your son."

"Sounds like you're the one needing prayers."

Perry pressed the off button and sank in the chair.

"That man at the door for you, sir?"

Perry looked at the guard. "Yes, I should be on my way." He stood up and watched the guard walk toward the door. When the guard wasn't looking, he dropped the cell phone in a wastebasket.

Nothing was said until their sedan squealed away from the curb into the southbound traffic on Lakeshore Drive. Gray-suit looked over his shoulder at Perry. "Who were you talking to?"

"Can't say."

"Let's see your cell phone."

Perry shrugged. "I lost it. Had to borrow one from the guard."

Gray-suit glared at him. "Got the CD?"

Perry reached into his jacket pocket and pulled out the envelope. He handed it to gray-suit and watched him rip it open.

Gray-suit turned away from Perry and glanced at the driver. "Step on it, I'm calling in."

Perry watched gray-suit lift a PC from his briefcase and place it on his lap while snatching a cell phone from his pocket. Gray suit punched a dialing code and pressed the cell phone against his ear.

"It's me. We have the CD."

Perry clenched his fists while gray-suit inserted the CD into the laptop. Gray-suit leaned forward and stared at the screen, his hand holding the cell phone against his ear.

"Looks like a bunch of soldiers in a dark room. Someone's asking them questions … Yeah, it's pretty clear except for the shadows. They look real shook … Bodies? No, I don't see any, but they keep looking to their right and breaking down … Okay, transmitting now."

Gray-suit closed the cell phone and slipped it in his pocket. He didn't bother ejecting the CD when he completed the transmission and returned the laptop to its briefcase.

Perry leaned forward. "Where are we going?"

"We're here."

Perry looked out the window in time to see their car swerve into a deserted industrial park. The sedan sped across the empty parking lot into an abandoned warehouse where two cars sat beneath one of the rusted beams. Perry stiffened as the sedan eased to a stop.

Gray-suit climbed out of the car and pulled Perry's door open. "Get out."

Perry was halfway out the door when gray-suit's fist slammed into his gut, dropping him to his knees. He let out a groan and gripped his stomach, but gray-suit wasn't in the mood for hysterics. He seized Perry's shoulder and yanked him up like a rag doll.

"You're in big trouble, Mr. Ambrose." Gray-suit's left fist dug into Perry's ribs, dropping him again. Perry doubled up in pain, gasping for air. When he looked up, gray-suit was holding out the cell phone.

"Someone wants to say hello." Gray-suit bent down and jammed the phone into Perry's hands. He backed away and glared at the grimacing reporter.

Perry crawled against the car and held the phone against his ear.

"Mr. Ambrose?"

The harsh voice crackled in Perry's ear. "Yeah?"

"What are you trying to do?"

Perry grimaced. "I think you know, but for the record, I mailed a duplicate CD to a friend for safekeeping. If they don't hear from me in a few days, they have instructions to mail everything to the media along with my letter of explanation."

Perry listened to the man's strained breathing. He waited a few more seconds before throwing his final punch. "Did you get that, Mr. Smith?"

"Who?"

"Sorry, I mean, Mr. Jordan. Or is it Charles Mootley? Blast, we both know it isn't Clyde Burble."

"Damn you!"

"Sorry, just doing my job."

"You little bastard. Give the phone to my man, you little piece of crap."

Perry sneered at the phone. "Nice talking to you, Mr. Jordan. Say hello to Claire for me. Oh … sorry, I mean, Charlene. Then again, it's hard to talk to the dead."

"Give him the fucking phone!"

Gray-suit lunged at Perry and snatched the phone out of his hand. He held the phone against his ear and backed away. "It's me … Yes, sir. Happy to." He jammed the phone in his pocket and nodded at the other three men.

They spread-eagled Perry on the hood of the car. The punches were more than powerful, they were surgical. First, to the ribs and groin. Then to the face. Perry screamed plenty, but they were just getting started.

He could barely see through his swollen eyelids. His mouth was full of blood. He spat on the broken concrete floor and felt a knifing pain in his kidneys from someone's shoe. He rolled on his back and felt one of them yanking off his jacket. Then came the ripped shirt sleeve and stinging pain in his arm. A massive fist seized his collar and jerked him into a sitting position. He couldn't see the man, but he knew it was gray-suit.

"Pleasant dreams, scumbag."

Gray-suit's fist caught him square on the jaw, driving him backwards against the concrete floor. His head was on fire. He could see hell! He let out a primordial scream. His eyes filled with psychedelic images, and that terrible ringing in his ears. It would be a long night in Chicago.

CHAPTER 24

SHOCK

Jordan suppressed a smile and placed the newspaper on the desk. "I'll be damned. That's one I didn't expect."

She nodded and stared at the headline—

Chief of Staff and FBI Director Killed in Fatal Accident, President Visibly Shaken During Press Conference

He leaned toward her. "You okay, Missy?"

She lowered her head. "Kingston left a wife and two daughters. I know that pain."

Jordan eased back in his chair and stared at the window. "The President must be a basket case. He and Wiley were very close. Came up the political ladder together. No replacement for that kind of trust."

She pushed out of her chair and walked around the desk to the window. It was a beautiful summer morning at Lake Warnock. Blue sky, gentle breezes, the lake rippling through the trees, but she didn't notice. Her mind was on the front page photograph of the twisted, melted hulk that was once an SUV.

Jordan stood up and eased beside her. He rested his hands on her shoulders and spoke softly. "Sure you're okay?"

She stared at the lake. "It doesn't make sense."

"What?"

"They died on a fishing trip."

"So?"

"Who goes on a fishing trip with someone they hate?"

He patted her shoulders. "They were probably trying to work something out. It's no secret the President wanted Kingston off the payroll. Easier to settle things away from the office."

She turned toward him and pointed at the newspaper lying on the desk. "I've seen too much war, Matt. That SUV exploded before it went off the road."

"Now really, Missy—"

"For god's sake, look at the photo. They're digging melted metal out of the trees. The road's black with scorch marks." Her eyes burned into him. "That's blast heat. I've seen a hundred like it."

He grasped her arms. "Easy, Missy. It was an accident, pure and simple. Now snap out of it cause we have work to do. We need to hit them now, before they recover."

She started to speak, but he raised his hand for silence. "Where's the reporter?"

She folded her arms and looked down. "He made the exchange and took off."

"That's confirmed?"

She nodded. "Jess called me this morning. Ambrose made the exchange and took off."

Jordan's face reddened. "I don't trust that little bastard. I've seen his kind before. He'll sell his soul to the highest bidder."

She sighed. "He's not going to try anything. He has what he wants."

"What about the video?"

"All there."

"And the interviews?"

She shrugged. "Jess is working on the first telecast."

His anger faded. He backed away and stared at her with glistening eyes. "My god, do you know what this means? We'll be at thirty percent by month end. Then the debates and—" He grimaced and clutched his chest.

"What's wrong?"

He groaned and pressed his clenched fist against his heart. His body slumped against the desk.

"Matt?" She rushed beside him and gripped his arms.

"I'm okay. Just a little dizzy."

She stroked the sweat off his brow. "I'll get a doctor."

"No!" He pulled her against him. "Hold me, Missy. Hold me tight."

Her eyes welled up with tears. "Please, let me get a doctor. If anything happens to you—"

He held her in his arms. "Never mind me, Missy. You're the only one who matters. Your time has come, Claire. We're in your hands … all of us." He couldn't contain himself. He buried his face in her shoulder and broke down.

"Oh, Matt." She melted against him and felt his sweat on her cheek. He was breathing hard, his arms pulling her close. She could feel his member hardening against her. She pressed her lips to his ear and whispered softly. "Oh, my darling. I'm sorry. I'm so sorry."

They clung to each other while the waves of passion surged through them. When it was done, he kissed her on the lips and staggered out of the room.

She collapsed against the desk and saw the star shells and rockets streaking across the night sky. Then the artillery blasts and tracers, and screams of dying soldiers and civilians. And through it all, she saw Matthew Jordan's reassuring face, the face that sustained her, the rock that kept her whole.

She glared at the window and felt the words spew out of her mouth. "My god, we're going to win."

CHAPTER 25

THE TRANSMITTER

"How are you feeling?"

The voice echoed in Perry's ears. He opened his swollen eyes and squinted at the blurred face peering down at him.

"Can you hear me?"

Perry could see him now. The man wore a surgical gown with a stethoscope dangling from his neck. He had a handsome, youthful face with curly brown hair and brown eyes.

The doctor grasped Perry's wrist while glancing at his watch. "Things clearing up a bit?"

Perry tried to sit up, but froze from a sharp pain in his right side. He felt the doctor's hand press him down.

"Better watch those ribs. You've had a rough time."

Perry collapsed on the pillow and stared at the ceiling.

"You're at Urban Clinic in Old Town. I'm Doctor Manzar." He patted Perry's shoulder. "How about you?"

Perry ignored him.

Manzar sat on the stool beside the bed. "You were in pretty bad shape when the police brought you in. They found you lying in a street near here. We checked for ID but your pockets were empty, except for this note." He opened the crumpled paper and held it in front of Perry's face—

I don't like threats. One wrong move and my men finish what they started.

Cordially,
Mr. Smith

Manzar nodded at the paper. "Know what it means?"

"Perry shook his head."

Manzar stuffed the paper in his pocket. "It would really help if I knew your name."

Perry stared at the white ceiling. *No ID? Empty pockets? Blast, he doesn't have a clue. Don't blow it, chum. Anonymity is your only hope.*

Manzar leaned toward him. "The police want to talk with you, but I told them to hold off until your vital signs stabilize."

Perry looked at him. "What happened?"

Manzar sighed. "That's what we'd like to know. Three cracked ribs, a concussion, cuts and bruises. Looks like no organs are damaged, except for a bruised kidney. You'll have quite a headache for the next twenty-four hours. Can't be walking around with a concussion." He hesitated while manipulating Perry's jaw. "You lost a lower right bicuspid and some blood. Two black eyes and a deep cut over your right ear. Nine stitches if I recall." He forced a smile. "You took some hard punches. Good thing they stopped."

Perry took a painful breath. It was coming back. The beating and interrogation. The injection and hallucinations while they tried to squeeze it out of him. He still felt the plastic cell phone jammed against his ear with Mr. Smith screaming at him—

Who's your contact, Ambrose? Talk or you're a dead man. Think I'm playing games? You're in it up to your neck and there's no way out. Talk, goddammit! Where did you send that CD? Who is he? Who the hell is he!

Perry felt the doctor's hand on his wrist.

"You okay?"

He stared at the doctor and fought his racing heart. No time to figure things out. Just go with your best shot and hope it works.

He looked at the ceiling. "I'm Clarence Harris. I was in town on business. Stopped for a nightcap at a local bar and got lost on my way back to the hotel."

"Which hotel?"

"I don't remember. It's a bloody fog." Perry tried to grasp his forehead but the doctor pulled his hand away.

"Go on, Mr. Harris."

"I was headed for a cab stand when the blokes jumped me. Must have been three of them. I fought back but they were all over me. I remember one of them fumbling for my wallet when everything went black."

"You're English?"

Perry smiled through his cracked lip. "How did you guess?"

Manzar leaned closer. "What about the note?"

"Blast if I know. Maybe they thought I was someone else."

"I see." Manzar straightened up and gave Perry a quizzical look. "I neglected to mention something."

"Yes?"

"When we took a blood sample for the transfusion, we found traces of pentothal and LSD in your system. Seems a little exotic for a mugging."

Perry looked away.

"One other thing, Mr. Harris. I noticed a healed bullet wound in your left arm. Not well treated from the looks of the discoloration." Manzar paused and lifted a small envelope out of his pocket. "I was checking the wound for infection when I spotted something on the X-ray. At first, I thought it was a bullet fragment. Then something strange happened."

Perry's bloodshot eyes locked on him. "Strange?"

"The object emitted a signal of some sort. Picked it up on the X-ray." Manzar opened the envelope and dropped something into his palm. "Hope you don't mind. I removed this from your arm."

Perry squinted at the tiny object in Manzar's palm.

"I'm not much for espionage, but under the magnifier it looks like a small transmitter." Manzar grasped the object between his thumb and forefinger. "So tell me, Mr. Harris. What do you do for a living?"

Perry squinted at the tiny wafer. *Think fast, chum. In another minute, he's going to invite the cops in for a chat.* He grimaced and reached for his forehead. "I'm a little dizzy. Think I'm blacking out."

Manzar snatched Perry's wrist. "It's the concussion. We have to be careful with that."

"Need to rest. Need to clear my head." Perry turned away from Manzar and closed his eyes.

He felt Manzar check his pulse and push off the stool. Manzar placed something on the medical table beside the bed before turning off the light and walking out of the room.

He heard Manzar arguing with the cops outside the door. The corridor echoed with their harsh footsteps when they stormed away. Then Manzar's instructions to the ward nurse to check Mr.

Harris' pupils every fifteen minutes and call him if the life sign monitor showed anything unfavorable. Then they were gone.

Perry's eyes snapped open. He sat up in the darkness and gripped his spinning head. *Pull yourself together, man. You have to get out of here."*

Nurse Bentley checked the patient at 11:14, exactly fifteen minutes after Dr. Manzar's instruction. Nothing unusual noted. Pupils dilated, no fever, life signs stable. Patient appeared in deep sleep. She flicked off the light and closed the door.

If Bentley had dropped in a few minutes earlier, she would have been shocked to see her patient staggering through the darkness with a flashlight in his hand, a little souvenir from the medical table beside his bed.

Though giddy from the painkiller, Perry had found the envelope Dr. Manzar left on the medical table, and had removed its tiny micro-transmitter. He nearly collapsed when he stood on the bed and dropped the tiny object into the overhead lamp fixture. If the damn thing still worked, its new location might buy him time to break free of the scum that nearly beat him to death in that deserted warehouse.

Bentley's second visit came at 11:29. No change in vital signs. Pupils dilated. Patient resting comfortably. She turned off the light and exited the room.

No time to lose. She would be back in fifteen minutes. Perry climbed off the bed and staggered toward the hamper beside the door, the life sign sensors straining against his arms and chest.

No options left. He ripped off the sensors and stared at the monitor's flat line while praying it wasn't linked to a central monitor at the front desk.

He reached into the hamper and dug out his damp trousers, shirt, and sport jacket. Slipping on the trousers almost dropped him to the floor. Then the shirt, its torn right sleeve spattered with blood, but his sport jacket would cover it. He slipped on the wet jacket and jammed the flashlight in an outside pocket.

Next his socks and shoes, placed neatly on the floor beside the hamper. His last act was to unravel his head bandage and drop it in the hamper.

He was nearly out the door when the dizziness overtook him. He gripped the knob and felt his legs giving way. *Fight it, Ambrose. No turning back now.*

He pressed his head against the door and took slow, deep breaths while praying for the dizziness to pass. No guarantees with a concussion. One minute you're up, the next you're out cold.

The corridor was deserted except for a laundry cart outside the men's room. He gritted his teeth and rushed for the exit door at the rear of the corridor.

Perry pushed through the door and staggered into the stinging rain. He stumbled past the two ambulances parked in the lot and shuffled toward the flooded street.

He managed to cover two blocks before the dizziness became intolerable. He ducked into an alley and collapsed on a pile of trash bags, his face buried in his hands. He heard a clap of thunder and everything went black…

He awoke to the sound of traffic echoing off the alley's brick walls. He raised his head and grimaced from the bright sunlight shining in the alley. It was high noon in Chicago. He had slept twelve hours.

He rolled over and sat up on the bags, his hands gripping his head. The dizziness was gone, but his body ached from head to toe. His tongue probed the gap between his lower right incisor and molar. Blast, he hated dentists.

The trash bags were surrounded by deep puddles of rain water. He could see cars and pedestrians darting past the alley entrance. From the sun's high angle, it must be lunch time in Chicago. He gripped his sore stomach. Blast, he was hungry.

He leaned toward the puddled water and peered at his reflection. The face looking up at him was in pretty bad shape with swollen eyes and puffed cheeks. Add the abrasions and scowl, and he resembled a boxer who had gone one round too many.

He rubbed his forehead and took a deep breath. Maybe best to go back to the clinic and talk to the cops. At least he could get some food and medical attention.

His scowl deepened. *Forget the bloody clinic, Ambrose. There are debts to be paid and it's time to collect. So get off your bruised bum and start begging. All you need is a few bloody quarters.*

He let out an agonizing grunt and stood up in the puddle, his hand resting against the brick wall. *Not so bad, chum. Beg some quid, hit the nearest shelter for some warm food, and you'll be good as new. Now get moving.*

He started down the alley and hesitated when his foot struck a newspaper floating in the puddle. He bent toward the newspaper and stared at its black headline—

Chief of Staff and FBI Director Killed in Fatal Accident, President Visibly Shaken During Press Conference

He reached into the puddle and lifted out the soaked paper while trying to focus on the article below the headline. A fire engine flashed by the alley's entrance, its siren echoing off the brick walls, but he didn't hear it. He was recalling the voice he'd recorded two nights ago at Lake Warnock—

Hell, how do you think I feel? Not easy whacking your best friend. At least I have some consolation knowing that sonofabitch in DC no longer has a chief of staff and FBI director.

"My god, Mr. Smith. Did you do this?" He dropped the newspaper in the puddle and staggered down the alley.

CHAPTER 26

INDEPENDENCE DAY

Josh Barden was sprawled in his favorite leather chair with his feet propped on the desk when his intercom went off with an annoying buzz. He sat up and pressed the talk button. "Yes?"

"Jess Wilkin is on the phone, sir."

Barden's eyes lit up. "Wilkin?"

"Yes, sir."

"Put him through."

"Yes, sir."

Barden gripped the mug on his desk and took a healthy sip of coffee. He took a deep breath and snatched the buzzing phone. "Barden here."

"Hi, old buddy."

"Hi, Jess. How goes the battle?"

"Things are heating up. Thought I'd give you first shot at a major speech."

Wilkin's words hit Barden between the eyes. He lost his grip on the cup and let out a loud "Shit!" as hot coffee spilled across his desk.

"Something wrong?"

"Sorry, just a minor accident." Barden pushed his chair back from the dripping coffee while fumbling with the phone. "Did I hear, major speech?"

"That's right."

Barden gripped the phone. "The troop interviews?"

"No."

"No interviews?"

"Not yet, Josh."

Barden sank in his chair. "Then why the speech?"

"Can't say, but you won't be disappointed."

Barden stared at the coffee dripping off the desk. Since Claire Minton's explosive performance at the *Ritz Carlton*, he'd waited for a magic call from Jess Wilkin that would propel him to even greater heights than his top floor office in the famed WNN building. Anchoring the telecast that exposed the *Freedom Square* interviews would guarantee WNN a huge sweeps victory and assure Josh Barden another lucrative promotion — but it wouldn't be today.

"You there, Josh?"

"I'm here."

"Interested?"

"To be honest, I expected the interviews."

"Patience, old chum. Everything in its proper time. Just work with us and you'll get first rights."

Barden sighed. "Where's she giving the speech?"

"Lincoln Memorial."

"Lincoln, eh? When?"

"Three o'clock."

Barden's head snapped up. "Today?"

"That's right."

"Hell, it's July Fourth. The Mall concert's tonight. Potomac Park will be a mob scene."

"Right on, buddy. Can't think of a better time and place."

Barden glanced at his watch. "Cut me some slack, Jess. It's after ten. That only gives us a few hours. Why not use our studio? We can project the memorial on a blue screen. Saves lots of time and money."

"Sorry, Josh. This is too important for special effects. We need the memorial and we need it today. Too many people involved. Can't change things because of crowds and short windows."

Barden stroked his forehead. "How much air time do you need?"

"Fifteen minutes."

"That's all?"

"Yes."

Barden frowned. They both knew he had no choice. "Okay, we'll be there at three, but it better be good."

"I think you'll like it. Oh, one other thing."

"Yeah?"

"Please bring a wide-angle lens. Claire won't be alone."

"I surmised that. How many others?"

"Fifty-three."

"Fifty what?"

"There's actually one more, but number fifty-four can't make it today. Gotta go. See you there."

Barden placed the phone in its cradle and stared at his window's sweeping view of Atlanta. This would be candidate Minton's second media appearance in twenty-four hours, the prior one being an expression of condolences to the beleaguered President.

He glanced at his watch. Ten twenty. It would be a real scramble to set up the three o'clock telecast, but he knew it was the only way to guarantee WNN's first shot at the *Freedom Square* interviews.

He muttered a curse and reached for the intercom.

"*Yes, sir.*"

"Aileen, put me through to Sam Hirschberg. I don't care where he is or what he's doing. Tell him it's hot."

"*Yes, sir.*"

"And book the corporate jet for a flight to Washington, DC. We need to be there by one o'clock."

"*Today, sir?*"

"Yes, dammit! And please get someone in here to wipe this coffee off my desk." Barden released the button and collapsed in his chair, his eyes glaring at the window.

****

Barden and his three-man crew arrived at the Lincoln Memorial at two thirty on July 4th after a frenetic chartered flight and commute to the historic landmark.

The reflecting pool below the memorial was surrounded with milling tourists and picnickers waiting for the evening's festivities. Throngs of visitors climbed the memorial's steps toward the imposing statue of Honest Abe, their cameras in hand, their eyes locked on the bearded face peering at them from behind the Doric columns. And of course, there were the usual protestors, two dozen of them marching along the two thousand foot reflecting pool with placards blaming the President for not lifting a finger to stop the Mideast war.

A line of security police stood off to the side, their eyes trained on the protestors, some of whom had begun shouting at the tourists. Through the trees, Barden could see the police vans and squad cars lining Henry Bacon and Daniel French Drives. One hostile move and DC's police would be on the protestors in the blink of an eye.

Barden glanced at his watch. Two forty-five and nothing visible except police, demonstrators, and tourists. He folded his arms and squinted at the Washington Monument rising into the blue sky beyond the reflecting pool. One of the gawking tourists gave him a friendly wave, but he didn't notice.

Barden swiped his foot at a stray candy wrapper, his eyes filled with anger. He looked up at the blue sky and muttered a curse. What the hell were they going to do, drop her in a parachute? A cheap photo-op that would make Claire Minton into more of a charlatan than she already was? Come on, folks, who's running this bleeping show?

He yanked the cell phone out of his pocket and scrolled the speed dial list for Jess Wilkin's name. He was about to press Wilkin's number when he heard the sirens.

He squinted through the trees at the column of limousines rumbling down Route 50 accompanied by a flying wedge of motorcycle police. The first limo veered onto Henry Bacon Drive and eased to the curb across from the parked police vans. The other limos filed into the vacant spots behind the first limo until the line of parked cars stretched beyond the trees.

As if on cue, an army of security agents sprung from the limos, taking positions at the curbside passenger doors. After a sequence of nods, the agents pulled open the rear passenger doors and backed away as the occupants stepped out of the limos into the bright sunlight.

Barden watched Claire Minton smooth down her pinstripe suit after climbing out of the first limo. Jess Wilkin joined her, his right hand shading his eyes while he scanned the memorial. Wilkin snatched a cell phone from his pocket and held it against his ear.

Barden flinched when his cell phone went off with a loud ring. He fumbled with it and pressed it against his ear while staring at the column of blue and gray suits climbing out of the limos.

Wilkin's voice crackled in his ear. *"You there, buddy?"*

Barden frowned. "I'm here. We're looking down at you from the tenth step of the memorial."

Wilkin squinted at Barden and his camera crew. *"Got that wide-angle lens?"*

Barden frowned. "I've got it."

"Great, Josh. Now please back off the steps and focus on old Abe. Our security guys will clear away the touristas."

Barden stared at the line of limos. "What's with the army?"

"You'll know in a minute."

Barden watched Wilkin slip the cell phone in his pocket and whisper something to a security agent. Seconds later, the throng of suits followed Claire Minton and her campaign manager through the trees with a wall of police and security agents clearing the way.

When Claire Minton began her walk up the memorial's steps, Barden was already on the air, interrupting all WNN broadcasts for a "breaking story." He stared at her from the base of the memorial while speaking to WNN's hundred million viewers.

"I'm not sure what candidate Minton is up to, but I recognize some interesting faces in the entourage following her up those steps." He glanced at the monitor on his left. The camera had zoomed on a gray-haired man with a deep scar on his forehead. "That's Senator Marty Zamboni, folks. Haven't seen much of him in recent months. He looks well since the operation."

The camera switched to a youthful, Kennedy-like face following Zamboni up the steps. "The young representative from Michigan. Many say Samuel Pierce will be the Democrat's leading candidate for senator in two years, and beyond that, the presidency."

The camera shifted away from Pierce while targeting faces in the column of dignitaries ascending the steps. Barden pointed out Congresswoman Edith Hackenworth from North Carolina, Senator Jacob Friendly from Texas, Congresswoman Mindy Shankton from Florida, Senator Forest Takawa from Hawaii, Congressman Bernie Zelton from Vermont, and many others as Minton's entourage continued their methodical walk up the memorial's steps.

When Minton reached the top step, she turned toward the crowd and smiled, her hands clasped in front of her, and the shouts began.

"Hey, it's Claire Minton! Can you believe it?"

"Hey, Claire, we're with you, honey! All the way!"

The demonstrators lowered their placards and began cheering along with the tourists. Sensing something big, Barden ordered his crew to pan the sea of faces straining to see the woman standing beneath the statue of Abraham Lincoln.

The fifty-three senators and representatives took positions on the steps below her, their hands waving to the crowd below, their handsome faces gleaming in the sunlight.

Barden felt a hand on his shoulder. "What do you think, buddy?"

Barden turned and saw Jess Wilkin smiling at him. Instinctively, he raised his microphone and guided Wilkin into the camera's view. "Well, look who's joined us. It's Claire Minton's campaign manager, Jess Wilkin. Can you enlighten us, Jess?" He extended the mike toward Wilkin.

Wilkin looked up at the fifty-three people standing on the steps below his candidate. He nodded reassuringly and leaned toward the mike. "This is a wonderful day, Josh. Better to let Claire do the talking." He patted Barden's shoulder and backed away, his eyes focused on his candidate.

Barden knew Wilkin's little back step was a signal for candidate Minton to begin speaking. He nodded to Sam Hirschberg while pointing a trembling finger at the woman atop the steps. He watched Hirschberg swivel the camera away from the crowd until it was locked on her.

An aide handed Minton a wireless mike and backed away. She raised her hand for silence while staring at the sea of humanity gathered below her. Slowly, the cheers subsided until the only sounds were whispers rustling through the crowd.

The warm breeze ruffled her short-cropped hair. She lifted the mike and spoke the words that would change the face of American politics forever.

"I am honored to stand below this great man on the two hundred forty-fourth birthday of our nation. God bless this land and its people."

A mighty roar erupted from the thousands of onlookers. Minton lowered her mike and acknowledged their cheers with a smile while milking the moment for everything it was worth.

Barden stared at the spectacle taking place around him. He looked up at the woman standing beneath the statue, and he suddenly knew history was being made.

She raised her hand for silence and listened to the cheers fade. Then that graceful, regal gesture as she lifted the mike to her lips.

"On September seventeenth, I will engage my two opponents in a great debate. It is important I enter that debate with your trust that I am more than a spoiler or dealmaker. That is why I have come here today with my friends from the Congress."

Barden whispered in his microphone while his cameras panned the crowd. "This is incredible. Look at their faces. People of every ethnic and racial makeup, every age and sex, all of them mesmerized by the woman standing beneath the statue of Abraham Lincoln."

Barden hesitated while the cameras closed on her face. "I'm just a reporter, America, but I have a feeling something profound is about to happen."

Minton swept her hand over the fifty-three people standing below her. "These are your elected representatives, America. They come from every diversification known to man. Black, white, yellow, red, male, female, young, old, straight, gay, Christian, Jew, Muslim, Hindu, Buddhist, and even atheist. Fifty-three people who are different in every way … save one."

She lowered the mike to let her words reverberate through the mass of humanity standing beneath her. Slowly, deliberately, Claire Minton raised the mike as if signaling her audience that the final, decisive blow was about to be struck.

"I never expected to come this far. I was content to help my brothers and sisters in Kansas. I never envisioned I would be standing before you today." She lowered her head and waited for the perfect moment. The crowd was frozen, their faces locked on her. Some had begun to cry. Others could only nod while waiting for the grand finale. The hell with patriotic songs and fireworks, this was the best show of the day.

Her head snapped up. "I've seen poverty and pain. I've seen war and death. I've seen a great nation humbled by incompetent leaders and greed-driven money merchants." She took a deep breath and glared at the crowd. "Well … are we ready to end it? Are we ready to pull them down?"

Barden felt the microphone vibrate from the deafening roar that rose from the crowd. The police barricades strained against the sea of humanity pressing toward the woman standing atop the steps.

Minton raised her right hand and screamed into the mike. "These fifty-three brave Americans are prepared to work with me to lead this nation to a better world. We'll reject the corrupt elite that have taken over our government. We'll bring home our brave men and women who have been betrayed by the profiteers and their puppets. Yes, my fellow citizens, these brave Americans standing before you have sworn their allegiance to a new direction. They have shed their Democrat and Republican cloaks to join America's true party. A party that will speak for the forgotten souls that built this nation. A party that will embrace all who seek a better life for themselves and their families. A party without barriers to religious, ethnic, racial, or sexual orientation. The people's party! America's party! The Heartlanders!"

Barden stared at her while the cheers echoed off Lincoln's statue. He tried to find the words to describe it, but he could only listen to Claire Minton's final exhortation.

"JOIN US, AMERICA! JOIN THE BRAVE SOULS STANDING WITH ME ON THESE HALLOWED STEPS! WE WELCOME YOU! WE EMBRACE YOU! JOIN US NOW! JOIN THE HEARTLANDERS!"

She lowered her head and bowed to the thousands of citizens charging the memorial, their fists shaking, their voices exploding as they broke through the police barriers.

Barden pulled his crew back from the stampede. He managed to blurt out, "It's getting ugly down here. The crowd has broken through the barricade and is rushing toward the woman at the top of the memorial. Riot police are racing toward us from the trees. I'm not sure—"

The transmission went dead when someone knocked over Sam Hirschberg's camera.

****

The President stared at the television screen. A WNN newsman was describing the melee that had broken out at the Lincoln Memorial. It appeared that Josh Barden and his crew were safe, as were Minton and the fifty-three rebel congressmen. Reports of injuries were coming in from eyewitnesses to the scuffles that had broken out between the massive crowd and riot police. Tear gas and stun guns were being employed to restore order to Potomac Park. Tonight's festivities had been cancelled.

The President pressed the remote's off button and leaned back in his leather chair. He stared at the empty seat across the desk, his eyes filled with tears. "I need you, Jack. What the hell should I do?" He lowered his head and listened to the clock ticking on the mantle.

His head snapped up, his eyes staring at Lincoln's portrait, and he knew what must be done.

"The troops, idiot! Get to the troops!"

CHAPTER 27

DUBUQUE

arry Zimmerman's dairy complex was located eight miles southeast of Dubuque on a slope overlooking the Mississippi River. At forty acres, Zimmerman's sprawling dairy farm and pasteurization facility were well-known throughout the Midwest, as was its feisty owner.

Old Harry had started the business forty-five years ago with a small pasture and barn, five cows, and a business degree from the University of Iowa made possible by the GI Bill. Today, his Holsteins grazed the pastures of twenty thousand farms in Iowa and neighboring Wisconsin with his famed "HZ" brand burned into their butts.

Harry Zimmerman was a billionaire, but no one would ever guess from his worn dungarees, distressed leather boots, gingham shirt, and straw hat. Every morning, he could be seen walking through his dairy plant, his trained eyes studying the pasteurization equipment while he shot the breeze with his workers.

And there were goodwill trips too, launched from Harry's private airstrip behind his Victorian mansion. Twice a week, Harry's *Cessna* would hopscotch across Iowa and Wisconsin, dropping in on a dozen of his loyal farmers to personally hand them a generous check while pressing the flesh and talking about families, neighbors, and next year's crop outlook. Of course, there was always a farmer's co-op representative standing nearby with a camera to capture the neighborly handshakes for the local newsletter.

Yes, the farmers loved Harry for his generosity and humble ways. And why shouldn't this ex-Vietnam War fighter pilot be humble? With his dairy profits soaring, Harry Zimmerman was living the American dream.

Most people have two sides, and Harry was no exception. That's why on this July 4th he honored Matthew Jordan's request to host a very private meeting at his mansion. Only six people were invited — six very special people.

It was ten o'clock at the mansion and the socializing was done. After a first class barbecue filled with boisterous laughter and backslapping, no words were spoken as Harry and his six guests watched the last of Dubuque's fireworks from Harry's porch. It was a reverent time, a solemn time.

The air smelled from cigar smoke as Jebb Wheatly and Barnie Holdren savored the Cubans stuck in their mouths. Charles Mootley gulped down his moonshine gin and let out a contented sigh. Mervin Boyle stared at the fireworks while recalling his nights in Vietnam. The others just leaned against the porch railing, their eyes gazing at the flashing sky.

Harry felt a nudge and glanced at Matt Jordan. He jammed his cigarette in an ashtray and pushed away from the porch railing. "Well, gents?"

The others nodded grudgingly and followed Harry, Jordan, and Charles Mootley into the mansion.

Harry's second floor conference room sported a twenty foot oak table that fit comfortably in the spacious oak paneled room.

Twin ceiling fans rotated above the table, making Harry's air-conditioned room quite comfortable for his guests.

The walls were plastered with photographs spanning Harry's lifetime. Everything from a young lieutenant standing beside his F-4 to an old man receiving last year's dairyman of the year award in Madison, Wisconsin.

There were no family pictures because Harry had never married. When asked why, his famous quip was, "Never had time. Guess I love my cows too much."

They spent the first twenty minutes sipping coffee while watching a video of Claire Minton's earthshaking speech at the Lincoln Memorial. Harry's six guests gave approving nods as cheers erupted from the DC crowd. And while Claire spoke, the men seated around the table couldn't help noticing Matthew Jordan's proud smile.

Harry lifted a remote and clicked off the video. He placed the remote on the table and clasped his gnarled hands. "Well, quite a day." He smiled at his comrades. "I'm gonna ask Matt to take over since this little gathering was his idea." Harry smiled at Jordan and eased back in his chair.

Jordan leaned forward, his green eyes studying the men seated around the table. Aside from Charles Mootley on his left, he hadn't sat with his comrades in almost four months.

His tone was firm and confident. "Things look pretty good. From everything we know, Claire'll enter the debate within four points of the President and almost ten ahead of Hawley." He smiled. "And heaven help those wimps when she takes them on."

The room rustled with one-liners.

"Right on, Matt."

"It's about time, dammit."

"Go get 'em, Claire."

Jordan pushed back from the table and folded his arms. "When it's over, Claire'll be dead-even with the President, and Hawley will be history." He glared at his listeners. "But that isn't enough. With Hawley broken, the President's men will pull out all the stops. Best we can figure, he'll be back in the lead by Election Day, maybe by five points."

Jordan stared at their somber faces. "We can't let it slip, men. We've come too far. We need to finish the job."

Jebb Wheatly leaned forward and looked Jordan in the eye. "What do you mean, finish?"

Jordan frowned. "You know what I mean."

Wheatley shook his head. "No way, Matt. I was willing to go with you the first time, but not again." He looked at Jordan with pleading eyes. "They're our boys, Matt. We can't betray our boys. They're not the enemy."

Jordan's eyes flickered. "You think I'm enjoying this? If there was another way, don't you think I'd take it?"

Charles Mootley cut in. "This is tough, but Matt's right. If we can put one more nail in that scum's coffin, we'll run him out of the White House and replace him with one of our own. We can't back down now. We've come too far."

Jordan waited for a reaction, but there was none. He squinted at the portly man nodding off at the far end of the table. "Mike, you still with us?"

Michael Tabor nodded.

"You with me?"

Tabor shook his head. "We're playing with fire, Matt."

Jordan glared at him. "You didn't answer my question."

Tabor took a strained breath. "It'll cost a lot more this time. The government's clamped down on security since those missiles disappeared." He scratched his bald head and gave Jordan a sheepish look. "We'll have to go through the Chinese for this one."

Jordan clasped his hands. "How much?"

Tabor shook his head. "Ten, maybe twelve billion." He sighed and listened to the shocked whispers.

Jordan nodded. "So be it, old buddy. You get to your Chinese contacts and tell them to set it up."

Tabor looked at him in shock. "You serious?"

"Deadly." Jordan leaned toward him, his green eyes glistening. "And make sure your contacts tell that scum, Jihawri, that this will be the last time. One final, decisive blow to finish the job." He leaned closer. "Clear?"

Tabor sighed. "Yeah."

Jordan's face twisted in a scowl. "I want Jihawri to promise nothing will happen after the attack. I don't want any butchery or fanatic shit. When Claire takes over, she'll force the first withdrawal in March, and that'll be the end of this damn war."

Tabor nodded.

Jordan's green eyes burned into him. "You make sure my message gets through to that scum. If any of our troops are attacked during the withdrawal, if any of Jihawri's maggots so much as harm a hair on one of our boy's heads, you tell that scum Claire Minton will blacken his sandbox with thermal nukes that'll send him and his heathens to hell."

Jordan waited for a response. "Got that, Mike?"

Tabor sighed. "I got it."

"Good, cause I'm gonna get some shut eye." Jordan stood up and turned for the door.

"Hold it, Matt."

Jordan squinted at Mervin Boyle.

"How do we come up with that kind of money?"

"Guess."

Boyle eyed the others. "Yeah, we sort of surmised that, but how do we get our money back?"

Jordan folded his arms and smiled at Boyle. "My, my, Merv, haven't you become the doubting Thomas."

Boyle looked him in the eye. "I'd like to know." He nodded at the scowling man seated beside him. "Since Barnie's in this, I suspect he does too."

Jordan eyed Barnie Holdren. "That right, Barn?"

Holdren puffed his cigar. "That's a lot of dinero, compadre. Two, three billion each." He nodded. "I want Claire to win, but just for the record, I want my money back."

Jordan smiled. "You guys disappoint me. Think I'd throw us into this mess without payback?"

They stared at him.

"Ethanol, gentlemen."

Charlie gave him a puzzled look.

Jordan smiled. "When we pull out of Iran, it'll set off a world-wide panic for oil. Damn prices will hit three hundred a ton." He shrugged. "Great time for alternate fuels, gentlemen. Just in time for next summer's driving season. Lots of grain to feed all that demand for ethanol. Lots of good Iowa grain."

Jordan stretched his arms and yawned. "You'll get your money back in grain sales. I figure a twenty billion dollar windfall. That's a hefty profit. Not bad for winning back our country."

Holdren collapsed in his chair. "I'll be damned."

Jordan stretched his arms. "Just sign on the dotted line, boys. It'll all be fine." He walked out of the conference room while his six colleagues stared at each other.

CHAPTER 28

JULY 6TH

The massive *Chinook* landed in Tehran's "safe zone" at 01:14 in the darkness of July 6th. In seconds, it was ringed by a cordon of heavily armed guards under orders to defend the chopper at all costs.

With a protective cap of *Apaches* hovering overhead, the guards moved toward the chopper's exit door, expecting to see a general or cabinet member emerge from the red-lit interior. They were stunned when the President of the United States stepped on the exit ramp, his hand raised in a reassuring gesture, his face beaming despite the jet lag and late hour.

The President was ushered into an enormous *Apache* hangar along with his entourage, which included General Augustus Cook, Chairman of the Joint Chiefs of Staff, and Edwin Hammel, Secretary of Defense. Also accompanying the President were Jerome Wittington, National Security Advisor and Peter Atkins, Director of the CIA.

The brightly lit hangar was packed with a thousand coalition troops and their commanding officers. Ranks ranged from private to colonel. Every effort had been made to select a representative cross-section of the hundred thousand troops deployed throughout the war-torn country.

A mighty cheer went up from the troops when the President stepped onto the podium and gave his audience a rousing smile and thumbs up. Overhead, a dozen video cameras panned the throng of cheering grunts, transmitting images to a nearby van where intelligence personnel studied the sea of humanity while watching for any threatening move.

Two-dozen armed Marines lined the hangar's interior, their fingers locked on the triggers of their M27's. Their stern faces glistened beneath their camouflaged helmets while they scanned their thousand cheering comrades. Any hostile move would trigger an action message through their headsets that would launch the Marines into the crowd with guns blazing, and heaven help any innocent grunt who didn't heed their cries to hit the deck.

The President fought a wave of emotion while waiting for the cheers to subside. He glanced to his left where Hammel and Cook were seated, then to his right while managing a nervous smile for Wittington and Atkins.

The President looked down. For the first time in his thirty-year political career, he was without his closest friend and advisor. He was standing in front of the world's finest military force and for the first time in thirty years, he was scared.

The hangar fell silent except for a few scattered "OO-rah's." The President rested his hands on the lectern and unfolded his notes. He looked at the sea of desert brown and spoke in a deep, resolute tone.

"I came here with a heavy burden in my heart, but as I look into your strong faces, I feel the pain fading away."

The hangar exploded with cheers. The President raised his hand and nodded while waiting for the cheers to subside.

"Like many of you, I have lost a dear friend, but like all of you, the battle goes on."

"OO-rah! Give 'em hell, Mr. President!" The cheers were deafening as the President lowered his head and composed himself.

That was the President's finest moment on this dark, ominous morning in Tehran. Unfortunately, it was all downhill from there with the usual rhetoric about the war against terror, protecting the homeland by fighting the terrorists on their own soil, etcetera, etcetera, etcetera. Some of the troops were yawning when the President finally raised his hand and saluted the finest military in the world. The applause and OO-rah's were there, but not with the same vigor.

Then came the blunder that never would have happened with Jack Wiley at his side. Instead of throwing himself into the sea of cheering soldiers, the President followed his screen of secret service agents and military guards to the exit where he re-boarded the *Chinook* with Cook, Hammel, Wittington, Atkins, and Occupation Forces Commander, General Malcolm Taylor.

The six men would spend the next hour reviewing strategy while their audience dispersed to their barracks, awaiting reassignment to the battlefield. The President's unintended snub had left an indelible scar on the United States military—

He doesn't care! None of them care! We're all dead men!

The six men squeezed into a makeshift conference room aboard the *Chinook* while going over a post-mortem of the recent insurgent attacks on the oil complexes in Arak, Kermanshah, Isfahan, and Qom. No mention was made of the recent altercation between the President and General Cook. After some peace-making by Secretary Hammel and the late Jack Wiley,

General Cook had personally delivered a signed apology to the President and resumed his duties as joint chiefs chairman.

Damage from the coordinated insurgent attacks had been devastating. Over five hundred coalition troops had been killed and another four hundred wounded. One hundred twenty oil workers were dead with at least that many wounded. Twelve *Apaches* had been downed from XGA99 rocket hits, their crews vaporized. Five F-18's had been blown out of the sky by the new XGA99's, their pilots dead.

Impairment of the oil wells and refineries ranged from severe to total. Estimated recovery time, six months. Estimated economic impact, forty dollars per barrel. Odds of a similar attack — high. Insurgent losses were estimated at two thousand — but who cared?

The President sank in his black leather seat while staring at the typed brief. "My lord."

General Cook leaned forward. "We've retaken the lost territory, but they still have the missiles."

The President ignored Cook and looked at Hammel. "What about the media?"

Hammel shook his head. "So far, no leaks. It looks like Kinkaid was the only embedded reporter involved."

The President leaned toward him. "You're sure about no leaks?"

Hammel sighed. "No, sir."

The President looked down at the paper. "What do we do?"

General Cook leaned toward the President and spoke softly. "If there was any other way, sir. If there was any other choice." He straightened up and looked the President in the eye. "You know my position."

The President leaned back in his seat, his tired eyes locked on the general. The fierce anger was gone, replaced by a statesman-like demeanor. "General, if I authorize the use of field nukes, I must notify the Russian president, not to mention the Japanese, Chinese, Brits, French, Germans, Saudis, and a dozen others. We'll be condemned by every nation sworn against the use of nuclear weapons."

Cook glared at him. "Yes, sir."

"I know it's difficult, General. That's why I came here tonight." He placed the paper on the small table in front of him. "We need another approach."

Cook lowered his head.

The President looked at Jerome Wittington, his NSA director. "Jerry, can we make contact with Jihawri and his boys?"

Wittington stared at the President. "Sir, you want to talk to the insurgents?"

The President nodded. "I'm convinced it's our only way out. If we can open secret negotiations, we'll put an end to this madness and bring our boys home." He hesitated. "And we'll eliminate this damned third party threat to the nation."

General Cook stared at the paper lying on the table. "Then … we're pulling out?"

The President nodded. "It's our best bet, General. Your men and women have done their nation proud. I'll make sure they're given the honor they deserve."

Cook fell silent while the President deliberated with Frost, Wittington, and Hammel. It was more than a cold shoulder for the nation's top military officer. The President was sending his military a clear, unspoken message. We're giving up, gentlemen. We're in a war we can't win and it's time to cut and run.

Sorry about the eleven thousand dead, but you did your nation proud.

The meeting ended abruptly at 02:51 when the President glanced at his watch and rose to his feet. The final insult came when he asked General Cook to stay behind with the troops to give a speech commemorating the 244th anniversary of our nation's birth, two days after its occurrence.

The President bid Generals Cook and Taylor farewell while reassuring them he would keep them in the loop once negotiations began. The two shaken generals shook the President's hand and exited the chopper.

Cook and Taylor watched the *Chinook* rise into the night sky accompanied by four *Apaches*. They stood motionless, their eyes fixed on the fading choppers.

Taylor rubbed his stiff neck. "I could use a drink. How about you, Auggie."

Cook nodded. "Let's make it a bottle. Got any Kentucky moonshine?"

"Whole case."

Cook smiled and gestured toward the armed convoy parked beside the hangar. "Lead the way, Malcolm."

They climbed into an APC and headed for CENTCOM headquarters while trying to digest what had just happened. It would take their armed convoy an hour to reach the towering Atlantis complex, an hour that would seem like eternity.

They were at two thousand feet in the Elburz Mountains when Cook peered through the APC's armored slit at the flashes to the south. "Looks like some heat down there."

Taylor squinted at the flashes. "They're hitting Qom again."

"Can't we nail them?"

Taylor frowned. "We do, but they keep coming back."

"What about the missiles?"

"Nothing since last week, but I smell something."

Cook gripped his bouncing seat. "When?"

"Don't know." Taylor hesitated. "Can I speak freely, Auggie?"

Cook shrugged. "It's your whiskey."

"We're gonna lose."

Cook sighed. "Well, you sure have a way of getting to the point." He hesitated and chose his words carefully. "When's the last time you met with us?"

Taylor gave him a surprised look. "The chiefs?"

Cook nodded.

Taylor shrugged. "Never."

Cook smiled. "I think it's time you come home for a visit. We're having a pre-election powwow in October. The twenty-fourth, if I recall." He nudged Taylor. "I'd like you to fly in and give us your appraisal."

Taylor nodded at the flashes. "Appraisal? Hell, I just did."

Cook locked his black eyes on Taylor. "I mean a broader appraisal."

"Broader?"

Cook nodded. "The political situation and all that. How it all comes together in the eyes of a field general. Where we're going as a nation."

Taylor's eyes widened. "Nation?"

"Yes … something like that. And be direct, Malcolm. We could use that just now."

Taylor took a deep breath. "Yes, sir. I'd be honored."

Cook patted his friend's hand. "Good, I'll set it up. How's your golf?"

"Golf?"

Cook nodded. "We need an escape. Looks like it'll be at a private club in New Mexico."

Taylor leaned back in the bouncing seat. "My sand game has improved."

Cook smiled and stared at the flashes.

CHAPTER 29

JIHAD

Six weeks had passed since the President's unexpected visit to Tehran — six weeks of hell for the beleaguered coalition forces. Despite fierce air strikes and artillery bombardments, the enemy had gained formidable ground in the north and south while the battle-weary coalition troops clung to their tenuous positions in the cities. Armed with increasingly sophisticated weapons, the emboldened insurgents stepped up their attacks on Arak, Qom, Kermanshah, and Isfahan in the south while their brothers launched raids on Gorgan, Now-Deh, and Mashhad in the north.

Skirmishes were breaking out everywhere in the embattled country, each one lasting only a few seconds as insurgent snipers fired on their targets before disappearing into the darkness when fire was returned. The insurgents seemed to be probing the coalition's defenses, as if working to a plan.

The increased insurgent activity hadn't gone unnoticed by CENTCOM. Coalition troops guarding Tehran's safe zone had been beefed up, as had the armaments protecting Fortress Atlantis in the Elburz Mountains to the north. With the presidential debate only one month away, there were concerns of a major insurgent thrust, and everyone was on edge.

On the home front, Claire Minton's campaign manager had released the first two video interviews with Corporal Joey Matafuco and Private Rafael Cambria, promising that the remaining two interviews would be aired in time for the September 17th debate.

Anchored by WNN's Josh Barden, the Matafuco and Cambria interviews ignited the nation's television screens like gasoline poured on a fire. The President's popularity plummeted to twenty-eight percent as the enraged American public vented their wrath on their crippled leader.

When the President's Press Secretary, Sandy Meyers, phoned WNN's CEO, Franklin Carlton, to express his outrage at the televised interviews, Carlton laughed while retorting in a confident, assured voice, "Sorry, Sandy. Times change, and so do presidents. WNN's job is to get out the truth, and that's what we will do."

With the Mideast death count at eleven thousand, and no relief in sight, WNN's shocking telecast set the stage for a stunning clash between Claire Minton and the President in the upcoming debate. It was a dark time at the White House. The President knew it would take a miracle worker to save his sinking ship, but that miracle worker was dead.

Seven thousand miles to the east, dawn was breaking in the hills above Tehran. It was 0550 on the morning of August 21st, and Sergeant Virgil Benedict was leading his four man rifle squad down the rocky slopes along the Darakeh River.

At two thousand feet, they could see Tehran stretching below them in the haze, its ancient mosques and minarets intermixed with gutted office buildings and homes. The air smelled from smoke, although no fires were visible. In fact, it seemed unusually quiet without the usual bursts of small arms fire.

"Take five." Benedict raised his right hand and eyed his four comrades. He slung his M27 and looked up at the towering peaks to the north known as the Elburz Mountains. Above the peaks, twin vapor trails streaked across the cobalt sky as two F-18s executed their morning run over the great city.

Benedict felt the hillside tremble as the jets flew over his head before breaking right into a steep climb. He took a nervous breath and stared at their silhouettes fading into the morning sky. It was 0551 in Tehran and all was still except the wind whistling through the peaks.

"Quiet morning, eh, Sarge?"

Benedict glanced at Corporal Chacon. "Too quiet, Corporal."

Chacon shrugged. "Hell, it's Isis' day off. They're probably praying in their holes."

Benedict knew what his corporal meant. Today was Friday, the Islamic day of rest. He frowned and shook his head. "Forget that religious crap, soldier. There's no religion out here. They'll kill you today like any other, so keep your eyes trained on those rocks. Never know if one of the ghosts snuck through our lines last night. Hell, he could have you in his crosshairs right now."

Benedict watched Chacon grimace and check his clip. The other three did the same, their young faces showing the strain of battle. Their patriotism and boldness were gone, replaced by ashen faces and glazed eyes. Their confident swagger had become a slow, tedious pace for these soldiers had seen the deadly force of mines and roadside bombs, and each knew their next step might be their last.

Benedict cradled his M27 and squinted down the rocky slope. "Victor squad should be coming up to relieve us in a few minutes, so don't start shooting at the wrong guys. Just keep your eyes open and—"

He reeled from a terrific blast. "Down!"

Benedict dropped on the rocks and watched his four comrades do the same. He crawled past them and squinted at the plume of black smoke rising from the city's north quadrant.

Chacon crawled beside him. "What the hell was that?"

Benedict grimaced. "Don't know. Looks like—"

Two staccato blasts shook the hillside, followed by three more.

"What the hell?" Private Willis crawled beside his two comrades, followed by Privates Esterhaz and Mallard.

A dozen blasts rocked the hillside as smoke and flames billowed from the north quadrant. The air crackled with small arms fire.

Benedict rolled on his back and pressed the transmit button on his headset. "Tango Team to Mother. What's going on down there?" He waited for a response but only heard another half dozen explosions.

Chacon pulled out his field glasses and focused them on the flames. He adjusted the focus and lurched upward. "God, Sarge, there must be a thousand of them!"

Benedict gripped Chacon's arm. "Who, dammit?"

"The fucking ghosts! They're running down the streets firing at everything in sight!" Chacon clutched the binoculars. "They're hitting the safe zone!"

Benedict snatched the glasses from his corporal and rolled on his stomach. He peered through the smoke and fires while trying to focus the glasses on the north quadrant. Through the smoke, he could see the insurgents charging through Freedom Square, only a few hundred yards from GHQ. Some were dropping from the intense coalition fire, but they kept coming, their weapons blazing.

A terrific explosion shook the hillside. Then another. Benedict aimed the glasses down the slope where five men were scrambling up the rocks toward them. "Here comes Victor squad! Maybe they'll know—"

Benedict reeled from a blast of heat. He buried his face in his arms as rocks and chunks of earth rained down on them.

"Dammit, Sarge! What the hell's going on?"

Benedict ignored Private Willis and clutched the glasses with his trembling hands.

Chacon gripped his arm. "Where are they, Sarge? Where's Victor squad?"

Benedict peered at the smoking crater two hundred yards below them. He lowered his head and forced out the words. "They're gone, Corporal. They're gone..."

Another dozen blasts shook the safe zone. Benedict rolled on his back and tried again. "Tango team to Mother. What the hell's going on?"

A desperate voice crackled in his ear. *"We've got big trouble, Tango. At least two thousand ghosts coming at us from Freedom Square. We're trying to focus our fire on them, but they're really coming. Only a few yards to the perimeter. Hell, they're breaking through! Here they come, goddammit! Gotta go!"*

Benedict pressed the headset against his ear. He could hear cries and small arms fire crackling through the opened line. He rolled on his stomach and focused the glasses on the fires burning through the plumes of smoke. "Tango to base. Can you hear—"

A deafening explosion rocked the hillside. Then another. Benedict felt a hot blast against his back. He rolled over and looked up at Fortress Atlantis, his face frozen in shock.

Benedict wasn't the only one peering at the mountain fortress. Chacon and the others stared at the flames and black smoke billowing from CENTCOM. Overhead, twin vapor trails arched downward into the smoke and flames, their source unknown.

Benedict pressed his transmit button and glared at the inferno above his head. "Tango Squad to CENTCOM. Awaiting orders. Please advise." He listened to the static and glared at the inferno.

Chacon pressed against him. "For god's sake, what should we do?"

Benedict pushed him away and pointed a harsh finger at his face. "We stay right here. We stay here until we get orders."

Chacon gestured toward the fires. "But, Sarge—"

"Shut the fuck up!" Benedict gripped Chacon's flak vest and pointed his trembling finger at the inferno one thousand feet above them. "What's wrong with you, soldier? You in a hurry to die?" He watched Chacon slump on his elbow, his glazed eyes staring at Fortress Atlantis.

****

General Taylor was nearly to CENTCOM's communication center when the two impacting GG100 missiles blew away Atlantis' fortified steel doors only two hundred yards behind him. Taylor and his three man escort dived into a cross tunnel and covered up as the wall of flame surged past them, spreading death through the complex's labyrinth of tunnels and chambers.

When Taylor looked up, his eyes stung from toxic fumes. The air smelled from gasoline. Everything was pitch black. It was becoming hard to breath. The only sounds were explosions and blood-curdling screams echoing off the tunnel walls.

The shaken general clenched his fists. "We can't stay here. Let's make a break for the entrance." He gasped for breath and tried to stand but one of the guards pulled him down.

"What the hell—"

The young man shoved an oxygen mask into Taylor's hand and blurted out, "Use this, General."

Taylor glared at him. "Who are you, soldier?"

"Hammer, sir. Lieutenant Hammer."

"Now you listen to me, Lieutenant—"

Before Taylor got out the words, the young lieutenant scrambled to his feet and yanked out a small flashlight. He shined the light through the smoke until it reflected off a metal chest at the end of the tunnel. He charged toward the chest, his arm covering his nose and mouth while his other hand held the flashlight.

"Where the hell are you going, lieutenant!" Taylor slipped on his mask and rose to his feet. He looked down at the other two masked guards and choked out his words. "Stop him! He doesn't have a mask!"

The two shaken guards stood up and started toward Hammer, but it was too late. Lieutenant Hammer threw himself against the metal chest, his face contorted from the lack of oxygen. He ripped off the cover and flung three hot suits at the three men peering at him through the smoke. He was reaching for a fourth mask when a back draft caught him square in the face.

Hammer gripped his throat and collapsed on the rock floor, his lungs seared from the toxic, superheated vapor. By the time they got to him, he was dead.

The insurgents had planned their attack with uncanny precision. Utilizing two of their remaining GG100 missiles, their devastating vapor bombs knocked out the coalition's central command headquarters in a matter of seconds.

Three thousand feet below, two thousand screaming Isis warriors overran Tehran's safe zone in a frightening display of human will. Despite losing ninety percent of their command, the incensed *jihad* fighters inflicted heavy casualties on the coalition while dealing a fatal psychological blow to Operation Scorpion and the President of the United States.

At least, that's what the surviving embedded journalists reported to their global news organizations on that same day. What they failed to report were the one hundred hand-fired rockets the insurgents launched into the coalition's ranks while charging at them in human waves.

The new "Panda 499" rockets had worked well, vaporizing the coalition barricades with explosions rivaling the military's most powerful RPG's, yet no mention was made of these new high-tech weapons — and for good reason.

No one knew what a "Panda 499" was. How the hell could they? The damn things were built and tested in China from smuggled United States prototype designs.

And the method of transfer to Hassan Jihawri's insurgent army? Let's just call it a warm and fuzzy donation from clandestine arms merchants funded by a small consortium of billionaires in the United States, an anonymous group of seven men who last met in a private home outside Dubuque, Iowa on July 4th.

It took an hour for the fire brigades to quell the vapor-induced flames. When it was done, ninety-seven men and women were dead, over three quarters of CENTCOM's personnel. General Taylor was one of the eighteen fortunate survivors, his life owed to a valiant young lieutenant who gave his life that his commander might live.

In the nights to come, General Taylor would be haunted by the face grimacing at him in the smoke-filled tunnel, the face of a young man who would never hold his child or play with his grandchildren, the face of our nation's finest, sacrificed in a futile war to feed the profiteers and their political puppets.

FACE-TO FACE

The 767 touched down at noon, its silver wings gleaming in the sunlight. There were no bags to be claimed, so it only took Perry ten minutes to hustle down *United's* concourse to the public transportation exit.

It was hot in Los Angeles with hazy blue skies and the usual smog. LAX's crowds had thinned considerably since the morning commuter rush, but the heaviest traffic was yet to come.

It was Thursday, September 17th, and Los Angeles was bracing for an onslaught of media and VIP's not unlike the Academy Awards, except for one difference. Only one award would be given tonight and its recipient would probably become the next President of the United States.

The taxi driver looked into his rear-view mirror and spoke in broken English. "Where to, mister?"

"Fifteen-three-sixty-five, Harmony Road. In South Central off Crenshaw."

The driver pushed down his meter flag and accelerated into the airport traffic.

Perry leaned toward him. "I need to be there by two."

"No problem." The driver veered between two cars and sped down the exit ramp toward Century Boulevard. From the look of his well-dressed passenger, a timely arrival would mean a big tip. The driver smiled to himself. Why would a white guy want to go into South Central? *Tu es loco, señor.*

Perry gazed at the traffic while recalling the day two months ago when he staggered out of the alley, his eyes blurred from the concussion, his body quivering with pain. He would never forget the tortuous walk to North Lake Shore Drive and the Mercantile Bank. He could still see the guard's stunned face when he pushed through the revolving door into the busy lobby. He remembered the guard helping him to a chair while the bank's patrons stared at him in shock.

He recalled the bank manager's trembling voice when he stepped beside him and rested a hand on his shoulder.

We should get the police. You need medical help.

I need to withdraw some money.

Of course, but where do you live? They must be worried sick.

Then came his rush of panic when the manager picked up the desk phone. He needed that money, but if the cops took him in, the Chicago media might get hold of it and that would mean his bruised face smeared on every TV screen in Chicago. It would only be a matter of time before Jordan's goons tracked him down.

The guard tried to restrain him when he bolted off the chair, but he shoved him aside and charged for the door. He could still hear the manager's pleading voice when he staggered through the revolving door into the bright sunlight.

Please sir! I've called for paramedics! You're in bad shape! You need help!

The last thing he remembered was a woman's horrified face when he brushed past her before ducking into an alley.

The next week was a blur. By some convoluted twist of fate, he managed to dodge the cops, but in doing so, he deprived himself of badly needed medical attention. Condemned to the life of a rat, he wandered the streets of Chicago begging for his next meal.

In those seven days, life became quite simple for Perry Ambrose. Forget Claire Minton, Matthew Jordan, and the bloody election. The only thing that mattered was survival.

For seven days and nights, he begged for money and ate anything he could shove down his throat while cowering in Chicago's alleys. When an occasional druggie jumped him, he fought back like an animal until the pig gave up or clobbered him. He must have been beaten two or three times during that week in hell — but he survived.

When his head finally cleared, he checked into a shelter and got a warm shower, some decent clothes, a plate of human food, and badly-needed sleep. The only drawback was the vivid nightmare of his father pointing that gnarled finger at him.

I warned you, Perry. I warned you, boy. You picked the wrong bloody road. What did you expect? You go to the states with big plans and end up cowering in the bloody shadows with no money, cracked ribs, and a failed life. My lord, boy, what the bloody hell are you going to do?"

"We're here."

Perry blinked at the driver.

"Fifteen-three-sixty-five, Harmony Road." The driver flipped up the meter flag and shoved the cash tray through the bulletproof glass. "Thirty-one sixty."

Perry reached into his jacket pocket and pulled out his wallet. He placed two twenties in the tray and shoved the tray toward the driver. "Come back in an hour."

"No problem, mister."

He didn't hear the taxi pull away. His eyes were locked on the red brick tenement across the street. In the past two months, he'd phoned Julia Kramer seven times. Now, he would finally see her face-to-face, his last living link with Terell Kramer and that horrible morning in Tehran. He took a deep breath and walked across the street.

He was climbing the tenement's front steps when she pushed through the weather-beaten entrance door.

She wore a white blouse with a powder blue skirt and dark blue apron. Her black hair was tied in a bun. It was like she had jumped out of the video.

She forced a nervous smile. "Mr. Ambrose?"

Perry nodded.

She eyed the bangers glaring at them from across the street. "Welcome to the hood, Mr. Ambrose. You better come inside."

When they reached her second floor apartment, Perry could see she was straining. He leaned toward her and spoke softly. "Are you alright, Mrs. Kramer?"

She shrugged and inserted her key in the security lock. "We can sit in the dining room."

Her flat was well-groomed and rather pleasant given the location. Polished wood floors sprinkled with rugs, a small sitting room complete with couch and TV, and a surprisingly spacious living room with sunlight streaming through the curtained window. The air smelled from floral spray.

They sat at an antique dining table that looked like it had come from the old south. Perry ran his finger across the polished walnut surface and smiled.

"Like it?"

Perry nodded. "Reminds me of home."

"England?"

"Yes."

"Get back there much?"

Perry's smile faded. "My parents are dead. I haven't even seen my dad's grave."

She leaned toward him. "I see lots of pain in your face."

Perry sighed and pulled an envelope out of his jacket pocket. He reached across the table and placed it in front of her.

"What's that?"

He nodded at the envelope. "My thanks. You can give me back the CD now. I won't be needing your help any longer."

She picked up the envelope and opened the flap. Her eyes widened. "What is this?"

"Two hundred thousand dollars."

She dropped the envelope on the table and waved her hand at it. "No, sir. I'm not taking no hush money. All I want is the video of my boy."

Perry leaned toward her. "That money is clean, Mrs. Kramer. I respect you too much to give you unclean money."

She scratched her head. "Lordy, lordy, you must be a rich man."

Perry dropped back in his chair and stared at her. "You keep the CD, Mrs. Kramer ... and the money."

She looked down at the envelope. "I saw my Terell and the other boys on TV. Gotta admit I didn't believe you when we first talked." She chuckled. "Damn near fell out when I saw that president lady show my Terell to the whole country." She looked at Perry, her eyes glistening. "That meant a lot to me, Mr. Ambrose."

Perry nodded. "And to me, Mrs. Kramer."

She glanced toward the kitchen. "I made some tea. Would you like a cup? I know you English like tea in the afternoon. Don't have no crum—"

"Crumpets?"

"Yeah, them things, but I do have some homemade oatmeal cookies."

Perry glanced at his watch. "I should be going."

"Ain't you gonna watch the debate tonight?"

"Maybe."

She leaned toward him and rested a soft hand on his arm. "Those men are still after you, aren't they?"

"I'll be fine."

"Mr. Ambrose, can I tell you something?"

He nodded.

"I see so much pain in your eyes. You should go back where you came from. Maybe visit your dad's grave and make peace. I think it'll make you feel better."

He smiled and patted her hand. "I'll consider it."

"Before you go, will you do me a favor?"

"If I can."

"Will you sit with me and watch my boy one last time."

They spent the next twenty minutes in the sitting room, their eyes glued to the TV. He heard her whimper when Terell appeared on the screen, and he felt tears well up in his eyes. Her warm hand slipped over his and he felt the pain lift from his heart.

CHAPTER 31

COUNTDOWN

"Ten minutes, Mr. Barden."

Josh Barden ignored the young man standing at the dressing room door. His eyes were focused on the notebook computer in his lap. He'd gone through the words twice during the makeup session, but he wouldn't be content until he completed a final pass.

Barden was flipping the page icon when his cosmetician dabbed his cheek with her makeup brush. He frowned and looked away.

"Sorry, Mr. Barden. Can't let them see you sweat."

Barden was in no mood for quips. He swiped at the darting brush, but the persistent young lady managed a final dab before backing away to admire her handiwork.

Barden glared at her. "Are you quite done?"

"Yes, sir." She snatched the paper bib off his neck and dropped it in a wastebasket.

"Your jacket, sir."

Barden glanced at the tailor standing beside him with a gray suit jacket in his extended hands. He heaved a frustrated sigh and stepped off the stool.

"Just take a second, sir."

Barden heaved another sigh and placed the notebook computer on the stool. He slipped his arms through the jacket's sleeves while staring at the computer's screen.

The tailor draped the jacket on Barden's shoulders and stepped back, his eyes studying the smudge of powder on Barden's pants. "One second, sir." He snatched a whiskbroom off the dressing table and brushed the powder away.

Barden snatched the computer off the stool and snapped it shut. He buttoned his jacket and stared at the dressing room mirror. "Well?"

The tailor folded his arms and smiled. "Fit to kill, Mr. Barden. You'll have them eating out of your hands."

Barden took a final look in the mirror before turning to the attractive young woman standing at the door. He took a deep breath and forced a smile. "Guess it's time."

Cindy Jameson returned the smile. "Yes, sir."

Barden and his assistant followed their police escort through the dimly lit corridor, their footsteps echoing off the concrete walls. Barden's heart skipped a beat when they made the final turn toward the ramp leading to the stage.

A security guard stood at the ramp, his imposing stature blocking their path.

"Your badge, sir."

Barden took a nervous breath while fumbling for the VIP badge on his lapel. He unclipped the badge and handed it to the guard.

The guard passed the badge through a hand held scanner and stared at the scanner's mini-screen. He nodded at Barden with stone black eyes. "Go ahead, Mr. Barden. I'll give this back to you when you're done."

Barden stepped on the ramp and felt a hand pat his shoulder. He looked back at Cindy who was standing behind him, her eyes filled with tears. He could barely hear her soft voice.

"Give 'em hell, Josh. For my brother and the others over there."

Barden nodded and headed up the ramp on shaky legs. He squinted at the bright light shining through the ramp's opening, and he suddenly felt very much alone.

Only seconds now. He could hear the buzz coming from the auditorium where ten thousand whispering voices echoed off the convention center's towering ceiling, their eyes focused on the empty stage with its three lecterns and opposing table and chair.

Bob Quigley stepped through the light and looked down at Barden, his face glistening with sweat. "How are you doing, boss?"

Barden nodded, his hand clutching the notebook computer. A bead of sweat trickled down his forehead. He flicked it away and took a final deep breath.

Quigley pressed his finger against his headset and raised his right hand. "Ten seconds."

Barden watched Quigley's fingers count down the final seconds, and it hit him. The games he'd played to get here no longer mattered. When he walked through that portal, he would step into the ages. In the next ninety minutes, he would preside over the most critical debate in the nation's history. It was his show now, and he must not fail.

"Three … two … one…"

Barden nodded and stepped into the light.

★★★★

Steven Zimmer placed the tiny earpiece on a napkin and extended it to the President. "Here you go, sir. It's all checked out. Works like a charm."

The President eyed the tiny receiver before giving his new chief of staff a stern look. "I see you just climbed on the bandwagon."

"Sir?"

"The guys telling me to stick it in my ear."

Zimmer forced a smile while watching the President snatch the receiver from the napkin and wedge it in his left ear.

The President was turning away when he noticed Zimmer crushing the napkin in his fist. "Little souvenir?"

Zimmer looked down at the napkin. "No, sir. Nothing like that."

The President sighed. "It's okay, Steve. After the election, that napkin will be quite valuable. That's what happens when a standing President gets booted out of office."

Zimmer dropped the napkin on the floor. "We'll not have that talk, Mr. President. Maybe in four years when you give me something for posterity."

The President knew he was lying, but what choice did his new chief of staff have? They both knew Zimmer wasn't thrilled when they asked him to replace Jack Wiley. It wasn't chemistry or anything like that. After thirty-four years of government service, Steven Zimmer was quite capable of tackling a tough job.

The problem was motivation. Tough to walk away from a cushy professorship at Yale to be thrust back into politics at a time like this. With riots breaking out in the cities, the nation mired in recession, mutiny overseas, and protests at home, Steven Zimmer was being asked to work a miracle.

The President was snapped from his thoughts by a rap on the door. "Yes?"

The door opened and Jigs Tornquist popped his head in the room. "Ten minutes, Mr. President. We should be going."

The President nodded at his lead secret service agent. He looked Zimmer in the eye and sighed. "Any last thoughts?"

"Just be yourself, sir. Hawley will snap at you a few times, but he's harmless. I suspect he'll drop out after the debate."

The President's eyes flickered. "Never mind Hawley. What about the vampire on my left?"

Zimmer nodded. "I've studied her, sir. She likes to counter-attack, so don't let her get under your skin. She has a knack for unsettling her opponents and picking them apart when they lash out. Just make your points and ignore her sniping." Zimmer gave him a reassuring smile. "Broad shoulders and all that. Be a statesman, sir." He shrugged. "After all, you *ARE* President of the United States."

The President took a calming breath. "Just tell your prompters to go easy on me. It'll be hard enough warding her off without them shouting instructions in my ear."

Zimmer walked to the door and grasped the handle. "There will be no shouts, Mr. President. The voice you hear will be mine. Calm, collected, and surgical."

The President smiled at him. "Glad you're with me, Steve." He strode forward and followed his chief of staff into the corridor.

****

Seth Hawley's limousine pulled into the Los Angeles Convention Center's VIP entrance at 6:35 PM, only twenty-five minutes before the debate. A little close, but Hawley didn't need any last minute prepping or face dusting. With only twenty-one percent of America's voters behind him, Hawley didn't have a riverboat gambler's chance of winning the election. To put it politely, the pressure was off.

He watched the press corps snap photos of his limo as it sped through the security gate. Gentleman that he was, Hawley managed a beaming smile and hand wave before his limo disappeared into the parking garage. Might as well go out in style. No hard feelings and all that. Next stop, a good lake, good fishing pole, and six-pack.

"You have a call, Seth."

Hawley looked at Brad Forester who was holding out his cell phone. "Who this time?"

Forester smirked. "Cedric Marshall wants to wish you luck."

Hawley seized the phone and placed his hand over the mouthpiece. "That's the third call in fifteen minutes. First Luke, then Callup, now Marshall." His blue eyes locked on Forester. "How about you, Brad? Want to join the mourners?"

Forester knew what he meant. With all hope lost, Sam Callup, Cedric Marshall, and Lucas Mansted had decided to let their candidate dangle from his noose until after the debate.

Their reasoning was simple. Claire Minton's dramatic surge to the top had convinced them she was a clear and present danger to everything they had built in the Middle East. With Hawley hopelessly behind, their one hope was to shift their support to the President in a last-ditch attempt to thwart Minton and her Heartlanders from taking the White House.

Party affiliations no longer mattered. It was war now, the classic war between the rich and everyone else, and no pompous bitch was going to upset that apple cart.

Hawley removed his hand from the mouthpiece and placed the phone against his ear. "Hello, Cedric. I trust all is well with you?"

Forester watched his boss cringe with Marshall's every word. When it was done, Hawley mustered his diplomacy and maintained a civil tone.

"Thank you, Cedric. We'll give it the old college try. You never know about these things. We might get lucky. Talk to you soon." Hawley slammed the cell phone on the seat and glared at Forester.

Forester looked down. "I'm sorry, Seth. I never thought it would come to this."

Hawley sighed. "Well, you certainly warned us, old chum. She's a real tiger. They should have listened to you and put in Santene."

Forester shook his head. "It wouldn't have mattered. She would have chewed him up and spit him out."

Hawley smiled. "Know something?"

"What?"

"Maybe she deserves it. After all, politics *is* brutal. Survival of the fittest and all that."

A uniformed guard rapped on the window. "They're ready for you, Mr. Hawley. They're telling me ten minutes."

Hawley nodded at the guard. He reached for the door handle and felt Forester grip his arm.

Forester looked him in the eye. "For the record, you *were* the best man."

Hawley smiled. "Thank you, Brad. That means a lot." He pushed open the door and stepped into history.

✴✴✴✴

Jess Wilkin chugged his scotch and put the empty glass on the cocktail table. He sighed and pushed off the couch, his eyes trained on the woman standing at the foyer mirror. "Well, guess it's time."

Claire backed away from the mirror and smoothed her pin-stripe skirt. She turned around and struck a pose. "Good?"

Wilkin smiled. "The best." He snatched his attaché case off the floor and gestured toward the door of their plush suite.

She took a calming breath. "How long do we have?"

Wilkin glanced at his watch. "Half hour, but I don't want you rushing over there. Better to settle in a bit before you go onstage."

She nodded and broke into a smile. "Know something?"

"Hmm?"

"I feel good tonight. Best I've felt in months."

Wilkin returned her smile. "You should. You have the best team in the country at your side, not to mention the best campaign manager."

She stepped against him and gave him a hug, her blue eyes staring at the balcony window with its sweeping view of LA's glittering skyline.

Wilkin gave her a squeeze. "Must be love."

Her grip tightened. "I couldn't have done it without you, and Matt, and the others. It's a great day, Jess. For Mom, and Dad, and—" She choked.

Wilkin stroked her back. "I know, Missy. It's been a hard road, but we're almost home. After tonight, this country won't be the same." He gripped her shoulders and eased her away. "We're going to do it, Claire. We're going to shake those rotten apples out of the tree."

They were nearly out the door when Claire's cell phone went off. She lifted it out of her jacket pocket and scanned the calling number.

"Important?"

She nodded. "Clear the way. I'll just be a minute."

She watched him close the door before pressing the phone to her ear. "Matt?"

"You okay, Missy?"

"I'm good. Never felt better."

Jordan's voice broke. *"You give 'em hell tonight, Missy. I'll be with you every step of the way."*

She smiled. "Are you at the lake?"

"Hell, no. I'm standing outside this chicken coop they call an auditorium. I've got Charlie and Harry with me. We got lucky on VIP passes."

Her eyes brightened. "You're here?"

"You better believe it. We'll be sitting in the rafters like three roosting chickens. If you hear any cowboy yells, it'll be us cheering you on."

"Oh, Matt, I love you so much."

Wilkin stuck his head through the door. "Gotta go, Claire."

Jordan's voice crackled. *"That Jess?"*

She brushed away a tear. "We need to get over there."

"God bless, Missy. I'll keep the champagne chilled." The phone clicked.

She stood for a moment, her hand grasping the phone, her eyes staring at the lights of LA. Then she was gone.

CHAPTER 32

THE DEBATE

"We interrupt our scheduled programming to bring you tonight's presidential debate between the candidates of the Republican, Democrat, and Heartlander parties. Code Zero and The Kurlins can be seen next week at their regularly scheduled times."

With that introduction, television screens across the nation switched to a magnificent aerial view of Los Angeles complete with glittering skyscrapers, klieg lights, and hovering choppers.

The camera closed on a sprawling glass building at the intersection of Pico and Figueroa. It continued to close on the building's fountain entrance where a few limousines were still dropping off their well-dressed passengers. A dwindling line of VIP's could be seen presenting their passes to the police at the building's glass entrance doors.

Had the camera closed a bit more, it might have caught the faces of Harry Zimmerman, Charles Mootley, and Matthew Jordan as they flashed their passes at the police before stepping through the glass doors en route to their catbird seats.

The scene switched to a cavernous auditorium, its tiered seats filled with spectators clad in everything from tuxedos to sport jackets. Except for some scattered side conversations, all eyes were focused on the empty stage at the front. Across the nation, people stared at their TV's while listening to the omnipotent voice coming through their speakers.

"Ten thousand VIP's and media representatives have packed the Los Angeles Convention Center for tonight's debate. They have come from across the nation and overseas to witness this landmark event. Only seconds now. You can feel the electricity."

The camera locked on the blue-curtained stage with its three empty lecterns and opposing table and chair.

"Our host will be Josh Barden, WNN's lead anchor and famed war correspondent whose best-selling book, Memoirs From Hell, is available at bookstores everywhere. Ladies and gentlemen … Josh Barden."

The huge audience crackled with applause as Barden strode onto the stage grasping the notebook computer. He paused at the moderator's table and acknowledged their applause with a nod.

Barden placed the notebook computer on the table and looked at the camera. "Good evening, America. We live in a turbulent time. Our troops are engaged in a brutal war. Our nation is mired in deep recession. Our people search for an answer. In that spirit, WNN is proud to host tonight's debate between the three leading contenders for President of the United States."

The audience reacted with shouts and applause as their tension reached the breaking point. After months of sparring and mud-slinging, the long-awaited confrontation had come. With two of the candidates deadlocked in the polls, and no further debates scheduled, the next ninety minutes would determine the next President of the United States.

Barden looked across the stage at the right curtain. "They come to us from Charleston." He extended his hand toward the curtain and watched Governor Hawley step onto the stage amidst a burst of applause and scattered cheers. He waited for Hawley to take his place at the right lectern before proceeding.

"The White House."

The hall exploded with cheers and jeers as the President of the United States stepped through the center curtains in his traditional navy blue suit and red tie. The President waved at the audience and strode to the middle lectern.

"And Kansas."

The roar was deafening as Minton's supporters rose to their feet and unleashed their fury. Claire stepped onto the stage from the left curtain and took her position at the left lectern. She gripped the lectern and looked down while soaking up the cheers. Then came the flashing eyes, smile, and affectionate wave, perfectly timed to send her supporters into a frenzy.

It took a minute for the demonstration to subside. Barden waited patiently until the last shout echoed off the hundred-foot ceiling. He glared at the camera and spoke in a firm, resolute tone. "Ladies and gentlemen, this is a crucial moment in our nation's history that must not be disrupted by emotional displays. I will therefore deal harshly with any excessive outbursts or shows of partisanship. As citizens of this great country, we must respect our candidates' words. Only in this way can we make an informed decision." Barden hesitated. "In other words, I'm asking you to put a lid on it." He grinned while listening to the rush of laughter.

Barden clasped his hands and stared at the camera. "Tonight's debate will be divided into three parts, each focusing on a critical national issue. In the next ninety minutes, we will discuss the war, recession, and future of our nation in this complex, dangerous world.

Barden hesitated. "Each candidate will be given five minutes to answer my question, with an additional five minutes allotted for challenge and rebuttal. I will closely monitor expended times to ensure a fair and balanced debate."

Barden turned toward the three candidates. "Are we in agreement?" He waited for their confirming nods. "Then let us begin."

Barden sat down with his back to the audience. He opened his notebook computer and stared at the center lectern. "Good evening, Mr. President."

The President forced a nervous smile. "Good evening, Josh."

Barden looked at the notebook. "Mr. President, forty-eight months ago you promised an aggressive withdrawal of our forces from the Middle East. Instead, we find ourselves engaged in three ground wars in Afghanistan, Iran, and Syria. Our Middle East troop count has doubled from fifty thousand to one hundred thousand. Our dead have increased from four thousand to eleven thousand. Our wounded and maimed are three times that. The coalition has all but collapsed. There is evidence of mutiny among our battle-weary troops. Worst of all, the consensus of every major military strategist is that we are losing." Barden hesitated. "How can you defend that record, sir?"

The President nodded while listening to the voice crackling in his ear. He took a slow, pained breath and looked at the camera. "The most difficult job a president has is sending America's finest into harm's way. Eighteen months ago, this nation was attacked for a second time on our soil. Despite every effort to protect our homeland, we are again confronted with the harsh truth that an evil and formidable enemy is bent on destroying everything we cherish."

He paused and listened to the voice in his ear. "No one regrets the loss of American lives more than me, but if I pull our troops out of the Middle East under a delusion that the enemy will throw down their arms, I will expose this nation to a threat greater than anything we can imagine." He looked at the audience. "We have no choice but to persevere."

Barden listened to the silence. "You have something to add?"

The President shook his head.

Barden looked to his left where Claire Minton had raised her hand. "Go ahead, Ms. Minton."

She turned toward the President with a look of disbelief. "That's all you have to say?"

He nodded and gave her a courteous smile.

"Mr. President, eleven thousand American soldiers are dead. Our brave men and women are at the breaking point with mutiny in their ranks. The recent insurgent offensive in Tehran has destroyed any morale we had left." She hesitated. "Surely, Mr. President, you and your corporate profiteers have been made rich enough by this unjust war. Why not end the damn thing and heal this grieving nation?"

The auditorium reverberated with shocked whispers and jeers, but she ignored them. Her eyes were locked on his reddened face. She leaned toward him. "Mr. President?"

His fingers dug into the lectern, but there was no response.

"I see." She looked down for a moment before locking her eyes on the camera. "My fellow citizens, I stand before God to make this pledge. If I am elected President, I will end this terrible war in my first three months in office."

The auditorium exploded. The roar was deafening. Barden rose to his feet and waved for silence in a vain attempt to control Minton's enraged supporters. He glanced at his watch and looked at her with pleading eyes.

She smiled and raised her left hand.

Barden stared at the crowd in shock. Except for a lingering cough or two, the auditorium returned to silence as Minton's crazed supporters lowered their fists and dropped into their seats. A simple hand gesture had quelled five thousand screaming supporters in a few seconds.

Barden resumed his seat and looked at Seth Hawley who was staring at the audience with the same startled expression.

Barden leaned toward the mike. "Governor Hawley, have you anything to add?"

Hawley shook his head.

The next question was directed at Claire Minton, a simple request to explain how she could redirect the thirty billion in monthly war expenditures to national welfare programs while absorbing the hundred thousand troops returning home from the war.

Barden leaned toward her. "I don't get it, Ms. Minton. Every major economic study has refuted your plan, insisting that it is impossible to transition from a war-to-peace economy for less than triple the money you would recover from pulling our troops out. In other words, the experts say your thirty billion per month savings is only one third of what would be needed. Please explain your reasoning." Barden pushed back from the mike and stared at her.

Candidate Minton ignored the camera and looked Barden in the eye. "You're correct, Mr. Barden. Ending the war is only a third of the solution." She hesitated. "In my first six months in office, I will ask Congress for emergency tax legislation aimed at the oil and reconstruction cartels that have profited from this criminal war. The rest of the money will come from anti-waste and anti-corruption legislation that will be enacted by Congress with the help of my fifty-three Heartlander brothers and sisters."

She turned toward the audience and shrugged. "That should do the job."

As if on cue, the Heartlanders rose from their seats in a burst of cheers. And while they cheered, Claire squinted through the lights at the upper balcony. She couldn't see him, but she knew he was there, cheering her on with the rest of them.

When the display finally ended, Barden glanced at the timer and looked at the President. "Your thoughts, sir?"

The President took a deep breath and looked at the woman on his right. "You make it sound easy, Claire. I wish it were that easy." He hesitated. "Did you ever consider what would happen if we pulled our troops out?" His face reddened. "Islamic fundamentalists would overrun the three nations and convert them to a terrorist-led theocracy." He leaned toward her. "The free world would be confronted with a unified terrorist regime bent on destroying Israel, the United States, and every non-Islamic culture on the planet. There would be no end to their attacks. It would only be a matter of time before they acquired weapons of mass destruction with the will to use them." He leaned closer. "On us, Claire ... on us."

He straightened up and turned toward the audience. "As long as I am President, I will commit every resource we have to preventing that nightmare."

Barden looked at the audience. All eyes were frozen on the President. The huge auditorium was dead silent. Barden looked at Hawley. "Do you have anything to say, Governor?"

Hawley shook his head.

"I have something to say."

Barden looked at candidate Minton who was glaring at the President. "Go ahead, Ms. Minton."

The debate had reached its first confrontation, the ultimate clash of wills. Minton's blue eyes locked on the President's. No turning back now. Whoever blinked first would lose the election.

Minton fired her salvo. "I have served in both Gulf wars, sir. I have shed blood for my country and have carried my wounded comrades home. I have stood at the graves of my fallen brothers and sisters, and offered my prayers to their grieving families." She hesitated. "I must tell you, Mr. President. No one despises war more than a soldier. No one searches for peace more than a soldier. No one hates a corrupt government more than a soldier." Her eyes burned into him. "I have faced the enemy and I have faced you, sir, and I regret to inform you that I respect my enemy more."

The President was livid. He ignored the voice screaming at him through his concealed earpiece.

"Ignore her, sir! Look the other way! Do not respond!"

He raised his hand and pointed a trembling finger at her. "Excuse me, candidate Minton. Did you just call your president a traitor?"

She stared at him.

His face reddened. "I'm waiting for your answer, candidate Minton."

She smiled. "The difference between us, sir, is that in my world you would be put against a wall and shot, while in your world you just get voted out of office so you can go home and count your money."

The auditorium shook with shouts and applause. All eyes were on the trembling man at the center lectern.

The President couldn't contain himself. "How dare you! Do you know who I—"

Barden cut him off while raising his hands for quiet. "Let's move on. I think we know where you both stand." He ignored the President's stunned glare and looked at Hawley. "Well, Governor, anything to add?"

Hawley stared at the two candidates on his right. "Mr. Barden, if it's alright with you, I'd like to leave the stage to sit with the audience." He listened to the welcome rush of laughter.

Barden smiled and leaned toward him. "You know, we're thirty minutes into this debate and you still haven't offered anything."

Hawley smiled. "I'm afraid to." He listened the laughter.

Barden glanced at his notes. "Well, let's see if we can help you overcome that shyness, Governor. Ready for a question?"

"If I must."

"The polls show you hopelessly out of the race. Many wonder why you haven't dropped out. Your southern support base seems to have fled the scene in favor of the two candidates on your right." Barden shrugged. "Why stay in?"

Hawley sighed and rested his elbows on the lectern.

"Are you alright, Governor?"

"Yes, except for the deep pain in my heart."

Barden's smiled faded. "You mean, because of the polls?"

Hawley straightened up and stared at the camera. "To be frank, I was going to withdraw from the race last week when something came to my attention that is so grievous, I can't find the words to express it."

Barden sensed an opening. "Take your time, Governor. From my clock, we owe you ten minutes."

Hawley looked down and composed himself. The auditorium had fallen dead silent.

Hawley looked at the President and forced out the words. "Sir, I regret to inform you that Jack Wiley's death was not an accident."

The President stared at him in shock.

Hawley took a deep breath and listened to the stunned whispers in the audience. "Your chief of staff and FBI director were assassinated, Mr. President. I have undeniable evidence they were executed by Michigan militia under orders from one Charles Mootley, a high-ranking member of the Kansas red leg militia."

Barden fell back in his chair, unable to speak. He could see the President clutching the lectern like he was about to topple over — and the President wasn't the only one. Candidate Minton looked like a ghost, her face drained of blood, her widened eyes locked on the governor.

Hawley pulled out his handkerchief and patted away a bead of sweat. Across the nation, two hundred million shaken Americans were staring at him along with the ten thousand in the auditorium.

Hawley mustered his courage and continued. "There is more, sir. Far more. Your two men were killed because they had acquired hard evidence that a U.S. based militia organization is supplying our Middle East enemy with high-tech weapons, some of which are still classified." He paused and shook his head. "Jack Wiley and Zachary Kingston lost their lives trying to get that message back to you, sir. God rest their souls."

Barden listened to the shouts coming from the audience.

"Liar! Stooge! He's a goddamned liar!"

"No, hear him out! Who the hell do you think you are!"

Barden knew he only had a minute before all hell would break loose. He rose from his chair and faced Hawley while gesturing toward the audience for quiet. "Those are strong words, Governor. Can you prove them?"

Hawley looked Barden in the eye. "I have the evidence, sir, and will present it at a news conference following this debate."

Barden tried to speak, but Hawley cut him off with a raised hand.

"Please, sir, I only have a few seconds." Hawley nodded at the enraged audience. Police could be seen at the exits.

Barden nodded and dropped in his chair.

Hawley leaned toward the mike and looked at the stunned woman glaring at him from the far lectern. "Ms. Minton, do you know Matthew Jordan?"

Her eyes glazed over. She could feel her heart slamming against her ribs.

"Ms. Minton?"

She stared at him, unable to speak.

Hawley turned to the camera. "I have irrefutable evidence that Claire Minton is the adopted daughter of Matthew Jordan, leader of the Kansas red leg militia and orchestrator of two arms deals with the Islamic insurgents. Mr. Jordan is personally responsible for the death of one thousand American soldiers. He also approved the assassination of Jack Wiley and Zachary Kingston."

Barden didn't hear the fights breaking out in the auditorium. He didn't see the riot police charge into the audience. His eyes were locked on the three pallid faces in front of him. The last thing he remembered were the secret service agents rushing the President and his two opponents off the stage.

CHAPTER 33

LAX

"Incredible, the bloke's gone daft."

Perry smiled at the stunned man seated on his left. He sipped his gin and tonic while studying the crowd of onlookers huddled behind him. All eyes were focused on the fifty-inch television screen above the bar.

An inebriated woman brushed against Perry and placed her drink on the counter. "It's a damn publicity stunt. Hawley's just trying to drag Minton down. He and his alpha males can't accept a woman president, so they make up a story to destroy her." She glared at Perry. "Don't you agree?"

Perry nodded. "You could be right. Let's listen to what the governor has to say." He avoided her dirty look and stared at the TV screen where Governor Hawley had stepped to a lectern. A sea of reporters faced the governor, their raised hands clutching recorders and digital cameras.

Hawley's face glistened in the hot lights. He took a calming breath and rested his arms on the lectern. His voice was subdued. *"I am truly sorry for this press conference, but it must be done."* He paused while the reporters snapped their photos. The media room echoed with snapping camera shutters.

Hawley gripped the lectern and leaned toward the microphone. *"Let me first say that I am withdrawing my candidacy, effective immediately. To seek the presidency after what I am about to reveal would cast doubt on my honor. I want to assure my fellow citizens that I place my love of country above any personal goal. I will therefore complete my term as Governor of South Carolina and retire to private life."*

Hawley nodded at the projection screen beside the lectern where a young girl's photograph appeared. *"I want to assure you that everything I am about to reveal is based on hard, undeniable evidence. For what it's worth, I wish it weren't so."*

Perry listened to the reporters' stunned reaction as Hawley displayed the Cadmore photos while explaining Claire Minton's diabolical link with Matthew Jordan and his Kansas red leg militia. He sipped his gin and watched Hawley describe Jordan's ties to a covert militia group bent on putting their chosen candidate into the White House at all costs.

Someone tapped his shoulder. He turned to the man on his left who was well into his fourth martini.

"Sorry, old chum. Don't mean to disturb you, but do you believe any of this rot?"

Perry shrugged. "It's hard to say. What do you think?"

The man shook his head. "These bloody politicians will sell their souls for that chair in the White House." He gulped his martini. "At least thieves have some honor, but these chaps will do each other in at the drop of a hat."

Perry smiled. "Well, you have a point. It does seem a bit over the top, but you never know about these things." He raised his hand for patience. "Let's hear the chap out."

The man smiled. "I take it, you're from my neck of the woods?"

Perry returned the smile. "I'm from England."

The man nodded. "From that accent, I bet you're from Wales."

Perry chuckled. "Well done. Born and raised. How about you?"

The man gestured to the bartender. "London, and I'm certainly glad to be returning home. With all this unrest, things look a bit sticky over here."

Perry nodded. "Amen to that."

The man burped. "You're headed back to Wales?"

"Actually, to London."

"Ah, visiting a loved one perhaps?"

"Nothing like that, but I must admit this trip will be rather exciting." Perry leaned toward him. "I've come into a bit of an inheritance that's changed my life."

The man's eyes widened. "Good for you."

Perry leaned closer. "I've decided to change careers."

The man slapped his leg. "Good-oh! How exciting for you."

"Yes, sir?"

The man looked at the bartender. "Please, old chap. A fresh gin and tonic for my friend and a double martini for me."

Perry nodded. "Thank you."

The man shrugged. "So tell me, what kind of career change are we talking about?"

Perry raised his hand for quiet. Hawley had turned toward the photograph of Matthew Jordan embracing candidate Minton. The governor spent the next few minutes describing the close relationship between Jordan and his adopted daughter. The sexual inference was clear.

The reporters were in a frenzy when Hawley unleashed his bombshell. The video screen behind Hawley switched to a schematic view of two missiles.

Hawley's voice strengthened as he turned toward the schematic. *"These are declassified blueprints of our newest combat missiles, the GG100 and XGA99. Two months ago, these missiles were launched against our own troops in Iran. Five hundred brave men and women died in the resulting fiery hell. Last month, we lost six hundred more brave souls in the insurgent assault on Tehran's safe zone. The insurgents were armed with the latest hand-held RPG's, this time imported from China."*

Hawley hesitated and took a sip of water. *"Yes, my fellow citizens. Eleven hundred of our finest Americans have died at the hands of Islamic insurgents supplied and trained by global arms merchants."* He leaned toward the camera, his blue eyes on fire. *"Let me be clear on this. Our troops were killed by our own weapons, smuggled to the terrorists by a global arms network that received several billion dollars from Matthew Jordan and his covert militia group in our United States."*

"Great Judas Priest!" The inebriated man slammed his fist on the bar, his glazed eyes locked on the television screen. The crowd behind Perry fell dead silent. The inebriated woman on his left stared at the screen in shock, her hand gripping an empty glass.

Hawley took a calming breath while eyeing the reporters. *"When you leave this press conference, my aides will provide you with a copy of a recording made at Claire Minton's Warnock Lake estate outside Lawrence, Kansas. The voice will be a bit tinny, but we've confirmed it belongs to Matthew Jordan after receiving word that Jack Wiley and Zachary Kingston were dead, victims of a militia hit ordered by Jordan."*

The reporters lowered their cameras, their stunned eyes locked on the man at the lectern. One of them shouted, *"What about your source? Who's your source?"*

Hawley shook his head at the reporter. *"I can't give you that, but I will provide hard evidence that the man behind all this is Matthew Jordan."*

The reporter shrugged. *"How?"*

Hawley glared at the reporter. *"Through a voice print and confidant's testimony."*

"Confidant?"

Hawley nodded. *"A man called Clyde Burble."*

The room exploded with questions.

"Who?"

"Where is he?"

"Have you met him?"

"Why isn't he here?"

Hawley raised his hands. *"Please, let me finish."* He waited for silence before forcing out the words. *"Matthew Jordan ordered the assassination because Wiley and Kingston had uncovered his illegal arms deal with the terrorists. Their contact was a disgruntled militiaman named Clyde Burble. Mr. Burble was assassinated on the same day as Wiley and Kingston."*

Hawley watched the room erupt as two reporters darted through the doors to place calls to their networks. He gestured for quiet and spoke over the din. *"Ironic an American entrepreneur would lower himself to killing our own troops for political advantage, but that's where we are."* The Governor glared at the reporters. *"And Matthew Jordan is not the only one. If there ever was a time for vigilance, it is now."*

Hawley pointed to the projection screen where two faces appeared. *"I've turned everything over to the President. It is essential that Matthew Jordan and Charles Mootley be apprehended with all haste and that they be brought to trial for high treason."*

Hawley sighed and stared at the camera. *"God bless this nation and its people."* He strode off the stage amidst the chaos and flickering lights.

"Blast!" The man beside Perry gulped his martini and slumped on the stool.

Perry looked down at his gin and listened to the conversations going on behind him. He was about to take a sip when an attractive woman patted his shoulder.

"Mr. Woolsley?"

Perry turned toward her. "Yes?"

"Your plane will be departing in fifteen minutes." She handed him a ticket. "Everything is checked. I can escort you to the gate if you wish."

Perry nodded. "Thank you. Be with you in a minute."

"Time to go?"

Perry turned to the man on his left. "Yes, must run." He extended his hand. "Pleasure talking with you."

The man shook Perry's hand. "Maxwell Hanston. Let's get together for a drink in London." He handed Perry a business card. "I'm in real estate. Perhaps you'll be looking for a property."

Perry looked at the card and smiled. "Good timing, Mr. Hanston. I'll be seeking a flat near the Thames, and pursuing a leased building that I can renovate a bit."

"Yes?"

"I'm looking to start a pub there."

Hanston broke into a beaming smile. "Good-oh! I'll be in touch, Mr.—"

Perry pulled out a business card. "Woolsley ... Marion Woolsley." He handed Hanston the card and pushed off the stool.

"Say, old chap. You never told me what kind of work you do."

Perry smiled and picked up his briefcase. "I was a journalist of sorts, but I grew tired of it. I think I'll enjoy this new venture. Have a good flight, Mr. Hanston."

"And you too, old chap." Hanston watched the black-haired Welshman walk out of the bar. He smiled and gestured to the bartender. "One for the road, please. I must toast that man's success."

CHAPTER 34

CHAOS

"Director Frost is here, sir."

The President spun his chair away from the window and pressed the intercom button. "Send him in, Kate."

"Yes, sir."

The door swung open revealing Clarence Frost grasping a black attaché case. Frost looked nervous as he stepped into the oval office. Not the best image for the nation's acting FBI director.

The President rose from his chair and broke into a smile. "Come in, Clarence." He watched Frost stride toward him. "Would you prefer the couch?"

"The desk will be fine, sir." Frost reached across the desk and shook the President's hand.

"Good to see you, Clarence."

"Yes, sir."

The President released his grip and gestured to the chair facing the desk. "You said it was important?"

"Yes, sir."

The President waited for Frost to sit down before slipping into his chair. He leaned forward and rested his hands on the famed chestnut desk. "So, what do we have?"

Frost opened the attaché case and pulled out a silver folder. He placed the folder on the desk and trained his black eyes on the President. "Sir, I worked for Director Kingston nearly seven years. I was shaken by his death as I'm sure you were by Mr. Wiley's."

The President gave him a pained nod.

Frost looked down at the folder. "I'm sure you're aware that Zach became a bit insecure after you took office."

The President was in no mood for subtlety. "Get to it, Clarence."

Frost nodded. "Zach and I worked closely together. He trusted me with everything." He paused. "That changed after you took office."

"The insecurity thing?"

"Yes, sir. To put it bluntly, Zach trusted no one from that point forward."

"Not even you?"

"Correct, sir."

The President sensed something. He eased back in his chair and softened his tone. "Want a drink?"

"No thank you, sir."

"Then please proceed, Director Frost."

Frost nodded. "Zach had a habit of storing his confidential notes in the organization's underground vault. Top security status, accessible only by him … with one exception."

"Exception?"

"Yes, sir. In the event of Zach's death, the notes were to be given to you."

The President's eyes widened. "Me?"

"Yes, sir … or your successor."

The President looked at the folder. "They're in there?"

"Yes, sir."

"How did you get them?"

Frost sighed. "It's the way he set it up, sir. They were on my desk this morning … in that silver folder."

"You knew nothing until this morning?"

"Correct, sir."

The President scratched his head. "Forgive me, Clarence, but this is a little hard to take. It's been three months since Director Kingston's death. Why so long before these notes get to me?"

Frost nodded at the folder. "It's explained on the first page, sir. I guess Zach wanted to ensure his family was financially secure before passing the notes to you."

The President frowned. "I see … the trust thing again."

"Yes, sir." Frost slid the folder toward him.

The President slipped on his reading glasses and started to open the folder. He glanced at Frost. "Have you read the contents?"

"I scanned them, sir."

The President looked him in the eye. "And you consider them important?"

Frost leaned toward him. "Mr. President, I consider them frightening."

The next ten minutes were silent except for the clock ticking on the desk. Frost watched the President's face redden as he leafed through the folder's fourteen pages.

The President fell back in his chair, his eyes locked on his FBI director. "How much of this can you confirm?"

Frost sighed. "I know that Zach had made contact with a disgruntled militiaman named Clyde Burble, but that's about it." He hesitated. "Except—"

The President leaned forward. "Go ahead, Clarence. Whatever you have."

Frost looked down at his clasped hands.

"Come on, Clarence. This is no time for diplomacy."

Frost's head snapped up. "Three months ago, Zach asked me to take a stroll with him. He liked to take an afternoon stroll along the Mall, but never with anyone." He looked down. "I had a bad feeling. Thought I was going to be fired."

"Fired?"

Frost nodded. "Things were pretty shaky after Zach's confrontation with Mr. Wiley."

The President gave him a startled look. "With Jack?"

"You didn't know?"

The President shook his head.

Frost eased back in his chair. "The way I heard it, Mr. Wiley was very upset because Zach lost track of a reporter who had acquired some damaging information about the war." He shrugged. "I suspect it had to do with Claire Minton's video of the Tehran incident."

The President clenched his fists. "Tell me about your stroll with Director Kingston."

Frost nodded. "He was very cryptic. Kept talking about an important trip he was taking the next day, a trip that would determine our jobs."

"And this stroll was when?"

Frost stared at him. "July First, sir. The day before my boss and your chief-of-staff were killed."

The President sank in his chair. His mind flashed back to the late night meeting at the Pentagon and the ride back to the White House when Jack Wiley told him that he would be out of touch for a few days. He sighed and looked at Frost. "Did Director Kingston say anything else?"

Frost nodded. "He became irritated when I started asking questions. I remember him raising his hand and blurting out that the trip could change the election."

The President looked down. "I see."

They sat motionless, their eyes locked on the opened folder. The President finally broke the silence. "Have you corroborated Hawley's evidence?"

Frost nodded. "It all checks out, sir." He eyed the folder. "And now we have this."

The President closed the folder. "Thank you for coming, Clarence. I know this wasn't easy. You've done your nation a great service."

"Thank you, sir, but there's one more thing."

"Yes?"

"I went down to the vault this afternoon. I have a contact there. Just wanted to see if he knew anything about the folder."

"Go on."

Frost's black eyes locked on the President. "The folder I received was the second copy."

"Second?"

Frost nodded. "The first copy was mailed to an undisclosed party last week."

The President looked at him in shock. "Last week?"

"Yes, sir."

"Can you trace it?"

"No, sir. My boss was very good at his job."

The President looked down. "Director Frost?"

"Yes, sir?"

"Could that recipient have been Governor Hawley?"

Frost sighed. "I think so, Mr. President. If I may speak freely..."

The President nodded.

"I think Zach wanted to level the playing field between you and the governor. I think he wanted to destroy Claire Minton and her third party. I think he believed it was for the good of the nation."

The President sighed and rose to his feet. "Thank you, Clarence."

"Yes, sir." Frost stood up and shook his hand.

The President waited for Frost to leave the room before pressing the intercom. "I need you in here, Steve."

The President spent the next hour in seclusion with his new chief of staff, Steven Zimmer. All appointments were rescheduled as the two men tried to piece together the revelations of the past twenty-four hours.

The deeper they went, the more frightening the scenario became. It was more than Hawley's evidence or Frost's silver folder. It was also Zach Kingston's startling explanation of the clandestine missile deal communicated to the President beneath the Pentagon in the wee hours of July 2nd.

Chief-of-Staff Zimmer put down his coffee and leaned back on the couch. He rested his head against the cushion and rubbed his tired eyes. "Let me try to piece this together. We have Claire Minton snatched from an adoption home by an entrepreneur named Matthew Jordan. Claire is raised by Jordan with the help of Kansas militia. She joins the army and becomes a war hero, congresswoman, and candidate for President of the United States, all under the watchful eye of her extremely rich stepfather."

"Go on."

"Jordan becomes a major force in the militia movement. He's driven by an insatiable passion to right the wrongs of a corrupt government and believes his adopted daughter can lead us to the promised land if she's elected president."

Zimmer sat up and looked at the President. "Jordan's obsession gets the best of him. He must not fail. He's willing to do anything to win."

The President leaned toward him, his eyes on fire. "Even kill American boys?"

Zimmer took a deep breath and nodded. "And anyone else who gets in his way."

"Like Jack?"

"Yes, sir. And Director Kingston. And Clyde Burble, Jordan's closest friend."

The President shook his head. "My god, Steve. How did it come to this?"

Zimmer shrugged. "Doesn't matter. We need to stop those lunatics now." He pointed to the opened folder on the cocktail table. "Mr. President, we must apprehend Matthew Jordan and Charles Mootley in all haste. I'm afraid they're just the tip of the iceberg, but we must start with them."

The President frowned. "What about Minton?"

"She must not be harmed in any way. If you do that, it could cost you the election."

The President gave him a startled look. "Election? The nation's on the verge of a militia coup and you worry about the election?"

Zimmer smiled. "I like those words, sir. We'll use them in tonight's speech."

The President glared at him. "Speech?"

Zimmer raised his hand for calm. "Mr. President, Claire Minton's candidacy is finished. With Hawley out of the way, you should go on television tonight and address the people. Tell them about the clear and present danger facing this nation from renegade militia. Tell them about the megalomaniac named Matthew Jordan who must be brought to justice before he kills more American soldiers. Tell them that we are still a democracy and nation of laws." Zimmer slapped his knee and stood up. "Yes, I like the ring of it. I'd better get started on your speech." He eased beside the President and patted his shoulder. "Stand strong, sir. You just won the election."

The President couldn't speak. He watched his chief of staff leave the room. The only sound was the clock ticking on the desk.

He looked down at the opened folder and brushed away a tear. "My god, Jack. You did it."

CHAPTER 35

LAKE MURRAY

"**G**ot one!"

Seth Hawley watched his stunned grandson strain against the bent fishing rod. He grabbed the rod and began shouting instructions. "Don't lose him, Jeb! Pull him in and reel! At-a-boy. Little at a time. Get ready now. He's a big one. Maybe a twelve pounder."

Hawley braced his foot against the rowboat's gunnel and tugged at the rod with his grandson. He waited for the striped bass to leap into the air before yanking the pole with a deft flick of his wrist. The fish flew into the rowboat, its glistening body flipping on the deck.

Jeb Hawley watched his grandfather snatch the beast by the gills while removing the hook from its mouth — and he wasn't the only one watching. Two secret service agents peered at the scene from their rowboat ten yards to the rear.

It had been a wonderful day at Lake Murray. For the first time in thirty years, Seth Hawley was at peace. In a few months, he would shrug off the chains of office and retire to his Charleston estate for a life of writing, fishing, and enjoying his grandson.

Hawley felt a warm hand on his arm.

"C'mon, Gramps, let's catch another one."

Hawley smiled at his beaming grandson and dropped the nine pounder in their catch basket. Maybe not quite twelve pounds, but an acceptable fish story for a grandfather and his grandson.

"Gramps?"

Hawley gave him the evil eye. "Okay, but first you have to make a pledge."

"You got it, Gramps."

"Raise your right hand and repeat after me."

Young Jeb raised his right hand in the air.

"I, Jeb Hawley, promise his gramps that he will never go into politics."

"Done deal." Jeb slapped his knee and shook his grandfather's hand.

They fished for another hour before pulling in their rods and heading back to shore, followed by their two secret service agents. The nine-pounder was all they had, but to Jeb Hawley, they had just snared Moby Dick.

They were climbing onto the dock when the governor's cell phone went off with an annoying ring. Hawley dragged the phone out of his fishing vest and flipped it open. "Yes?"

"Did you catch one for me?"

Hawley recognized Lucas Mansted's voice. "Can't say we did, but we have a striped bass that'll feed three hungry mouths. Come down and join us."

"No problem, Governor. We're already at the cabin with forks in hand."

"We?"

"Hope you don't mind. I drove down with Brad, Cedric, and Sam. Thought we might chug a few and have a little chat."

Hawley's face went blank. "You know I'm with my grandson."

"Sure do, Governor. We only ask thirty minutes and we'll be on our way."

Hawley sighed. "Thirty then." He closed the phone and felt his grandson tug at his pants.

"The fish, Gramps. We gotta clean him before he spoils."

Hawley patted Jeb's head. "Now Jeb Stuart Hawley, you know how to clean that fish. You get up to the shed and get started on him. I have some business, but it won't take long." He handed Jeb his knife. "And don't cut off any fingers."

"No problem, Gramps. Just don't take too long with them politicians."

He watched his grandson scoot up to the shed with the catch box dangling from his hand and fishing rod draped on his shoulder. A smile crept across his lips as he recalled the illustration in his collector's edition of *Huckleberry Finn*.

His smile faded. He slung his fishing rod on his shoulder and started toward the cabin, followed by the two secret service agents.

Two days had passed since he held the press conference. To put it bluntly, the nation was in chaos. With the war worsening in the Middle East, the media was swamped with cries for vengeance against the militias that had betrayed our country. There was word of a major television address this evening in which the President would decry the traitors named Matthew Jordan and Charles Mootley while rallying the nation against an internal enemy more hideous than the terrorists across the sea — all of it because Seth Hawley had cut a secret deal with a nondescript reporter named Perry Ambrose.

The governor opened the cabin door to find them seated at the oak dining table with forks in hand and sheepish smiles. He ignored their ill humor and shook their hands.

Lucas gestured to the chair at the head of the table. "We saved the best seat for you, Governor."

Hawley slipped into the oak chair and took off his fishing cap. "So, what brings you gentlemen to Lake Murray?"

Cedric Marshall nodded to Brad Forester who pulled a paper out of his briefcase and rested it on the table. Forester looked down at the paper and shook his head. "Incredible, Seth." He pushed the paper toward the governor.

Hawley read the numbers and looked at him. "Twenty-nine percent?"

Forester nodded. "I still can't believe it. You just pulled off the biggest surge in polling history ... like the Phoenix rising from the ashes." He leaned toward Hawley. "The people were shaken by your speech, Seth. They're looking for someone to lead them out of this madness, and that person is you."

Hawley looked at the others. "That's why you came?"

Sam Callup smiled. "I have to be honest. I thought it was over until this happened." He leaned toward the governor. "How did you get your hands on that blockbuster?"

Hawley put down the paper and stared at the three men smiling at him. "I don't get it, gentlemen. I'm out of the race. I've given my word."

Forester clasped his hands. "Look, Seth, none of us expected this. Hell, you damn near gave us heart attacks when you went your own way in the debate." He sighed. "You ignored my preps, you ignored Barden's questions, and you blew our minds with the biggest bomb in political history."

Hawley glared at Forester. "I did it for the nation, not personal gain." He watched Forester's face redden. "It's more than an election, Brad. We need to stop this nightmare."

Mansted leaned toward the governor. "Seth, I know you gave your word, but the nation's crying out for you." He gestured toward the others. "Hell, we can engineer your honorable comeback. It'll only take a few days to set it up. You'll stand there shaking your head while the party pleads with you. Then, at the perfect moment, you'll step out of the governor's mansion to tell the American people that you care too much for this nation to turn your back on them." His eyes grew misty. "And with the flag waving above your head, you'll pledge your commitment to your fellow citizens."

Forester chimed in. "I like that. Hell, you'll be at thirty-five percent by next week." He broke into a beaming smile. "What a launching point."

Hawley looked down at the paper. "What's the President's status?"

Forester pulled a second sheet from his briefcase and glanced at it. "He's eased up to thirty-four percent, but that was expected after Minton's collapse."

"And Minton?"

Forester looked him in the eye. "She's finished. Down to nineteen percent and falling."

Hawley stroked his chin. "So, I'm at twenty-nine, the President's at thirty-four, and Minton's at nineteen."

They nodded.

Hawley's eyes burned into Forester. "What about the other eighteen percent?"

Forester opened his hands in a pleading gesture. "They're up for grabs. If you jump back in, we can take—"

Callup cut him off. "Forget the damn numbers." He leaned toward Hawley and pointed a bony finger at him. "You can win this thing, Seth. Everything you've worked for is at your fingertips." His eyes glistened. "Seize the moment, man. You've earned it."

Hawley smiled. "And I'll have your support?"

"Of course, man." Callup glanced at the others. "One hundred percent. All the way to the White House."

Hawley's smile disappeared. "I've seen your support, Sam. It blows with the wind."

Callup threw up his hands and fell back in his chair. "Can someone talk some sense into this sharecropper?"

Mansted raised his hand for calm. "Seth, we've known each other forty years. I've never lied to you and I won't now. Until you dropped that bombshell the other night, we'd given up on you. Minton seemed impregnable. Our only choice was to tough out the debate and turn our support to the President."

Hawley smirked at him. "By jumping parties?"

Mansted opened his hands. "We had no choice."

If the Heartlanders take over this country, we're finished.

Hawley contained himself. He handed the paper to Forester and slipped on his fishing cap. "I need to help my grandson scale a big fish. It's been a pleasure gentlemen." He stood up and watched them follow suit.

Mansted stepped around the table and shook his friend's hand while looking him in the eye. "For the good of the nation, Seth. You said it yourself."

Hawley shook their hands as they filed past him toward the door. He followed them out of the cabin and watched then climb into their waiting limousine.

Marshall paused before ducking into the black car. He looked at Hawley and smiled. "Hope to hear from you, Seth. We need to move on this thing."

Hawley forced a smile and gave him a feeble wave. The message was clear. Don't turn your back on us, Governor Hawley. You just don't do that sort of thing.

Jeb had finished scaling the striped bass when his grandfather entered the shed behind the cabin. The young man put down the knife and stepped back from his handiwork. "You better bone him, Gramps. I'm not so good at that."

Hawley patted Jeb's shoulder and picked up the knife. He was nearly done removing the spine and ribs when Jeb spoke up.

"Have a nice meeting?"

Hawley nodded.

"They're not staying for the fish?"

"No, Jeb. They're gone."

Jeb tugged on his grandfather's vest. "You okay, Gramps?"

Hawley nodded while recalling the desperation in Lucas Mansted's face when he spoke the words—

If the Heartlanders take over this country, we're finished.

He smiled to himself. What kind of fool did they take him for? Hell, they didn't care if he or the President won the election. In either case, the arms merchant and oil baron would do what was necessary to prolong their windfall profits from the war. The only person that could shut them down was no longer a threat, but that wasn't good enough for Sam Callup, Cedric Marshall, and Lucas Mansted.

No, it must be thorough. Eliminating Claire Minton wasn't enough. The Heartlanders must be erased from our memory. No remnant of Matthew Jordan's third party threat must remain. Only in this way, could the profiteers protect their kingdom.

The sun was setting on Lake Murray when Governor Hawley and his grandson carried the boned fish to their cabin. They were inside the door when the governor looked back at the two secret service agents. He broke into a smile and raised the fish. "You gents hungry?"

They nodded and followed the governor and his grandson into the cabin.

CHAPTER 36

THE SMALLEST INSECT

Jess Wilkin leaned against the oak door and knocked a second time. "You okay, Claire?"

No response.

Wilkin frowned and opened the door.

She was standing at the bay window, her arms folded, her eyes gazing at the lake. The sky was overcast and thunder could be heard in the distance.

Wilkin edged beside her and stared at the raindrops spattering against the window.

She broke the silence. "Any word?"

Wilkin shook his head.

She looked at him with concerned eyes. "It's been two days."

"He'll be okay." Wilkin reached into his jacket pocket and pulled out a folded paper. "I've set up a press conference at five. This is your speech."

Her eyes flickered. "Cancel it."

"Claire, you have to speak up. You have to defend yourself."

She turned away. "I'll defend myself when I know the truth. Now cancel the damn thing."

Wilkin sighed and backed away. He placed the paper on the desk and glared at her. "We've come too far, Claire. You can't throw everything away because of their cheap lies." He turned and walked out of the room.

Wilkin waited until his car cleared the lodge before pulling off the road and opening his cell phone. Five minutes later, Claire Minton's cell phone rang. She lunged for it and pressed it against her ear. "Yes?"

"Hi, Missy."

She gripped the phone. "For god's sake, Matt, where are you?"

"Can't say. Better for both of us that way."

She squeezed the phone. "It's me, dammit!"

"I know, but you gotta trust me, Missy."

She rubbed her forehead and took a calming breath. "Is Charlie with you?"

"Yeah, but we're gonna split up. No sense making it easy for the President's boys."

She brushed away a tear. "Oh, Matt, what the hell's going on?"

"They're desperate, Missy. They'll do anything to stop us."

She mustered her courage and forced out the words. "What they said about Clyde, is it—"

"Of course not. From what we know, the FBI got hold of him and tried to cut him a deal." He paused. *"Hell, Missy, Clyde was my best friend. No way would he rat on his old drinking buddy."*

She stared at the rain. "Then who killed him?"

"I'm not sure, but it looks like the government boys did it. That's the way they operate. If you don't cooperate, you're dead."

She walked to the desk and dropped in the chair. She wanted to believe him, but something was eating at her, something very deep.

"You there, Missy?"

She looked at the window. "Jess wants me to speak tonight."

"Tonight? What time?"

She glanced at the paper. "Five, I think."

"That's good. You'll go on one hour before the President and point your finger at that SOB and his lackey, Hawley, and you'll tell the American people their lying President is the fat cats' last chance to crush our only hope for a better world." His voice broke. *"You do that, Missy … for me, and Charlie, and Clyde, and the Heartlanders."*

She sank in the chair. "When will I see you?"

"Soon, Missy. Soon…"

"Can I ask you something?"

"Be quick, Missy. I gotta go."

"Whose voice was on the recording?"

He hesitated. *"Don't know, Missy, but we'll find out."*

"She gripped her forehead. "That voice knew so much. He sounded so much like you."

"Gotta go, Missy. I love you, my little angel. Give 'em hell tonight. I'll be watching."

The phone clicked.

She sat at the desk staring at the rain-spattered window. Her mind drifted back to the Iraq war. She felt Corporal Tanner's warm blood on her hands when she dragged him to safety. Her legs ached from the bullet wounds. She heard the rock music blaring on the infirmary's radio when they operated on her.

Her eyes closed. She could see her mother waving to her from the porch of their farmhouse in the hot Kansas sun.

C'mon Missy. Got your favorite dinner tonight. Roast chicken, mashed potatoes, and peas, but you better hurry cause ol' Rob is mighty hungry.

"Oh god." She pressed her hands against her face and broke down. She hadn't cried since Rob died. It felt good to cry…

The phone startled her. She snatched it off the desk. "Yes?"

"Hello, Claire."

The English accent shot through her like a jolt of electricity. She sat up and gripped the phone. "Who is this?"

"I think you know."

"Perry?"

"It's me."

Her eyes flickered. "Where are you?"

"Not important. Just wanted to say goodbye. Never got the chance after your father's thugs worked me over."

She stood up, her face hot with anger. "Are you behind this?"

"I guess you could say that."

"My god, Perry."

His voice softened. *"I'm sorry, Claire. I've had time to think things through since the last time we were together."* He paused. *"You didn't know, did you?"*

She clenched her fist. "Do you know what you've done?"

"Yes."

"We had a deal. You took the money and betrayed us!"

His voice sharpened. *"Money?"*

"The two million, dammit!"

"Oh, I guess Mr. Jordan didn't tell you. His people removed the first million from my Chicago account. The second million … well … his blokes kept it after they bloody near killed me in that warehouse."

She gripped the phone. "Liar!"

"You don't believe me?"

She backed against the wall, her eyes glaring at the window. "For god's sake, Perry, you destroyed me and everything we've fought for."

She listened to his breathing. "Say something!"

He sighed and broke her heart. *"If you became president, your good intentions wouldn't matter. You're surrounded by jackals, Claire, and you're too brainwashed to know it. If you took power, Jordan and his militia would bring this nation down, and you couldn't stop them."*

His words burned through her. She clenched her fist and fired her final salvo. "My god, Perry, do you hate me that much?"

His voice trembled. *"I don't hate you, Claire Minton. You were my hope. I believed in you, like the other beaten souls. I believed you would make a difference."*

"And you honor that by sticking a knife in my heart?"

He sighed. *"We all have our little crusades. Yours was to right the nation's wrongs and avenge your family. Mine was to make sense of my screwed-up life."* His voice rose. *"But you and Mr. Jordan changed all that when you betrayed me and your country."*

"How can you say that? You of all people. You had everything."

"And you took it back."

She pushed away from the wall. "You speak of money now?"

"It was more than money, Claire. You took away my hope, and you made me bring you down."

"Damn your soul!"

He paused. *"Are you in Warnock?"*

She fought the anger raging through her.

His voice sharpened. *"At the window?"*

She collapsed in her chair.

"Look out the window, Claire. See any dead trees? Probably quite a few dead ones out there." He hesitated. *"Funny how that*

happens. A tree grows up from the earth, and somewhere along the way it forgets its roots. It gets so caught up reaching for the sun, some lowly insect brings it down."

The phone clicked and went dead.

CHAPTER 37

JUST LIKE TEHRAN

Jordan snatched his suitcase off the floor and gave the motel room a final look. "Guess that's it."

Charlie nodded while glancing nervously at his watch. "It'll have to be. We gotta be at the plane in thirty minutes." He eased open the door and eyed the blue SUV parked in the lot. "Come on, let's get the hell out of this screwed up country."

They were nearly out of the parking lot when Charlie pulled under a tree and yanked out his cell phone.

"What are you doing?"

Charlie frowned. "Harry told me to call him before we leave the motel. He needs to let the pilot know so the plane'll be revved up when we get there."

"Harry's not flying us out?"

Charlie glared at his friend. "Hell, no. Harry's got enough grief without flying America's two most wanted men across the Canadian border. The pilot's some guy named Sam, and that's good enough for me."

Jordan watched his friend punch Harry's cell code. "Hurry up, man. I don't like sitting out here in this damn daylight."

Charlie raised his hand in a calming gesture. "We're gonna be fine. Just stay cool. Tomorrow at this time, we'll be soaking up the nightlife in Gay Paree, and all this crap will be a bad memory."

Jordan squinted at the Mississippi River churning through the valley below them. He could barely make out the silver glint of Harry's dairy complex on the sunlit slope across the river.

He smiled to himself. Good ol' Harry. He'd pay him back for all his help when he got clear of this mess. Maybe buy him some new dairy equipment and a few purebred Holsteins — and personally hand him his multi-billion dollar check from the ethanol deal.

"Where the hell are you, Harry?" Charlie shook the phone and jammed it in his pocket. "Hell with it. We'll call him from France." He pressed the accelerator and skidded out of the driveway.

Jordan leaned back in the seat and stroked his silver hair. "Will we have time to catch Claire's speech?"

Charlie shook his head. "Maybe on the internet."

Jordan rubbed his forehead. "I feel so damn guilty, leaving her to hang out to dry in front of those fucking media vultures."

Charlie reached across the seat and patted his friend's arm. "She can handle it, Matt. She's seen worse than this." He skidded the SUV into a hard left turn and veered onto the main highway, unaware that two men were looking down at him from the slope on his left.

Roady glanced at the man lying in the grass beside him. "Hard to believe, ain't it?"

Hector shrugged. "We're not in the believin' business, compadre. We're in the doin' business." He lifted the RPG launcher into an upright position and rested his cheek against the sight.

Roady patted Hector's shoulder. "No other cars visible. You're clear, old buddy."

Hector waited for the SUV to pass below them. He centered the crosshairs on the passenger compartment.

"Got 'em?"

"Piece of cake, brother. Just like Tehran." Hector placed his finger on the trigger. "Sorry, Mr. Jordan. Nothin' personal."

CHAPTER 38

OCTOBER 24TH — WHITE SANDS

The SR72 *Aurora* touched down at White Sands with a screech of rubber before decelerating to a stop at the end of the runway. It had completed its eight thousand mile journey in only three hours.

The pilot's voice crackled in General Taylor's helmet. *"All clear, sir."*

General Taylor lifted his visor and unclipped his oxygen mask while studying the expanse of white desert. He frowned and shook his head. "I'll be damned."

"Sir?"

"I just flew eight thousand miles to land in another desert."

Captain Ryan Medford unclipped his mask and smiled.

A silver van pulled alongside the *Aurora* followed by a tow truck. Within seconds, the aircraft was ringed with white-suited technicians. Their supervisor watched his men push an exit ladder beside the cockpit before giving Medford a thumbs-up.

"Clear to exit, General." Medford flipped the canopy release switch and climbed out of his seat as two F-22s roared overhead, their wingtips rocking in a salute to the general.

Taylor followed Medford down the exit ladder onto the blistering tarmac. He dragged off his helmet and took a breath of desert air. The hot, dry breeze stung his lips. He tasted the grit between his teeth. It felt like Iran.

"Here comes your ride, sir."

Taylor stared at the black APC racing across the sand toward them. He turned to Medford and shook his hand. "Thanks for the lift, Captain. Hope to fly with you again."

Medford smiled. "My pleasure, sir." He snapped to attention and gave the general a proud salute.

Taylor snapped a salute in return. "Be well, son." He turned and walked toward the waiting APC.

They whisked him across the gypsum sand to a cluster of white bunkers surrounded by an electric fence guarded with Special Forces personnel. They were on military ground, off limits to anyone not carrying top-secret clearance.

Overhead, the darkening sky was etched with white contrails. Shockwaves echoed across the New Mexico desert as the world's most advanced aircraft cracked the sound barrier a final time before coming down.

Missile towers were visible to the north, and beyond them Trinity site where seventy-five years ago the first atom bomb lit the morning sky with a brilliance greater than the sun, and changed the world forever.

Taylor was climbing out of the APC when he heard a familiar voice.

"Hello, General. How was the flight?"

Taylor turned and saluted Augustus Cook, Five Star General of the Army and Chairman of the Joint Chiefs of Staff.

Cook returned the salute and shook Taylor's hand. He smiled while eyeing his friend of thirty years. "I must say, you look a little green about the gills, Malcolm."

Taylor shrugged. "My stomach's still in Tehran."

Cook patted his arm. "Sorry about that. I thought it best to get you over here fast, given the situation."

Taylor forced a smile. "Only problem is my stomach. It's still back there."

Cook swung his arm around Taylor's neck and nodded at the bunkers. "I can fix that, General. I've got a bottle of Kentucky moonshine in my quarters."

Taylor cracked a smile. "Lead the way, sir."

They adjourned to Cook's quarters for a healthy round of shots from the unlabeled bottle in Cook's desk. The moonshine was definitely what the doctor ordered. Taylor was into his third stiff shot when he stretched out his legs and smiled at his old friend.

Cook returned the smile. "Better?"

Taylor smiled.

Cook chugged his shot of moonshine. "The others are waiting for us."

Taylor's eyes widened. "The chiefs?"

Cook nodded. "All five of us. Jimmy stayed in DC to ward off the jackals."

Taylor knew he was referring to General James Wilcox, Vice Chairman of the Joint Chiefs. He sighed and sipped his moonshine. "That's a tall order for Jimmy."

Cook shrugged. "He can handle it. Besides, we don't need to be in DC to know what's going on. Hell, there's enough intel within fifty yards of this desk to hear a rat farting in Tehran." He leaned back in his chair and rubbed his tired eyes. "Hardest thing was sneaking out of Washington without some media jerk getting wind of it."

Taylor looked down at his glass. "So, where do I fit in?"

Cook looked him in the eye. "Like I told you in Tehran, we want your honest appraisal of the war."

Taylor sighed. "That was three months ago, Auggie. Things were bad then, but now they're—" He caught himself.

Cook leaned toward him. "Don't hold back, Malcolm. You tell us what's in your heart."

Taylor frowned. "Everything?"

Cook nodded.

Taylor chugged his moonshine and placed the empty glass on the desk. "I'd like to clean up, if that's okay."

Cook gestured toward the door behind the desk. "Use my bathroom. If you want to lie down for a few minutes, my billet's through the adjoining door."

Taylor smiled. "Nice and cozy. Afraid I'll run away?"

Cook reached across the desk and gripped his friend's arm. "I'm glad you're here, Malcolm. I need you just now."

Taylor's smiled faded. "That bad?"

"Worse."

Taylor sighed. "It's hard to keep up with things back there. Lots of rumors and media hype, but no cold, hard facts." His brown eyes glistened. "What the hell's going on?"

Cook released his grip and fell back in his chair. He stared at his friend with bloodshot eyes. "Hawley's little show really shook things up. I'm afraid the idiot started a prairie fire."

Taylor leaned closer. "The militia thing?"

Cook frowned. "It's damn serious, Malcolm. On September seventeenth, Governor Seth Hawley declared war on all state militias and that jerk in the White House followed suit with raids on militia camps across the country."

"Insane."

"Good choice of words." Cook shook his head. "Politics is one thing, but you don't beat up the militias. The way things are, it could start a damn civil war."

Taylor stared at his friend. "I heard about the shootout in Flint. Reminded me of Tehran."

Cook reached into a drawer and pulled out a pack of non-filtered cigarettes. He plucked one out and jammed it between his lips.

"I thought you quit."

"I did." Cook struck a match and lit the cigarette. He took a deep drag and blew the smoke at the ceiling. He took another puff and swallowed the smoke. "It's a mess, Malcolm. The President's in a dead heat with that rebel from South Carolina. The FBI's shooting it out with disgruntled militia and we're getting creamed in the Middle East." He stuffed the cigarette in an ashtray. "How's that for bad?"

Taylor looked down at the crushed cigarette. "What about Minton?"

Cook frowned. "She should've dropped out, but she keeps fighting. She's down to fourteen percent in the poles, but she won't give up."

"Anything on the two missing felons?"

Cook shook his head.

"What about the burned SUV they found in Illinois?"

Cook shrugged. "Nothing visible. No human remains except a charred toe nail. They're still trying to extract DNA." He glared at his friend. "Just the excuse Minton needed to pound home her message that the FBI is behind this whole mess. She keeps preaching that they killed Jordan to protect the real guys behind the arms deal."

Taylor smirked. "Including the President?"

"Who else. Hell, she's even thrown in Hawley as the President's stooge. Claims the whole thing is a conspiracy to discredit her. That the global profiteers will do anything to maintain their two party control of the nation. That this is an excuse to wipe out America's last bastion of freedom … its militia." He slammed his fist on the desk. "And while those three megalomaniacs fight for the presidency, they're leading us closer to civil war."

Taylor took a nervous breath. "It's spreading?"

Cook nodded. "Six recorded incidents of shootouts like the one in Michigan. One in Wisconsin, one in Florida, and the others in Ohio, Maine, Mississippi, and for Christ's sake, my own state of Kentucky." Cook pointed a gnarled finger at him. "But that's not the worst of it, Malcolm. When the Michigan thing got out of control, the governor called in the National Guard."

Taylor nodded. "I heard about that."

"Did you also hear that only two thirds of the guard reported for duty?"

"What?"

Cook snatched another cigarette and lit it. He took a deep drag and blew the smoke at the ceiling. "Fourteen militia members were killed in the shootout. When the FBI checked the bodies, they discovered nine of them were National Guard troops that failed to report."

Taylor sank in his chair, his eyes gazing at Cook.

Cook waved his hand in disgust. "Like I said, it's a real mess." He puffed his cigarette. "What about your side?"

"Sir?"

"The friendly fire."

Taylor frowned and rested his head against the chair. "We've had seventeen known incidents in the past month. I suspect far more weren't reported."

Cook grimaced. "The reason?"

Taylor shrugged. "Wrong words spoken at the wrong time, excessive cruelty by a superior officer, racial stuff, ethnic stuff…"

Cook's black eyes locked on him. "I asked for the reason."

Taylor rubbed his forehead. "Battle fatigue, stress, call it what you like." He looked at his commander with sullen eyes. "Our troops are burned out, Auggie. They've been out there too long. They've seen too much pain. They've killed too many people to know the difference between friend and foe." He leaned toward Cook, his eyes filled with desperation. "They're at the breaking point, Auggie. We need to get them home before they snap."

Cook stared at the exhausted man seated across from him. He nodded and glanced at his watch. "Get some shut eye. I'll delay the meeting until nineteen hundred hours."

The four joint chiefs were seated around a black circular table when General Cook led his friend into bunker three's conference chamber. The chiefs rushed out of their chairs and mobbed their returning warrior. Handshakes were brisk along with pats on the back and words of encouragement for the tired field general.

General Cook took his place at the table and gestured for Taylor to sit in the vacant chair on his right. True to military protocol, Taylor sat down and removed his cap, placing it on the table. The chiefs waited until he was down before following suit, the ultimate gesture of respect.

Cook eyed the four chiefs. "I've asked General Taylor to give his candid assessment of the situation over there." He glanced at his friend. "Malcolm?"

Taylor leaned forward and clasped his hands while trying to find the right words. He looked at the five uniformed men seated around him and felt a rush of nerves.

Something was wrong. He could see the strain on their faces. The tired eyes and furrowed brows. The taut lips and locked hands. These were men who had tasted war and all its evil — battle-hardened men who had attained their lofty posts through accomplishment, loyalty, sacrifice, and pain. Rock-solid commanders who knew the importance of a steadfast, confident demeanor. Not the type of men who would convey uncertainty to a returning field general, yet their faces betrayed them.

Chief of Naval Operations, Admiral Harley Ponton leaned forward. "Speak freely, General. You're among friends."

Taylor looked down at his clasped hands and forced out the words. "We're losing, gentlemen, plain and clear. If we continue this course, we'll be driven from Iran within six months."

Commandant of the Marine Corps, General Terry Kelsey looked Taylor in the eye. "And Atlantis?"

"Compromised, sir. Their missile attack destroyed our command and control infrastructure."

Kelsey pressed him. "But we've replaced the equipment? Things should be up and running by now?"

Taylor looked the bushy-browed Marine in the eye. "Yes, sir, our equipment is operational." He fought a surge of emotion. "It's the people, sir. We lost ninety-seven of our finest technicians in that raid." He looked down at his scarred palms while recalling his final moment with Lieutenant Hammer. "And we lost some good soldiers who gave their lives so I can be here today."

Kelsey dropped back in his chair, his face flushed with anger.

Army Chief of Staff, General Marv Denton leaned toward Taylor. "General Taylor, you're the best we have. Please give us your candid assessment of the reasons for this mess."

Taylor glanced at Cook while recalling the President's crushing words in the *Chinook* on July sixth.

Cook smiled. "Go ahead, Malc. They're aware."

Taylor stared at his friend in disbelief. The President's words were not meant to leave the chopper. He sighed and looked at the chiefs. "You gentlemen know about the smuggled missiles?"

The chiefs nodded.

"And the President's request to open negotiations with Jihawri?"

"They nodded."

"I see." Taylor stiffened and spilled his guts. "We have the finest military in history, but you can't win a war when you're betrayed by your own government." He leaned forward and looked them in the eye. "I may be out of line, but I've seen too many good soldiers fall because of that betrayal. If we don't nail the traitors behind those arms deals, we're finished over there."

"And over here?" Air Force Chief of Staff, General Harold Mitchell leaned toward Taylor.

Taylor looked Mitchell in the eye. "Yes, sir ... over here."

Mitchell eased back in his chair. "You said, nail the traitors. I'd like your thoughts on that."

"Sir?"

"How far should we go with that?"

Taylor gave him a puzzled look.

"I mean, what if the felons are in the government?"

"Government, sir?"

Mitchell nodded.

Taylor's stomach churned. What was Mitchell getting at? That was a question for the FBI or CIA, not a general in the field.

Cook patted Taylor's arm. "Harold just wants to hear your thoughts, Malcolm. We don't need to proceed down that path." He glanced at his notepad. "You're saying we can hold on for six months?"

Taylor nodded. "Yes, sir."

Denton leaned toward him. "Casualties?"

Taylor grimaced. "Based on what I see, we'll lose another eight to ten thousand."

The room fell silent as the five chiefs stared at their guest in shock. General Denton took a deep breath and leaned forward. "That many?"

"Yes, sir."

"Can't we cut our losses with air strikes?"

"No, sir, the enemy is too determined." Taylor hesitated. "And they have our missiles."

Denton dropped back in his chair. "Thank you, General."

No words were spoken as the chiefs looked down at their notes. Cook finally broke the silence. "We appreciate your candor, Malcolm. I assure you nothing will leave this room." He aimed a remote at the blue screen on the wall. "It's probably best we spend our final hour going over the battle zones." He pressed the remote and watched a map of Iran appear on the screen. A second button displayed an overlay of troop and equipment movements within the past twenty minutes.

Taylor spent the next hour standing at the map while answering tactical questions from the chiefs. When it was done, they rose from their chairs and stepped beside him for a final round of handshakes and pats on the back.

Cook escorted Taylor out of the bunker into the fenced compound. It was 2120 in White Sands and the air had cooled considerably.

Cook pulled out a cigarette and lit it. He took a deep drag and blew the smoke at the stars. "Are the nights like this in Tehran?"

Taylor shook his head. "Too much haze from the fires to see anything like this." He folded his arms and studied the bowl of stars.

Cook stomped out his cigarette and looked his friend in the eye. "The next few days will be difficult. You'll be asked to do something you won't like."

Taylor shrugged. "Nothing new there."

Cook shook his head. "We'll talk tomorrow when you're back in Tehran."

Taylor's eyes widened. "Tomorrow?"

Cook nodded. "I've arranged a return trip for you. They'll be coming by to pick you up in forty minutes. It's best you get back there."

Taylor gazed at him. "What's up, Auggie?"

Cook took a deep breath. "We'll talk tomorrow." He shook his friend's hand. "Good seeing you, Malcolm. Wish we had more time."

CHAPTER 39

THE DOCUMENT

General Cook strode into the conference room at 2212 hours with a black attaché case dangling from his hand. He took his place at the empty chair beneath the American Eagle and nodded at his four comrades. "Be seated, gentlemen."

Cook waited for them to sit down before easing into his chair. He placed the attaché case on the floor and rested his arms on the table.

General Kelsey leaned forward. "He's gone?"

Cook nodded. "He'll be in Tehran in three hours."

Kelsey stared at Cook. "Think he can handle it?"

Cook took a pained breath. "If not him … who?"

The four chiefs sat in silence, their eyes trained on their commander.

Cook snatched the attaché case off the floor and placed it on the conference table. He fumbled with the combination lock and pressed the latch.

They watched him open the case and pull out a black folder. He opened the folder, exposing a sheet of paper, which he placed on the table in front of him.

Cook eyed the paper while reaching into his jacket pocket for a blue fountain pen. He unscrewed the cap, his black eyes scanning the four chiefs. "I'll sign first."

He waited for their painful nods before positioning the pen over the paper. "Know this, gentlemen. If there were any other way..." He frowned and signed his name. "God bless the United States and all its people." He rested the pen on the paper and slid the paper to General Kelsey.

It took ten minutes for the paper and pen to complete their journey around the table. Each chief studied the paper carefully before signing his name. Admiral Ponton was the last to sign. He pushed the paper and pen to Cook and dropped back in his chair.

Cook capped the pen and returned it to his pocket while studying the five signatures. He nodded and placed the paper in its folder, then inserted the folder into the attaché case and locked it. He stared at the sealed attaché case for a moment, as if in prayer.

Cook stood up and waited for the others to follow suit. He slipped on his cap and gave the brim a firm tug. His eyes locked on the four men. "Tomorrow, this document will contain twenty-seven signatures." He glanced at his watch. "I'll deliver it to the President at twenty-three hundred hours tomorrow evening."

General Mitchell leaned forward and rested his hands on the table. "What about Taylor?"

Cook sighed. "I'll call him in the morning."

Mitchell frowned. "He'll comply?"

Cook glared at the Air Force joint chief. "Don't worry about General Taylor, Harold. You're the one with the tough job."

Mitchell took a deep breath. "Yes, sir."

Cook eyed the chiefs a final time. "God be with us." He snatched the attaché case off the table and walked out of the room.

CHAPTER 40

OCTOBER 26TH

Josh Barden was walking out of WNN's bustling lobby when he heard the guard at the front desk cry out to him. "Important call, Mr. Barden!"

Barden glanced nervously at his watch. He had to be at Hartsfield International Airport in forty-five minutes. If he missed his chartered flight, he'd blow the biggest interview of his life with the nation's newest hero and leading presidential candidate, Governor Seth Hawley.

It had taken Barden a month to set up the Hawley interview. With glory in his grasp, the nation's finest anchorman was being detained by a fat guard in a rented uniform with a black phone in his chubby hand.

Barden stormed to the desk and snatched the guard's phone. "This is Barden."

"Something's brewing, Josh. We need you up here."

Barden recognized Mason Parker's tremulous voice. He gripped the phone and vented his stress. "Are you nuts? I've got a twelve forty-five flight to Columbia, South Carolina." He pressed the phone to his lips. "Do you know what that means?"

Parker sighed. *"I'm sorry, Josh. This is really important."*

Barden glanced at the limo driver waving to him from the lobby's revolving doors. He took a deep breath and restrained himself. "For god's sake, Mason. What the hell could be more important than an audience with the next president?"

"Something's happening in Iran. Our troops are pulling back."

Parker's words shot through him. "Pulling back? To where?"

"Don't know, but it's across the boards."

Barden rested his hand on the desk. "What the hell does that mean?"

"The whole friggin' country. We've got units in full retreat from Tabriz to Bandar Beheshti."

Barden glanced at his watch. "Maybe they're redeploying. Nothing unusual about that." He heard Parker mumble to someone. Then a brushing sound as the phone switched hands.

"That you, Josh?"

Barden recognized Murray Klinton's voice. "Yeah, it's me. What the hell's going on?"

"I've run two computer simulations." Klinton hesitated. *"It looks like we're pulling out."*

Barden felt the limo driver's hand on his arm. He brushed it away and stared at the guard. "And you have confirmation?"

"No, but maybe the President's speech will shed some light on it."

Barden stiffened. "Speech?"

"He's going on at twelve thirty. Came out of the blue. The White House is telling us it's important."

Barden glanced at the driver. He lowered his head and frowned. "I'll be up in a minute."

Barden stepped into WNN's massive news center at 12:06 after placing an emergency call to his secretary—

"Tell them to hold the charter, Aileen. And tell Hawley's people I'm checking some troop deployments in the Middle East. Tell them I'll fill them in when I get there for the interview ... I don't know when! Just do it!"

Barden blew past Mason Parker and his staff while scanning the cavernous news center. He spotted Murray Klinton standing beneath the room's massive projection screen, his eyes focused on a flickering map of Iran.

Barden rushed beside Klinton and stared at the screen. "Well?"

Klinton pointed at the map. "Those white arrows are troop withdrawals. They're all pointed south except for the troops pulling out of Zabol and Zahedan." Klinton pointed at the two arrows in eastern Iran. "See how they converge southwest toward the other arrows?"

Barden squinted at the two angled arrows. "So?"

Klinton frowned. "If you ask me, our entire force is retreating to the Persian Gulf."

Barden glared at the ex-military intelligence officer. "Do you know what you're saying?"

Klinton nodded.

"When did this start?"

"A few hours ago, but no one paid attention until it became massive." Klinton looked him in the eye. "It's definitely coordinated."

Barden studied the map. "Are we under attack?"

Klinton shook his head. "Nothing visible. Our guys are just pulling back."

Barden stared at the arrows. "How far have they gone?"

"Ten to fifteen miles, depending on location."

"And you think it's for real?"

Klinton sighed. "We should wait for the President's speech."

Barden gripped his arm. "Come on, Murray. This is why we pay you. The hell with the President. Give me your best shot."

Klinton looked at the screen. "I don't like it. It's too sudden." He hesitated. "It's like they're clearing the battlefield for something big."

Barden stared at the flickering screen. He turned toward the anchor desk at the far end of the news center. It would only take a few minutes to replace Jodie Marshall. She'd be pissed, but so be it. This was a job for WNN's finest. The Hawley interview would have to wait.

CHAPTER 41

MY FELLOW AMERICANS

At exactly twelve thirty, WNN's cameras focused on Josh Barden seated at his anchor desk in the sprawling Atlanta newsroom. There were no introductions as Barden leaned forward and stared at the camera.

"Good afternoon, America. I only have a minute, so I'll cut to the chase. WNN's analysts have detected unexplained troop movements in Iran. After careful deliberation, we have concluded that these movements signal a possible withdrawal. To be blunt, it appears we might be experiencing a full scale retreat of our forces from Iran. We should know more in a few seconds when the President addresses the nation."

Seth Hawley put his coffee cup on the cocktail table and leaned toward the TV, his eyes locked on Josh Barden's face. He glanced at his watch and frowned. "Guess we won't be talking to him today."

"Yeah…" Brad Forester put down his papers and stared at the TV.

They had been engrossed in a last minute prep session for the Barden interview when the TV screen flashed with a "Breaking News" logo. They would have ignored it except for the unexpected image of Josh Barden seated at WNN's anchor desk.

Since Barden's recent promotion to director of programming, his anchor chair had been relinquished to Jodi Marshall, WNN's brilliant investigative reporter. Seeing Barden in that chair was more than a surprise for the stunned governor and his campaign manager since they were supposed to meet with Barden in one hour.

The screen displayed a picture of the White House followed by the Great Seal of the United States. A firm, omnipotent voice spoke in the background—

"We interrupt our scheduled programming to bring you a special address by the President of the United States."

The camera closed on the President who was seated at his oval office desk. The President's brown eyes locked on the camera.

"Good afternoon, my fellow Americans. As you know, we are in the nineteenth year of a difficult struggle in the Middle East. Our Iran campaign has entered its second year and our coalition forces are engaged in ongoing combat with Islamic fundamentalists in Afghanistan and eastern Syria."

He paused and clasped his hands.

"This has been a hard time for us all. Many brave souls will not be returning home to their loved ones. There is unrest in the land. America's patience is worn thin."

He hesitated while lifting a sheet of paper off the desk.

"In recent months, I have tried to open negotiations with all parties involved in the conflict, but to no avail. It appears that Iran is not interested in moving toward democracy, but instead remains a haven for terrorist regimes bent on destroying freedom."

Forester jumped out of his chair. "Can you believe this?"

Hawley raised his hand for silence. "Not now, Brad."

The President looked down at the paper. *"Under advisement from the joint chiefs of staff, I am therefore ordering the immediate withdrawal of all American forces from Iran. I have notified our coalition partners of my decision and they have assured me they will follow suit."*

Hawley glared at the screen. "My god."

The President lowered the paper and stared at the camera.

"I do this for the good of our people and in the hope my decision will bring unity to our nation and lay the framework for a better life for us all."

He hesitated as if mustering his courage.

"I have asked General Augustus Cook, Chairman of the Joint Chiefs, to explain the withdrawal timetable. Before relinquishing the microphone to General Cook, let me reaffirm my offer of negotiation to all participants in this bitter war, including Hassan Jihawri and all factions under his command."

Forester shook his fist. "My god, the idiot's committed political suicide! After eleven thousand dead, he's thrown in the towel!"

Hawley wasn't listening. His eyes were focused on the President's tear-streaked face.

"God bless you, my fellow Americans, and God bless the United States, and its Constitution."

"Yes, dammit! We have him!" Forester gripped Hawley's arm. "We're going to win, Seth! You're going to be the Prez!"

Hawley stared at the Great Seal on the screen. He could hear the phones ringing. Most likely Callup and the boys brimming with exuberance. After all, their man was about to become the next President of the United States.

Forester backed away. "Say something, Seth. For god's sake, we've won!"

Hawley looked down. His voice was barely audible. "Where's the Congress?"

"Who?"

"The Senate and House leaders?" Hawley looked at his campaign manager with sullen eyes.

Forester stared at the man he'd grown to respect. "What do you mean?"

Hawley looked his friend in the eye. "First, the President; then the chairman of the joint chiefs. Where are the elected members of Congress with their voice of approval?" He collapsed in his chair. "This isn't the way it's done." His face went blank. "My god, Brad. I don't think there's going to be an election."

CHAPTER 42

FIFTY-FOUR

She had spent the past month taking long walks around the lake, trying to cope with the pain tearing at her heart. Her two secret service agents had learned to give ground to the slim lady walking ahead of them. When she stopped along the shore, they fell back and looked the other way.

A month had passed since she last talked to Matthew Jordan. All attempts to reach him had failed. Charles Mootley had also disappeared, as had Harry Zimmerman and Matt's other militia brothers. It was as if they had vaporized.

In Washington, the FBI continued to test the DNA drawn from the charred SUV, but Claire Minton already knew the outcome. Her GPS trace of Matt's final phone call had placed him at an Illinois motel only three miles from the burned wreckage. It was just a matter of time before the DNA samples confirmed his fate.

She ruffled her hair and looked at the trees swaying in the breeze. The man she loved was gone, killed by the same ruthless profiteers that had sacrificed eleven thousand American soldiers to a war of attrition — profiteers bent on protecting their lucrative interests at all costs, even if it meant destroying America's last hope of dissent — its Heartlanders.

Her campaign had collapsed since Seth Hawley's crushing press conference. At fourteen percent, her only hope was to play the role of power broker by striking deals with both parties before her dwindling popularity took away her last card. There was only one problem. Neither candidate would talk to her.

With Claire Minton out of the race, the President had altered his campaign strategy. Desperate to overcome Governor Hawley's five point lead, he fought to regain the high ground by rallying the nation against its new internal enemy — its state militias. If he could distract America's war-weary voters from the Middle East for two more weeks, all would be well except for a few disgruntled NRA members and rednecks.

With his new chief of staff, Steven Zimmer, at his side, the President's strategy appeared to be working. For the first time in three months, pundits across the land were giving him the election by a nose.

More importantly, the profiteers were smiling again. The Callups, Mansteds, and Marshalls could relax and enjoy the show. It didn't matter who won. Their cash flow was safe. Order had been restored. America's two-party system was intact. Capitalism had triumphed.

Claire snatched a pebble off the shore while recalling the bedraggled, shoeless man who climbed into her limousine on that April night six months ago.

Was it possible? Could a washed-up reporter bring down the greatest third party movement in American history?

She squeezed the pebble and relived his final words—

A tree grows up from the earth, and somewhere along the way it forgets its roots. It gets so caught up reaching for the sun, some lowly insect brings it down.

"My god, Perry." She flung the pebble at the water and watched it skip across the surface before disappearing with a splash.

"Ms. Minton!"

She spun around. One of the agents was running toward her with a cell phone in his hand. He nearly tripped on the wet shore before skidding beside her.

The agent extended the phone. "Urgent call, Ms. Minton. We have orders to get you back to the lodge."

She looked at him with puzzled eyes while taking the phone from his hand. "Yes?"

"Get back here, Missy. We've got trouble."

"Jess?"

"Get back here now. The President's speaking. WNN says we're pulling out of Iran."

She looked at the lake in stunned silence.

They escorted her to a gray SUV parked in the trees. Jess Wilkin was waiting at the lodge's front door when the SUV skidded to a stop on the gravel. She was barely out of the car when he grabbed her arm.

"Come on, he's already started."

She ran up the steps behind him. "When did this happen?"

"A few minutes ago. No explanation or warning. WNN looks as surprised as everyone else."

They spent the next ten minutes in her study watching the President's heart-wrenching address to the nation. When the camera closed on the President's tear-streaked face, Wilkin glanced at her for a reaction, but there was none.

"I have asked General Augustus Cook, Chairman of the Joint Chiefs to explain the withdrawal timetable. Before relinquishing the microphone to General Cook, let me reaffirm my offer of negotiation to all participants in this bitter war, including Hassan Jihawri and all factions under his command."

Wilkin glared at the television screen. "I don't believe it. He's lost his marbles."

"God bless you, my fellow Americans, and God bless the United States, and its Constitution."

"Insanity!" Wilkin looked at her in shock, but she didn't respond. She seemed frozen, her eyes staring at the TV. There was no movement, no sign of emotion.

The screen switched to an aerial view of the Pentagon, followed by a close-up of General Augustus Cook seated at his desk. He sat beneath the Great Seal of the United States. The stars and stripes flowed from a standard on his right. On his left, four crossed pennants represented the Army, Navy, Air Force, and Marines.

Cook clasped his hands and spoke in a firm, resolute tone.

"My fellow citizens. Under orders from the President, the joint chiefs have requested that all American forces initiate an immediate withdrawal from Iran's soil. We do this in full concert with the President, and anticipate the withdrawal's completion within the week."

Wilkin fell back in his chair. He started to speak, but was cut off by the general.

"No one hates war more than a soldier. In the past months, it has become apparent that we are engaged in a politically motivated police action that does not fit the mold of America's fighting spirit."

General Cook leaned toward the camera. *"To be blunt, war is hell … the last resort. To subject the world's finest military to an ill-advised occupation is not the answer to global peace."*

Cook stiffened, his black eyes locked on the camera. *"The days ahead will be difficult. It is never easy to pull back from a conflict. I have instructed General Malcolm Taylor to withdraw our forces in all due haste. We anticipate a similar response from our coalition partners."*

Cook paused as the camera closed on his face. *"As our troops withdraw to embarkation points in the Persian Gulf, we expect the enemy to honor the rules of war. To put it simply, our soldiers have been ordered to avoid enemy engagement at all costs. We expect Hassan Jihawri's forces to honor the same truce. To do otherwise will be considered an act of barbarism, warranting unchecked retaliation."*

The camera pulled back. *"God bless you, my fellow Americans, and may God shine his guiding light on us all."*

Wilkin watched the screen switch to an aerial view of the Pentagon. "Damn!" He clicked the remote and flipped it on the desk.

He pointed to the stack of papers on the desk. "Your speech to the Illinois farmer's co-op. I wrote the damn thing to emphasize how the war has diminished our farm support program." He frowned and pushed out of his chair. "I need to write a new one."

She leaned back in her chair and forced a weak smile. "You're a good man, Jess. You go write that speech."

He snatched the speech off the desk. "Hell, I'll come up with something. After all, you did lead the protest against the war." He nodded. "Yeah, that's it. Your message finally got through. That idiot in DC finally woke up. Now, if I can just find the right words—"

She watched him walk across the room with his papers in hand. The door closed and all was still.

She hadn't used the dialing code since July 4th. She punched "R-E-D-L-E-G" and listened to the high-pitched whine. An automated voice answered.

"Please enter your security code."

She unlocked her lower desk drawer and fumbled through a file folder until she pulled out a sheet of paper. She placed the paper on the desk and punched its string of typed characters into the phone's keypad.

The line beeped followed by a curt, *"Stand by."*

In the nation's capital, General Augustus Cook was preparing to meet with his chiefs when his cell phone buzzed. He pulled out the phone and pressed the connect button. "Yes?"

"What's going on, Auggie?"

Cook hesitated. "Who is this?"

"Claire."

He sank in his chair. "Validate."

"It's me, Auggie. What the hell's going on?"

Cook frowned and pressed the phone to his lips. "Validate."

"Heartland."

He stared at the digital clock on his desk. "I have an important meeting. We should talk later."

"What are you doing, Auggie. This wasn't supposed to happen until I took over."

He nodded. "But that's not in the cards, is it?"

"You can't do this, Auggie. He's still the President."

Cook sat up. "Sorry, Missy. Too much at stake. Let's just say we've moved things up a bit."

Her voice sharpened. *"And you expect me to sit by while you take over the government?"*

He gripped the phone. "We ARE the government, Missy … AND the people … and it's been that way for two hundred forty-four years since the minutemen took up arms at Lexington and Concord."

"Auggie, you've gone too far. I never meant—"

His face reddened. "Stay out of it, Claire. In a few weeks, everything will be back to normal and you can have your election."

"No, dammit! You think I don't know what's coming? I was over there, remember? For god's sake, Auggie, there are innocent people involved. Come to your—"

"Sorry, Missy." He pressed the off button and jammed the phone in his pocket.

General Cook was nearly out of his office when he stopped to look back at the American flag. He stiffened and nodded at the flag. "For the heartland."

With the afternoon sun streaming through the window, Heartlander number fifty-four walked out of the most important office in the world.

CHAPTER 43

UNCHECKED RETALIATION

A day had passed since the President's shocking speech to the nation. It was 6:45 a.m. in Atlanta on Tuesday, October 27th.

At Peachtree Center, WNN's newsroom was silent except for the communications static coming from the quad speakers on the ceiling. Inside the cavernous room, a dozen technicians sat at twin banks of consoles, their eyes trained on their television monitors. Beyond them, the projection screen continued to display the map of Iran, its white arrows slowly converging on the Persian Gulf.

Josh Barden sipped his coffee while staring at the projection screen. He hadn't left the news center since yesterday's brief introduction to the President's speech. He took a slow, deep breath while listening to the static coming from the speakers.

God, he loved it. It was better than any narcotic, an out-of-body experience only an anchor could know, and he was the center of it, the eyes and ears of two hundred million viewers.

The projection screen flickered with static as WNN's top war correspondent, Rolff Stensen, attempted a live telecast from General Taylor's command vehicle south of Tehran. Taylor's two brigades were the last to pull out of Tehran after falling dangerously behind the other white arrows headed for the gulf.

With F-18's and *Apaches* flying air cover, Taylor had stepped up the pace. His half-mile column of humvees and transport vehicles were approaching Qom where they would board a troop train for the treacherous run over the Zagros Mountains to Kuwait.

Stensen was about to interview the general when the first enemy rockets struck Taylor's Alpha and Bravo brigades. The stunned reporter was suddenly caught in a mad scramble for shelter while trying to relay the chaos to the world's viewing audience.

"The column has veered away from Qom toward the open desert on our left. From the jarring inside our vehicle, we must be moving at fifty miles an hour. Through my view port, I can make out a Blackhawk helicopter descending on the desert, maybe a half mile ahead. It looks like they're waving us aboard. It's hard to know what's going on, but one thing's certain. With three thousand troops in the column, that chopper isn't big enough to carry three thousand soldiers out of this mess. My guess is the Blackhawk's come for General Taylor."

Stenson gripped an overhead support and lunged forward. *"I'm going to try to get a minute with the general if I can make it to the front of this humvee. We're moving pretty fast and I'm bouncing all over the place, so bear with me."*

The unsteady camera focused on Stensen as he hung on for dear life while easing toward the general who was seated in the front seat beside the driver. Stensen extended his mike while clinging to the general's seat. *"General Taylor, can you tell me—"*

The screen flashed as the humvee shook from a near hit, followed by two loud explosions.

"God, that was close. I think the last one hit the column. I'm squinting through the rear view port and can see flames coming from the convoy, maybe a half mile back."

The camera shook as it tried to focus on Stensen. *"I count three explosions to our left. There's another! I'm going to sign off until—"*

The screen went blank. Then came the "STAND BY" logo as WNN interrupted the telecast. Barden sank in his chair and stared at the stunned technicians looking at him from their consoles.

Confirmation reached WNN twenty minutes later. Rolff Stensen was dead along with Commanding General Malcolm Taylor. The general's humvee was within a hundred yards of the *Blackhawk* when it suffered a direct hit. Speculation quickly followed that the insurgents had used Stensen's transmission to target their missiles.

At the Pentagon, General Augustus Cook and his four chiefs glared at their projection screen while listening to the casualty reports coming in from Taylor's column.

Seventeen SCUD-type missiles had been fired from hidden sites in the rocky highlands above Qom. Three of the SCUD's had made direct hits on the convoy's rear.

Four GG100 missiles had been fired at the convoy from the Elburz Mountains. Two had made direct hits, killing six hundred helpless GI's. F-18 strafing runs had encountered a cluster of incoming XGA99 missiles, taking out two of the F-18's. The missiles appeared to emanate from Tehran.

And fresh news was coming in. Insurgent brigades were storming the streets of Tehran from the north, led by their holy leader, Hassan Jihawri. Sporadic attacks had begun in Qom to the south and in the hills to the column's west. Under fire from three directions, Alpha and Bravo's besieged brigades were being forced eastward into the Dasht-e Kavir desert, exposing them to certain death from Hassan Jihawri's remaining GG100 missiles, the ultimate disastrous conclusion to an impossible war.

Cook leaned toward the globe-shaped speaker on the conference table. "Can you hear me Colonel Lingstrom?"

"Yes, sir, but you're breaking up."

Cook leaned closer. "You're certain about General Taylor?"

"Yes, sir. His vehicle was struck by a direct hit. The Blackhawk rescue chopper was also taken out."

General Kelsey slammed his fist on the table. "Damn them to hell!"

Cook fought his emotions. "What's your condition, Colonel Lingstrom?"

"We're under heavy fire from the north, south, and west. Recon advises that we're cut off from the rest of southern command. It looks like the insurgents have singled us out for some kind of political statement." Lingstrom hesitated while conferring with his officers. Explosions could be heard in the background. *"We're headed east into the desert. It's our only option, sir."*

Cook's face reddened. "Negative, Colonel. I want you to dig in where you stand. Under no circumstance are you to change your position."

"Sir?"

"Do it, Colonel. That's a direct order."

Cook listened to the static. He knew Lingstrom was trying to get confirmation from his line superiors. Under no conditions was a senior field officer to take orders from the joint chiefs who were an advisory group to the President, and not in the chain of battle command.

"Sir, I'm unable to reach CENTCOM. I need confirmation from—"

Cook exploded. "Forget the damn confirmation! You've got ten minutes! Now dig in and dig deep!"

Lingstrom's voice was barely audible through the static. *"Yes, sir. Digging in."*

Cook leaned back in his chair and flicked away a bead of sweat. He looked at the Air Force general seated across from him. "Okay, Harold. Your show."

Mitchell nodded and placed a silver attaché case on the table. He opened it and lifted a red phone to his mouth.

The chiefs watched General Mitchell go through the familiar code routine. The room was silent except for Mitchell's muffled voice.

"Authenticate … America … Lexington … Concord … Alpha … Omega … Trinity … JCOS."

The phone gave off a beep followed by screeching static. Mitchell took a deep breath and spoke decisively. "Can you hear me Colonel Mayweather? … Yes, I hear you loud and clear."

Mitchell looked at the map of Iran on his console. "Targets as follows … Qom … Hamadan…" He hesitated and looked at General Cook.

Cook tightened his lips and nodded.

Mitchell took a deep breath and spoke his final word. "… Tehran."

Thirty seconds later, Colonel William Mayweather uncapped a red button and held his gloved finger above it. *"Missiles armed and programmed.*" He took a deep breath of oxygen and pressed the button. *"Missiles away."*

Twenty minutes later, Josh Barden and the WNN news team were shaken by an unexpected whine from their laser printers. Mason Parker and Murray Kimble were the first to read the *Reuter's* news flash. They looked at each other across the darkened news center, their faces frozen.

Barden watched the news center come alive with stunned whispers and gasps. He saw Kimble stagger toward him with the laser printout dangling from his hand. Kimble gripped the anchor desk and handed the paper to Barden.

"What's wrong, Murray? What happened?"

Kimble couldn't speak. He nodded at the printout in Barden's hand. Barden lifted the printout to the light and read it—

Reuters, London, 12:15:47 Greenwich Mean Time … three massive explosions have occurred in Iran … the affected cities are Qom, Hamadan, and Tehran … the explosions are believed to be thermonuclear … no confirmation or denial has been communicated from the President of the United States … the loss of life is anticipated to be catastrophic…

Barden lowered the printout and stared at the map of Iran. His words were barely audible—

"My, god … unchecked retaliation."

LONDON

Perry knelt down and placed the photo on the black granite. He smiled while staring at the stone's inscription—

HECTOR AMBROSE
1939-2012
Have one on me, mate...

He leaned toward the stone and spoke softly. "Hello, father. It's old Perry come home. I brought you a picture of our new pub. Thought it might cheer you a bit."

He leaned closer. "It's a great pub, father. Just like the old *Hunter's Bugle*, except it's on the West End. Near the theatres, and all that. Cost me an arm and leg, but it's worth it."

He stared at the photo. "Used to be a rundown liquor store, but we spruced it up prim and proper. Everything's brand spanking new, except the bar."

He rested his hand on the cold granite. "Cost me plenty, but I managed to salvage the *Bugle's* bar. The wrecking crews were getting ready to level the old *Bugle* when I stopped them. Paid them a bundle to dismantle the bar and lorry it to a craftsman who restored it good as new."

He patted the grave. "The bar looks great, father. All shiny and brassed-off. Sometimes, when it's late and we're closed, I look at the bar and see you standing there with that gray towel draped over your shoulder and that cigarette dangling from your mouth. I watch you squeeze off a pint for one of the blokes holding out a quid, and I feel good again."

He wiped away a tear. "I've named our new pub *The Cornered Fox*. Seems appropriate, don't you think? We're packing them in too, just like the *Bugle*."

He took a deep breath. "Sorry it took me so long to come home. I had some business to take care of, and..."

Perry tried to finish the sentence, but the moment caught him. He broke down and collapsed against the stone, his fingers clutching the granite.

After seventeen years, Perry Ambrose had come home. A bit late perhaps, but at least he and his old man would have this moment together.

There was so much he wanted to tell his father. Tales of dreams that became nightmares, friends that became foes, and revenge best served cold.

A barge's horn blared in the distance, its warning muffled by the thickening fog. It would be dark soon and the theatre patrons would pour into the *Fox* for a hearty meal before catching London's latest hit play.

By now, Josie and Christina had set the tables while Harry Doolings and his crew cooked up a feast of mutton, bangers, mashed potatoes, cod, chips, veggies, and Yorkshire pudding for the six thirty dinner rush. The tanks were filled with ale and the mirrored shelves behind the bar were stocked with the finest liquor.

Perry wiped his eyes and gave his father's grave a final pat. "Well, must get back for the evening rush. I'm glad we had this little chat. I'll come back tomorrow. Maybe split a pint with you." He broke into a tear-stained smile. "Blast, I'll even bring a flask of *Daniel's* so we can tie one on together."

He rose to his feet, his black Welsh eyes staring at the grave. "Be well, father. You're in my thoughts." He tipped his cap and walked out of the cemetery into the fog...

A NOTE FROM THE AUTHOR

Thank you for reading *Storm Rising* I hope you enjoyed reading it as much as I enjoyed writing it.

If you loved the book and have a minute to spare, I would really appreciate a short review of the book on Amazon.com. Your help in spreading the word is greatly appreciated. Reviews from readers like you are essential to the book's success..

~ Gary Naiman

*Storm Rising's ominous sequel has been released
in ebook format…*

HEARTLAND

It is 2021, and still no presidential election. The United States is torn by political upheaval, civil unrest, and increasing terrorist threats. Frustrated by hopeless overseas wars and its corrupt civilian leaders, the U.S. military has taken it upon itself to reset the nation's direction. Unfortunately, the power struggle between our military and elected officials has distracted us, and we are about to pay a dear price...

"What's going on? The sky's all lit up. I can't see..."
(final words of DC traffic copter pilot, 10:04 a.m., January 4th, 2021)

**Available on Amazon.com, Barnes&Noble.com, iBooks
and other ebook retailers**